CONQUEST

ESCAPE FROM WHEEL

MICHAEL SCOTT CLIFTON

BOOKS BY
MICHAEL SCOTT CLIFTON

The Treasure Hunt Club
The Janus Witch
Edison Jones and The ANTI-GRAV Elevator

Conquest of the Veil Series
The Open Portal
Escape From Wheel

Book Liftoff
1209 South Main Street
PMB 126
Lindale, Texas 75771

Interior's book design by Champagne Book Design
Cover design by Evelyne Paniez, www.secretdartiste.be
Resources:
Background/castle: Shutterstock
Clouds: are from my own photos
Stars: Shutterstock
Texture: www.deviantart.com/kuschelirmel-stock
Wings: Shutterstock
Horse male: Shutterstock
Horse female: Shutterstock
Bridle: www.deviantart.com/cyborgsuzystock
Male model: Shutterstock
Female model: Shutterstock

Illustrator: Nancy Durham, www.facebook.com/artistnedurham

Library of Congress Control Number Data
Clifton, Michael Scott
Escape From Wheel / Michael Scott Clifton
Magical Realism/Fiction.
Dragons & Mythical Creatures/Fantasy/Fiction.
3.Paranormal/Fantasy/Fiction
BISAC: FIC061000 FICTION / Magical Realism
FIC009120 FICTION / Fantasy/Dragons & Mythical Creatures.
2020913047

ISBN: 978-1-947946-63-7 (Ingram Spark Soft Cover)
ISBN: 978-1-947946-62-0 (Kindle Direct Publishing Soft Cover)

www.michaelscottclifton.com
www.bookliftoff.com

DEDICATION

"To my wife Melanie.
My ever present partner in everything I do."

"I can't go back to yesterday because I was a different person then."–Lewis Carroll, *Alice in Wonderland.*

PROLOGUE

MUURCH TRIED NOT TO SOIL HIMSELF.

He obediently followed the guard who led him across a polished marble floor. The color of obsidian, the quarried slabs formed a path ending at a pair of massive doors embellished with gold and silver leaf. Fully twenty hands high, they shielded entry to an inner sanctum he had only heard rumors of.

The throne room of Marlinda Darkmoor and Jack Morley—the Veil Queen and King.

Spaced at intervals, hammered brass bowls lined their path. Held aloft by the outstretched hands of sculpted figures—some human, some animal, some a melding of both—all contorted in various poses of agony. Within these bowls, flames flickered to illuminate the way.

Muurch passed one of the carved busts, a naked woman with pendulous breasts and a sharp, hooked beak rather than a mouth. The licking flames of the braziers cast his shadow on the figure. It stirred, eyes following his progress.

The Gatemaster gulped. Terror filled his veins like shards of ice. The razor-sharp needles pricked him with every step.

Why have I been summoned?

Since escorted from his post at the Gateway, this singular question occupied all his thoughts. As a young acolyte, he trained in the Dark Queen's caverns and had spent years there before his posting as a Gatemaster. But that was half a lifetime ago, and never once in all that time had he ever caught a glimpse of Marlinda…or Jack.

Now he had an audience…*with both*.

Muurch glanced at his guide, the sentry which accompanied him from the Gateway. A reptile's head, large as the fabled dragon lizards of the Katros Islands, rested upon the muscular shoulders of a man's body. A forked tongue flickered in and out of the creature's mouth, the iridescent scales merging with pale flesh.

Muurch thrust trembling hands in the pockets of his robe to conceal his fear.

The colossal doors swung open silently at their approach. Once inside, they whispered shut. Two guards stood inside, each a *meld* even more menacing than his guide. One wore the head of a ram, a pair of matched horns curling beside its head. Cloven feet *clacked* on the floor while a shaggy, fur-lined hand held an enormous axe taller than Muurch.

Tawny fur covered the other guard's entire body. Wicked incisors spilled from its feline mouth, and a pair of vestigial wings sprouted from between its shoulder blades. A paw armed with sharp claws clutched an iron-shod spear.

Both sentries struck the floor with the butt of their weapons.

"Kneel in the presence of the Queen and her consort!" the ram-headed guard boomed.

Muurch fell to his knees.

"Ah, our faithful servant, Muurch. Welcome, Gatemaster. Come forward and be received."

Muurch stood and forced his balky legs to propel him toward the sound of the voice. Before him, seated on a glossy marble throne, the Dark Queen gestured with one hand. Beside her sat her consort. Both wore garments of black silk. The Queen's floor-length gown accentuated a tiny waist, while her bodice strained to contain her full bosom. Hair, the color of night, cascaded past her shoulders. Her consort wore a pleated tunic and breeches, a gold cape draped over one shoulder. His long hair, a match for the Queen's own stygian shade, tumbled past his neck.

The pair's physical stature appeared to be rather ordinary. Of average height and weight, they hardly presented an imposing sight. But when his gaze met their eyes, all semblance to *ordinary* disappeared.

They oozed a dark evil which made the black marble floor look radiant by comparison. Insatiable hunger burned in their eyes, an appetite no amount of cruelty, murder, or slaughter could satisfy.

Muurch forced himself to tear his gaze away.

Perched on their heads were circlets of gold. Embedded with lodestones, the crowns glittered in the light. The Queen held a scepter, tapered at one end and flared on the other. Runes etched its entire surface, but it was what the belled end held which caused Muurch's breath to catch in his throat.

The orb.

At first glance, it looked rather commonplace, just a spherical knob on the scepter, but its power was legendary. He had never seen it, and in all his long life, never met anyone who had.

The Queen motioned to King Jack, and both stood. She smiled at Muurch, but no comfort came from the cold expression.

"What do you think of our audience room? I designed it myself." She tapped the wall behind the throne with the scepter. "I'm particularly fond of the façade."

The veneer thrust upward to the ceiling. Skulls of all shapes and sizes were fused to the bare rock. Other skeletal remains, mismatched parts of yellowed ribs, leg and arm bones, appeared as well.

The sight chilled Muurch.

The Dark Queen leaned forward. "Vanquished foes, our

enemies, all have taken their place here. Do you know why they occupy such a place of honor?"

Mute, Muurch shook his head.

"As a reminder of what happens to those who oppose us. This includes servants who displease us."

The Gatemaster's bowels clenched.

"Let me demonstrate." Marlinda inclined her head and the two guards stepped forward.

She pointed the scepter at one and then the other. With a *whoosh*, both creatures ignited. Within seconds, all that remained were ash and bones. The acrid odor of burnt flesh filled the room. Bile rose in Muurch's throat, and he fought to contain it.

With a flick of the scepter, the smoking bones of both sentries flew to the façade and with a *hiss*, merged into the rock.

The Dark Queen gestured at the Gatemaster. "Now, you must be thinking what our sentries did to deserve such a fate. And the answer is…*nothing*. They were loyal and wouldn't hesitate to give up their lives for us."

Marlinda walked toward Muurch. Jack followed behind and the two flanked the Gatemaster. "And of course, that is the point. They were sacrificed so you would know just how important the task is we are going to set before you."

The Dark Queen's eyes bored into Muurch. "There *will* be no failure."

The Gatemaster's teeth chattered. "Of course. What is your pleasure, my queen?"

Her icy smile returned. "Good." Marlinda crossed her arms. "Were you aware a portal remains open?"

"What? I'll close the magical gate immediately." Muurch felt the blood leave his face in a rush. Now he knew why he had been summoned. His scorched bones would soon join—

"Do nothing," Marlinda said, interrupting his thought.

Muurch blinked. "Nothing?" he stuttered.

Jack spoke for the first time. "Yes. Simply ignore the open portal."

"But why? The Empire may discover it. They'll send soldiers and, *gurk*—"

A strangled gasp escaped from Muurch as the Veil Queen's paramour lifted him off his feet and held him inches from his face. "You were chosen for your expertise on portals, not to ask questions!"

The Gatemaster managed a nod and the Dark King released him.

Marlinda moved closer and straightened Muurch's crumpled lapel. "There, there, good Muurch. We are confident you will use your considerable skill to make sure our raiders will continue to reave at will against the Empire's populace. As always, you'll open a gateway for them to pass through the Veil to plunder, retreat through it with their pillage and captives, then close it behind them. Oh, and one more thing."

"Yes, my queen," the Gatemaster rasped.

"No one is to know we had this conversation about the open wormhole. *No one!*"

"As you command, my queen."

Her face hardened. "Good. Because should you or any of your assistants tamper with this portal in any way, or should even one pair of inquisitive ears become aware of our discussion, your bones will join our collection...and it *will* be a prolonged process. You'll burn one inch at a time."

Marlinda waved her hand. "You are dismissed."

A guard escorted Muurch out, and the doors closed behind him.

His robe flapped like a bird in flight when he broke into a run.

CHAPTER 1

DOROTHEA, THE DUCHESS OF THE DUCHY OF WHEEL, POURED water into a crystal bowl.

She muttered words of power and touched the liquid with the tip of her finger. A languid ripple appeared, and her reflection stared back to reveal a pale face with ice-blue eyes. Tendrils of pastel-blonde hair dipped past the Duchess's shoulders, her full, blood-red lips pursed in concentration. More undulations disturbed the water, and then stilled.

Another face now stared at the Duchess.

Lord Rodric Regret flashed a cruel smile at Dorothea, ivory teeth displayed like a predator prepared to take a particularly juicy bite. Dark eyes cast a penetrating gaze from above a hawkish nose and narrow face. A crown of long black hair, plaited in a braid, looped across his collar.

"Dorothea. To what do I owe the pleasure? Especially since you banished me from Wheel less than a fortnight ago. Do you miss me already?"

The Duchess's mouth curled. "Your memory is as short as your self-control, Rodric. Or have you forgotten already your ill-conceived attack on the Duke's daughter, Alexandria? The very woman you are to be betrothed to?"

Rodric laughed. "Such fun, and yet my talents continue to be unappreciated."

"You are a fool!" Dorothea snapped. "However, I am in need of the very *talents* you boast of."

1

Rodric's eyes gleamed. "Oh, do tell. I'm all ears."

Dorothea snorted. "I'm afraid it doesn't involve torture or pulling wings off helpless insects."

A disappointed sigh escaped Rodric. "Very well. What is it you need?"

"A shade. One I can use to track Alexandria's movements."

"Why? You already have guards posted at her door every night."

"Because the Duke has given her permission to roam the city!" Dorothea barked. "And because I don't trust her! Since recovering from her fall she has behaved oddly...almost like she is a different person. She needs to be watched at all times."

Rodric tapped his lips. "Hmmm. I agree. She indeed seems changed. The Alexandria before the accident was more malleable." He leered and added, "And much more open to the concept of what it means to give *and* receive pleasure."

The insolent smile returned. "I'll decant a shade tonight. Be prepared to receive it by tomorrow."

Dorothea nodded in acknowledgement, and the watery image wavered and disappeared.

The Duchess pursed her lips. *"Don't ever try to match wits with me, Alexandria,"* she whispered. She picked up the bowl and hurled it against the wall where it shattered into a thousand glittering shards.

"Because you won't like the results."

Lost in thought, Alexandria Duvalier sat beneath an ornamental tree on the terrace. A cup of warm tea, untouched, sat forgotten near her fingertips.

Gardeners moved about the terrace pruning, pulling weeds,

and tending to the numerous flower beds. She stirred and eyed them uneasily.

Outside of Tell and Darcy, I don't know who I can trust.

Since rousing from the accident on Earth which left her in a coma, everything about her life had changed in an instant. She found herself on a new world with a new body and a new identity.

And faced with *new* problems and threats.

Mona Parker—her *former* self—was a plain and homely East Texas teenager, a penniless foster child bullied to the point of suicide by a rich and arrogant classmate. Her guardian angel, Thaddeus Finkle, appeared one night with a proposition;

Exchange a life with someone else.

Faced with the cruel bullying paired with her otherwise drab existence, the choice seemed easy. *What did she have to lose?* The next thing Mona knew, she woke from unconsciousness to find herself on the world of Meredith as Alexandria, a beautiful woman and the daughter of a Duke complete with servants and riches. Although Mr. Finkle refused to reveal the fate of the previous Alexandria, it didn't change the fact that her wildest dreams had come true.

Only then did she learn the cost of her bargain.

Trapped behind the Veil, a curtain of magic, the Duchy of Wheel was the last major province still unconquered by Marlinda, the evil creator of the Veil. The Dark Queen's brutal subjugation of the populace—ongoing for over a thousand years—was now almost complete.

But, bad as that prospect seemed, worse lay in store for her.

Attacked her first night on Meredith by her handmaiden, Darcy, the poor girl's body had been mystically commandeered by Rodric—a lord highly favored by her father, Duke Alton Duvalier. Via Darcy's body, Rodric's sadistic rage led to a brutal assault that almost killed her. Something snapped within her and a geyser of brilliant light pulsed from her. Like a high pressure hose, it hurled the commandeered body off and saved Alex's life. She still couldn't explain the eruption, and even now in bright sunshine, the experience continued to chill her blood.

The final evidence of her dire circumstances came last night. Given a magical book by Thaddeus Finkle, she found herself actually *pulled* into the volume. Instead of reading the book, it was like she became part of a video. *She* became part of the narrative, an eyewitness to the long ago history of the initial meeting between Marlinda and Jack. Now dubbed the Veil Queen and King, the poisonous fruit of this malevolent partnership became the magical barrier known as the Veil.

Alex reached for the tea and took a sip.

Still shaky from this surreal experience *within* her angel's book, she arose early and spent most of the morning lost in thought. No amount of meditation, however, could change her situation. Her only choice was to grab hold of her new life and move forward.

I am Alexandria Duvalier, heir to the Duchy of Dalfur…and I need to start acting like it.

No more "Mona" moments of indecision or fear of change. No more feeling sorry for myself. And most of all, no more dependency on Thaddeus Finkle…for anything! His last visit made clear, I'm on my own.

Her guardian angel—at times rude and condescending, and other times, warm and empathetic—never revealed more to her than snippets of what to expect.

Meredith is a world of magic and wonder where magic has replaced technology. But with dreams there are also nightmares.

He was spot on with his description…especially the nightmares. The fact he refused to elaborate further left her feeling she had been tricked into her decision to swap her old life for a new one.

Alex shook her head. *That isn't completely true. I wanted out of my old life...and I have only myself to blame if it didn't end in sunshine and roses.*

Frustrated, her fist struck the table and the teacup jumped and rattled.

The weather turned warmer, sunlight flickering through leafy branches. Clothed in a pair of tan riding breeches and a simple white smock she liberated from her sea of clothing, Alex felt comfortable for the first time since arriving on Meredith. Medieval ideas of appropriate women's attire prevailed here, and although sure to cause a stir among the Duke's stodgy court, she didn't care. She made a mental note to have the court seamstress make her more clothes suitable for riding.

Maybe I'll start a new fashion trend.

Earlier, she had sent Darcy to summon Tell, the officer in charge of her guard detail, so they could ride into Wheel. Since Rodric's attack with Darcy's hijacked body, the young lieutenant never strayed too far away. While waiting, she nibbled on a tray of scones.

On the table next to the sweet biscuits were books her hand-maiden retrieved for her. They chronicled the history of Dalfur, and contained maps of the entire region. Alex intended to pour over them at length until she knew the lay of the land and the rich history behind the Duchy. Although never a dedicated student back on Earth—she always considered history a dusty, pointless exercise—the stakes were higher now.

My life may depend on gathering every scrap of knowledge I can.

First, she needed to learn to negotiate the labyrinthian castle until she could find her way around without help. Next, read and learn everything she could about the region of Dalfur. Finally, she planned to explore Wheel, meet the city's people, and learn their ways and culture.

At the distinctive *click* of Tell's bootheels approaching the terrace, Alex rose from her seat. While she waited, the thought occurred to her that finding her way about the Duke's estate would be easy. The hard part lay ahead.

Determining who on this world I can trust.

◈

Jaw clenched, Tal hurled the bow away from him.

The arrow disappeared into the gray tunnel. A desperate gambit, he had no way to know if the missile would strike the murderous raider or simply be swallowed up by the Veil's magic. If he managed to escape, the *horde* leader would close the portal and all would be lost...their only chance in a thousand years to finally penetrate the accursed barrier gone in an instant.

The Prince and Heir to the Empire of Meredith squatted and watched with intense green eyes. He brushed a stray lock of copper-colored hair from his face, the powerful muscles in his arms and shoulders rippling as, impatient, he flipped his dagger into the ground only to repeat the process seconds later.

The gateway remained open.

Slowly, he stood on long legs, his attention riveted on the Veil. More moments passed.

The entryway into the enchanted boundary still lingered.

His eyes widened. Still no change.

The entrance beckoned.

Tal could stand the wait no longer. With a cry, he ran to a nearby horse cropping grass. He vaulted onto its back and grabbed the dangling reins. Ignoring the shouts of Bozar, he thundered toward the open doorway.

A dozen heartbeats later, he reached the tunnel...and charged into it.

Upon entry, a momentary disorientation came over him. Then just as quickly, it passed. Bent low on the horse's back, Tal steadied himself by squeezing his thighs against the beast's barrel. The smoky, swirling passageway flew past him. Although having the consistency of mist, the channel somehow still managed to support his weight and that of his mount.

Suddenly, he burst into the open. Bright sunlight assaulted his eyes and he blinked. When his vision cleared, he spotted a glorious sight.

The *horde* leader lay motionless on the ground, a shaft protruding from his body.

The last of the murdering scum from the Veil dead!

Tal slid off his horse and knelt beside the dead raider. A metallic flash at the edge of his vision caused him to turn. His eyes narrowed at the sight of a sprawled arm with the Artifact still clutched in a lifeless grip.

The key to the portal!

A commotion came from the gateway. Seconds later, his First Advisor, Bozar, galloped into the open with the garrison commander, Lord Gravelback, hard on his heels. They pulled up and stared at the sight of Tal beside the dead raider. Bozar, lean and sinewy, studied the scene from horseback with nut-brown eyes, the cinnamon-colored skin of his face pursed in concentration.

Gravelback chose to dismount and approach. Possessed of a barrel-like torso attached to powerful arms and legs, he moved with a fluid stride belying his large size. He stopped beside Tal. Several scars adorned Gravelback's weathered visage, his gray eyes taking in every detail of the dead raid leader.

Tal grinned fiercely and pointed at the Artifact. "The vermin died before he could close the portal." Jubilant, he reached for the magical object when Bozar's cry stopped him.

"Hold!"

Startled, Tal looked up to see his *Eldred* gesture for him to step away. "Do not disturb the body! We must do nothing to cause the Artifact to move."

Frozen in mid-reach, Tal stared at Bozar. "Why?" he snapped. "What harm can come from it?"

Gravelback answered before the First Advisor could reply. "Because even a slight shift might cause the grip on the Artifact to slip and release pressure. The portal could close."

Both men dismounted and joined Tal. He backed away, hands against his chest.

"I-I didn't think."

He swallowed and felt his face flush. *The only opportunity in a millennia to penetrate the Veil and my foolishness almost cost us that chance.*

Bozar gripped Tal's shoulder. "Do not think ill of yourself. If not for you, the way would never have remained open."

Gravelback agreed. "Aye. Your quick thinking slew Marlinda's pet before the murderous bastard could close the doorway."

The enormity of the event sank in, and Tal felt his heart soar. He bounded into the air and shouted, "We did it! The way is open! The Veil is finally breached."

Bozar's normally stoic composure slipped, and laughter spilled from his lips. Even Gravelback lifted his grizzled face to the sky and crowed in exultation.

After more celebrating, Tal collapsed on a nearby knob of rock. The culmination of the events of the past day and night left him drained.

Issuing from the enchanted barrier to pillage, murder, and carry off captives, a *horde* of raiders were surprised by Tal and his corps of flying cavalry. The running battle with the Veil raiders lasted most of the night to finally end with their defeat and total annihilation. Daybreak brought the realization the enemy's leader had somehow managed to escape. Too late, they discovered him hidden in their midst posing as a soldier of the Empire. By the time this ruse was revealed, the *horde* leader had stolen a horse, opened a portal, and fled through it—only to die moments later from Tal's hastily shot arrow. Then, the most important occurrence of all.

The discovery that the portal remained open.

Tal pulled his sword and held it before him, the sharp steel glinting in the light.

He chanted a familiar mantra, one he had mouthed countless times, "Blood shall be paid with blood. And one day, the Dark Queen's blood will paint my blade...this I swear."

He rose and sheathed the sword. *Much work lays before us...an invasion needs to be planned.*

The first step in the conquest of the Veil.

CHAPTER 2

BLUE EYES SPARKLED AT ALEX FROM HER IMAGE IN THE MIRROR. In only a week, the seamstress had produced a number of pantaloons—much to the consternation of Darcy. Her handmaiden expressed concern the attire was not appropriate for a *proper lady*... although the revealing dresses of the previous Alexandria apparently passed this test.

The irony was not lost on Alex.

She also ordered blouses which would match her "riding" attire. The slim fit accentuated her long legs, trim hips, and small waist. No doubt her new apparel would attract attention, but at least she didn't feel self-conscious anymore. Her former Mona self, shy with skinny arms and legs, never drew a second glance. Alex's voluptuous body couldn't be more different, and the exposed flesh most of her clothing revealed *always* drew eyes to her like a spotlight.

When combined with the former Alexandria's bad girl reputation, the two couldn't have been more dissimilar...and the present Alex had no desire to continue in her footsteps.

A knock at the door interrupted her reverie.

"Come," Alex called out.

Tell entered and stopped at the sight of her. "Are you ready," he stammered.

Alex smiled at his reaction. Tell's sun-bronzed face, like the books she studied, always told a story. His true thoughts never drifted far below the surface.

She looped her arm in his. "Let's go."

As they made their way to the stables, Alex reflected on the progress of the past week.

Their routine had been established after the first few forays into Wheel. First, an early breakfast, then into the city to explore and wander. After lunch—usually at a different establishment each day—more meandering. Finally, back to the ducal estate for dinner with the Duke and Dorothea.

Before turning in, Alex made sure she read and studied her books on Dalfur and the Duchy. With each new day, she would question Tell about the maps she scrutinized. Although she still had much to learn, Alex felt she had made significant progress.

Much to her surprise, she found Wheel to be a constant source of delight, and a distraction from the dangers lurking in the Duke's castle. Every day revealed something new about the metropolis and its citizens. The exotic sights, smells, the gaily decorated stalls and shops all combined to thrill her. This served to take her mind off her problems and the potential danger which seemed to lurk all around her.

On any given day, she might stop at a spice stall, wander through a goldsmith's shop, or even purchase a pair of boots from a cobbler. She tried to follow a different path each day in order to make new discoveries.

After negotiating the winding streets and alleys of the city in the elaborate ducal carriage, Alex found many of Wheel's minor avenues impassable. Too narrow for the coach, many times they were forced to walk long distances. Although Alex didn't mind the stroll, the time it took to navigate these pathways robbed her of what she really wanted to do—continue her exploration of the city.

Frustrated, several days earlier, Alex convinced Tell to let her ride a horse. After much reassurance to her father the Duke—he still remained fearful she could take another fall from the saddle—they no longer used the coach except when the weather threatened.

Unfortunately, in her former life on earth, she never so much as sat on a horse, much less ridden one. She hoped some sort of muscle memory remained from the former Alexandria.

No such luck existed for her.

Despite being provided with the gentlest mare Tell could find, Alex was bruised and sore after just a day of riding. Her muscles, unused to the activity, protested to the point she needed Darcy's help just to get out of bed the next morning. Doggedly, she kept after it, and after a few days, the act of riding began to feel more natural...and less painful.

The smell of hay and manure brought her back to the present, and signaled their approach to the stables. Grooms stood at the ready, their horses already saddled, and their escort, a pair of mounted guardsmen, waited nearby. One of the grooms placed a set of wooden steps next to Alex's horse, a gray mare named Lolly, and she stepped up and onto her mount. A short time later they rode through the castle gates and onto the main thoroughfare into Wheel.

They eventually stopped at a stand Alex discovered earlier in the week. Surrounded by fresh-cut flowers, the scent of a dozen different varieties surrounded the stall. Alex purchased an armful of long-stemmed flowers with enormous blue petals. She paid a young woman behind the floral stall a silver coin from her purse.

Money apparently wasn't a problem for the daughter of a Duke, and Alex took full advantage—her room always had fresh flowers now.

"Don't bother with any change," she said with a smile.

The girl's eyes widened. She curtsied. "Th-thank you, M'Lady."

Alex handed the flowers to Tell who in turn, passed the bouquet to a guard who placed them in a pannier hanging from his saddle.

Tell helped Alex up into her saddle. "What is your pleasure now?" he asked.

Alex placed her hand on his. "Can we go someplace new?"

Tell chuckled. "Of course. Why should today be any different?"

When Tell moved to mount his own horse, his hand momentarily brushed her thigh. Alex's skin tingled from his touch—and with it, confused feelings.

Am I falling in love with him? Is he falling in love with me?

She had never been in love…she didn't know what it felt like. She recalled her dream from the night before. It seemed so real! The mysterious man in this vision left her breathless with desire. While Tell elicited a certain attraction, *nothing* had ever affected her like this.

But isn't love—real love—more than just physical attraction?

She shook her head. What she needed was a friend, someone she could confide in. Darcy, her sweet handmaiden, would listen to anything she had to say…and then promptly share it with the cook, the stable groom, and anyone else she might cross paths with. A merry, compulsive gossip, the girl couldn't help herself.

That left Tell.

Her eyes settled on him. Puzzled, he cocked his head. "What's wrong?"

Alex swallowed and waved her hand. "Oh, nothing. Just some silly thoughts." She urged Lolly into a trot to forestall any further questions.

She led them deeper into Wheel than any previous foray. The sprawling city, home to over half a million citizens, contained numerous bridges spanning the meandering Misty River. They crossed the main bridge bisecting the city, carved statues of long dead Dukes flanking either side, and made their way into the eastern part of the metropolis. Following a now familiar pattern, Alex dismounted and strolled alongside cobbled lanes to stop and peer inside the windows of each establishment.

Near the noon hour, they came to a wide intersection which broadened to allow branching avenues to run along either side of a building. Constructed to conform to the forked boulevard, the structure was a three-story affair with a sharp angular frontage. It reminded Alex of the prow of a large ship.

A sign of unusual size and length ran from one side of the edifice to the other. Because of the structure's wedged façade, she had to ride first to one side of the building, then to the other to read the sign in its entirety:

Pandergast's Emporium: Antiques & Antiquities; Artifacts Bought, Sold, & Repaired; Sweets, Cold Drinks, & Ice Cream Parlor; Books, Parchments, & Scrolls Bought and Sold; Lodestones Bought, Sold & Re-Charged; Used Furniture & Apothecary Shoppe

Alex looked at the sign with undisguised curiosity. Even Tell looked on in amazement. The day had warmed considerably, and Alex's eyes lingered on the *Cold Drinks & Ice Cream Parlor* advertising.

"Let's stop here," she said.

Alex slid off Lolly and handed the reins to one of the guardsmen. She walked up to one of the doors straddling either side of the unusual building. She pushed the door open and a pleasant tinkle announced her entry.

As she began to enter the shop, a movement caught her eye. Startled, she whipped her head around but spotted only the building's shadow draped across the cobbled street.

Despite the bright sunshine, Alex felt a chill. *Am I imagining things?* With a shake of her head, she stepped inside.

Unseen, a dim shadow followed her.

CHAPTER 3

TAL STUDIED THEIR SURROUNDINGS. THE LAND LOOKED UNFAMILIAR.
"Strange. We traveled less than a league through the wormhole, yet this area bears little resemblance to the woodlands we left behind."

Low rolling hills spread out before them. Although pockets of trees appeared at intervals, grasslands were the dominant feature. A cloudless blue sky stretched overhead.

Gravelback looked up and squinted. "Aye. Even the sun appears higher than it should be."

Bozar turned slowly, his sharp eyes taking in every feature of land and sky. He nodded to himself.

"The theory is true. This proves it," he mumbled.

Tal frowned. "Eh? What theory?"

Bozar pointed at the swirling wormhole. "It has long been known the magic of the Veil distorts time and space. What isn't known is *how*. Without that knowledge, we have never been able to unravel its magic or find a way through."

The First Advisor waved a hand at the land around them. "Because of this distortion, we believe the foul magic of the barrier forces any entry or exit point to be angular rather than linear. The Dark Queen's Gatemasters know how to use this to control the placement and recall of the *hordes*."

Gravelback snorted. "For those of us who have not enjoyed a University education, pray enlighten us with a simpler explanation."

Bozar smiled. "I mean the wormhole doesn't follow a straight line-of-sight path. The portal can place raiders hundreds of leagues from the original gate they enter or exit from. The Veil Queen's sorcerers then manipulate this anomaly to choose locations from which *hordes* can raid—virtually anywhere along the Veil."

The grizzled garrison commander spat. "No wonder we can never predict where the murdering bastards will come from."

Tal took a new interest in their surroundings. After a slow pivot, he said, "We need a map."

Gravelback hurried to his mount and pulled a rolled parchment from the saddle. He tossed it in the air where it hung suspended. He touched the edge and it unrolled and expanded. Constructed of a thin vellum, the chart was blank and featureless.

"Location," he barked.

The map rippled. Suddenly, features appeared and flashed by with increasing velocity. A golden glow flared and when it cleared, a meticulous diagram of topographic features appeared. A blue flicker flashed on and off to indicate their location. Tal and Bozar joined Gravelback to study the map.

"Aerial," Tal commanded. Their location began to shrink as a birds-eye view appeared. Tal reached out and touched the map. It froze and he moved closer. He traced a line with his finger and then stopped.

His eyes widened and he jabbed at the map. "Look. Here is where we entered the wormhole, and here," he moved his finger down the chart, "is where we are now."

Tal shook his head. "We are at least four hundred leagues southeast of our camp."

They crowded closer to the chart.

After more manipulations and study, Tal, Gravelback, and Bozar stepped back and conferred.

Gravelback pointed at the map. "Markingham is the only city of any size in this entire area. Farther south are steppes and then the Sea of Sand…which means little water and food. Due north is Wheel, but it is five hundred leagues away through dense forest, across several rivers, and with one mountain range to negotiate."

The garrison commander looked up. "I say we make for Markingham. Although over a hundred leagues due east, it is a perfect staging location. With our army based there the Empire can—"

"Much needs to be done before any military action can take place, Lord Gravelback," Bozar quickly interjected.

The grizzled commander's eyes narrowed. "You are mistaken, First Advisor. I can have an expeditionary force ready in a matter of weeks."

Bozar inclined his head. "I'm sure you can, Commander. However, there are other considerations which must be decided first."

"What? What madness is this?" The garrison commander thrust a finger at Bozar. "The longer we wait the possibility for more raids and killings exists…and more victims that black-hearted bitch will take."

Bozar held the commander's enraged eyes calmly. "We still don't know how or why the portal remains open."

"The evidence is right before you! It lays dead at your feet! The Prince killed the raid leader before the portal could be closed."

"Too close to a Watch Tower to have been opened in the first place, and with no certainty it will remain so."

"Do not listen to him, Sire!" Face red, Gravelback turned to Tal. "We have waited so long, so many have been murdered, carried off into slavery or worse. We must have our revenge—"

"*Lord Gravelback!*" Bozar's countenance took on a steely expression. "You forget yourself."

The garrison commander's mouth opened and closed several times. Teeth gritted, he mumbled, "My pardon."

Bozar nodded. "We all want to end the monstrosity of the Veil and all it stands for. But to rush in without thought or planning is the height of folly."

Tal followed the exchange closely. Like Gravelback, he wanted to immediately plunge in and at long last, bring the fight to the Veil Queen and King.

Which is how I found myself here to begin with…my reckless actions.

The inner voice gave him pause. He sighed and nodded at Bozar. "Go on, my *Eldred*."

Bozar folded his hands. "Let us assume the Dark Queen is unaware of the open door through the Veil. What would happen once she discovers this?"

"The she-bitch would close it," Gravelback grudgingly answered.

"Knowing this, what should our first and most important course of action?"

This time, Tal answered. "Make sure the Veil Queen doesn't find out."

"Of course. Now, imagine the difficulty of moving an invading army through the magical barrier without Marlinda somehow catching wind of it. The Empire is infested with the Dark Queen's spies, particularly Meredith City."

"So these spies exist. So what?" Gravelback retorted. "It changes nothing. We send an army large enough to overcome anything the Veil filth can muster against us, and destroy them. What difference does it make if they see their doom coming with eyes open or shut? The result is the same."

Bozar ignored the outburst and continued. "Imagine further the consequences if this happens. Part of the army trapped once the Veil is again impenetrable? Part caught in passage and crushed when the wormhole collapses? Maybe the Dark Queen's own host waiting for our soldiers to appear so they can be slaughtered as they exit?"

Gravelback's face took on a deeper shade of red.

"Then there is the wormhole itself. Even if we manage to keep this a secret, the proximity of the Watch Tower may close it anyway. How a gateway managed to open so close to a Tower remains a mystery to me. Regardless, we *must* make sure it stays open."

Bozar turned to Tal. "As you know, I have already sent for Artemis Thurgood from the University where he teaches at the Royal Academy of Magic. He is an expert on the Veil and may be able to provide us with the answers we seek. What harm could come from waiting a few days to hear his findings?"

The grizzled commander slammed a fist into his palm. "Damn you, Bozar," Gravelback growled, "you weave words like your magic, with silken threads designed to entice and entrap."

A frustrated sigh escaped from his lips. "But…as much as I hate to admit it, you may be right. I suppose we must be sure before we proceed further."

A thin smile played across the First Advisor's face. "Thank you, Lord Gravelback. Now, we need to return. There is much to be done."

They mounted their horses, and one-by-one, entered the whirling tunnel to return. Tal, the last to leave, stopped and took one last look at the dead raider. He smiled and fingered his lodestone beads.

One more to add…with many more to come.

He turned and disappeared into the magical passageway.

CHAPTER 4

ALEX, WITH TELL AT HER SIDE, LOOKED AROUND, WIDE-EYED. A wonderful aroma came to her nose and she inhaled deeply. She couldn't quite place the delightful scent—like a combination of incense, spices, candy, old leather, and rose perfume.

A scarred, hardwood floor led to the ice cream parlor located directly in front of her. A polished wooden bar in a "V" contour flanked each side of the shop. Padded circular seats mounted on metal struts and attached to the floor ran alongside either side of the bar. Long wooden handles fastened to spigots jutted upward from behind the counter, while nearby, ice cream cones of every size and description formed pyramids.

Alex stepped farther into the shop, drinking in the wonderful sights and smells.

Multicolored candies of various sizes, shapes, and flavors rested in glass containers on one side of the wooden counter. Nearby, parfait glasses were grouped meticulously. Behind the wooden counter stood a large structure with a glass front. Frost decorated the glass and as Alex moved closer, she could see it held tubs of ice cream.

A sign located above the freezer advertised all the flavors of ice cream. Alex tried counting them all and gave up after she got past forty.

A small area in the otherwise crowded store contained several round tables and chairs...another area where patrons could sit and enjoy a cold drink or ice cream if they didn't want to sit at the counter. Alex looked at Tell, her eyes gleaming.

The young lieutenant chuckled. "I guess I'll take a seat while you make your choices." He walked to one of the tables and sat.

Alex moved to the bar and waited. The concession area appeared deserted and when she looked around, she could see no one. Puzzled she opened her mouth to call out, when a voice interrupted her.

"Be there in a moment." The sound came from the back of the store, and moments later, a figure appeared.

Alex's mouth dropped.

A small man walked toward her. Less than five feet tall, he look unlike any man she had ever seen.

Large, pointed ears swept up from either side of an olive green face. A few wispy hairs strayed from an otherwise bald pate, while merry eyes of lavender purple peered from an oval face. Flattened nostrils flared outward above smiling lips and a sharp, pointed chin. The "man's" head perched on a thin neck, and he wore an apron tied around a rotund waist.

"May I help you?" he asked.

Alex stared and stammered for a reply. Tell saved her from further embarrassment. "You're a…gnome?" He had stood and moved to Alex's side.

The little man chuckled. "In the flesh."

Wonder in his voice, Tell said, "I have never seen a gnome and only heard stories from my father and grandfather."

The gnome sighed. "Ah, yes. Sadly, we are not as numerous as we used to be."

He rubbed his hands together. "But where are my manners? My name is Pandathaway Pandergast, the proprietor of this store."

He took Alex's hand and placed it to his lips. "Welcome to my humble shop."

When he returned her hand, his eyes suddenly widened in recognition. "La-Lady Alexandria?" A guarded look momentarily flashed across his face before the ready smile returned.

The gnome rushed to move a table and chair next to Alex. "Please have a seat." He waved at the extensive list of offerings. "Do you see anything which interests you? Of course, it is on the house."

The diminutive gnome called over his shoulder, "Lillian, we have customers!"

A pair of swinging doors parted behind the bar and a female gnome exited wiping her hands on a towel. Golden brown hair, streaked with gray, was wound into a tight bun and placed beneath a scarf on her head. Twinkling brown eyes took in the scene before her. "What is all the excite—"

The tiny gnome spotted Alex. "Pandathaway! You didn't tell me the Lady Alexandria was our visitor!" Lillian scolded. She turned and asked, "How may we serve you?"

Intrigued by the diminutive pair, Alex answered, "Ice cream and a cold drink sounds delightful. However, your list is...impressive. Do you have any suggestions?"

Pandathaway hopped behind the wooden counter and described various confectionary combinations. When he finished, Alex chose a razzleberry sundae along with a drink the gnome called a *Cherry-Fizzle Surprise*. Tart yet sweet, the beverage was a perfect accompaniment to the mouth-watering sundae. Alex sighed with contentment when she finished.

Alex insisted on paying despite the gnome's protestations. While Pandathaway put the coins away, she asked, "How did you come by such a curious and lengthy sign?"

By this time, she and Tell were seated at the counter, and Pandathaway climbed onto one of the padded seats beside Alex.

"An excellent question, Lady Alexandria, and the abbreviated version is I established my shop when I retired from the Duke's service."

He scratched his chin. "Although it has been a number of years, I remember you as a young girl running up and down the Duke's estate, your nurse in desperate pursuit." His eyes crinkled in amusement at the memory.

Alex shook her head. "I-I'm, sorry. I don't remember you."

The gnome cocked his head and studied her. "Forgive me, Lady Alexandria, but there seems something different about you…I can't quite put my finger on it."

Lillian reached from behind the counter to slap him on the arm. "Her accident!"

Pandathaway threw up his hands. "Of course. Please pardon my insensitivity, Lady Alexandria."

The warm feelings Alex felt earlier evaporated. *He knows I've changed. But how? By his own admission he hasn't had contact with the ducal family in years.*

She cleared her throat. "There is nothing to forgive…and please call me Alex."

"Alex it is then" he said warmly. "As I was saying, I opened my shop when I retired from the Duke's service. I couldn't decide which type of business most interested me, so I finally decided I would open a shop which encompassed them all."

He leaned forward and chuckled. "Although there is certainly something to be said for specializing in only a few things, I *can* say it has kept me busy when business in one area is slow. When that happens, I pick up sales in another area."

"What he really means is that he is a stubborn old gnome who can't make up his mind!" Lillian called out from behind the bar. "Tell M'Lady the last time we had a vacation."

Pandathaway held up his hands in mock resignation, then stood and waved a hand at the store's interior. "Would you like a tour?"

Alex's eyes glowed. "I would love it."

Pandathaway guided Alex and Tell through the huge, multi-storied building. Every available space displayed an item for sale. Clothes lined rack after rack in one corner, mismatched furniture in another. Garden tools, used swords, crossbows, and other weapons were displayed side-by-side, and next to them, shelves holding glass containers of spices, tea, powders, and other elixirs. The scent of peppermint, cinnamon, and cloves, tickled Alex's nose. Although she could make out no rhyme or reason for their placement, the gnome seemed to know the precise location for every item in his store.

Late afternoon had fallen when Tell nudged Alex. The hours passed so quickly, she lost track of time. She sighed in disappointment as Pandathaway led them back to the front of the store.

I had such a good time.

They descended a flight of stairs and reached the landing above the street level of the store. Alex paused when she saw an unusual corkscrewed staff leaning against the railing. She picked up the staff and studied it. About five feet in length, intricate scrollwork embossed its surface end-to-end. Mounted on the knobbed end was a large blue lodestone. As Alex looked closer, she realized the staff had been divided into sections, the scrollwork filigreed in different colors.

Sensing a sale, Pandathaway approached Alex. "Ah, you have a Staff of the Test. It is used by Magisters at local magical Academies to test applicants. The Staff measures each student's potential for magic. They must pass the Test before they will be allowed to enroll."

He pointed to a collar of gray-black metal located halfway up the staff. "The student's magical aptitude must reach this level."

24

Intrigued, Alex looked at the staff with renewed interest. "How does it work? I mean, how can you tell if someone's magical ability has reached an acceptable level?"

The gnome smiled and pointed at the segments on the staff. "It glows to produce a luminescence in response to a student's magical potential. This radiance begins at the bottom and moves upward. How far up the staff the luminescence travels is in direct proportion to the student's latent talent for magic. It must rise to at least halfway in order for a student to be considered for enrollment."

Puzzled, Alex fingered the length of intricately etched wood.

"Here, let me show you," Pandathaway said, and instructed Alex to hold the staff with one hand at the top and the other at the bottom.

"Hold it straight out in front of you," he directed. "Now, close your eyes and concentrate."

Alex frowned. "What do I concentrate on?"

"Ah, that is part of the test. Just clear your mind of all thoughts and the staff will do the rest."

Alex dutifully let her mind drift, the wooden rod held out in front of her. This went on for so long, she heard Tell, impatient, clear his throat. Feeling foolish, she moved to put the staff aside when an odd sensation filled her. It was similar to the feeling she experienced when her former governess tried to penetrate her mind, and again when the Rodric attacked her with Darcy's body.

A part of her mind seemed to open a crack from which a brilliant shaft of energy poured. She staggered, and Pandathaway, close beside her, immediately grasped Alex's arm to steady her. Tell, quick to do the same, jumped to her side and held her other arm. She opened her eyes to see looks of concern on both their faces.

"Alex, what's wrong? Are you unwell?" Tell asked.

Alex felt her face flush at the worry she caused. She cast a rueful look at both Alex and the gnomish shopkeeper, then realized she still held the Staff of the Test.

It looked no different than before.

She handed it back to the gnome. "I guess I have no magical ability."

Pandathaway chuckled as he took the staff. "The lodestone hasn't been charged in years. Even Alabaster John himself couldn't have coaxed a reaction from this Artifact. It is a curiosity, nothing more." The shopkeeper leaned the length of wood back against the railing and led them down the stairs to the store's entrance.

"Please come again—"

The gnome whirled and crouched. He studied the area behind them, and his eyes narrowed as they came to rest on a pool of shadow at the foot of the stair.

Tell's hand flew to the hilt of his sword. "What is it?"

Pandathaway held his gaze a moment longer. Finally he turned and chuckled. "Oh, it's nothing, lieutenant. Just felt like we were being watched. I'm getting jumpy in my old age, I guess." Although the gnome attempted to make light of his reaction, he wasn't able to completely mask the concern on his face.

They exchanged pleasant goodbyes. Pandathaway and Lillian stood at the door and waved as they rode away.

A pang of regret filled Alex. She already missed the gnomish couple, and determined she would visit them again...soon.

She thought about the gnomish shopkeeper's reaction, and a persistent itch scratched at her back...like a hidden pair of eyes followed her every move.

It followed her all the way back to the ducal castle.

Pandathaway prepared to join his wife in bed.

He stifled a yawn as he pulled the cover back and climbed in. Their bedroom, located on the third and topmost floor, had been declared off limits by Lillian to the store's products, and so remained reasonably tidy and uncluttered.

Lillian looked up from the book she was reading. "The Duke's daughter seems like such a nice and pleasant girl…not anything like her reputation."

Pandathaway fluffed his pillow and collapsed on his back with a contented sigh. He stared at the ceiling. "She looks like Alexandria and sounds like Alexandria, but nothing about her is as I remember…. almost like a different soul inhabits her body."

Lillian frowned and she looked over at her husband. "Oh, Pandathaway, you can't be serious. She fell from a horse and suffered an injury, nothing more."

He shook his head. "I sensed something about her when she held the Staff of the Test. It felt like." He searched for words. "It felt like an ancient magic, rare and powerful."

He shrugged. "But of course, the staff showed no reaction to her touch and remained as dormant as a rock." He sighed and with a gesture, turned out his bedside lamp.

Pandathaway leaned over and kissed Lillian. "Forgive my ruminations, my dear. I'm an old gnome and given to flights of fancy. Goodnight."

Lillian placed her book aside and crossed her arms. "You don't fool me Pandathaway Pandergast. I've seen that look before, no matter how well you try to disguise it. Put this out of your mind or you won't get a wink of sleep tonight."

"No worries, my love. It has been a long day and tomorrow will be here soon enough." He turned over, and soon soft snores dribbled from his lips.

Lillian turned out her light and joined her husband in slumber.

Pandathaway felt someone shaking him.

"Wake up! Pandathaway, wake up!" Lillian whispered urgently.

Groggy, he mumbled, "Wh-what is it?"

"A light is on."

"Eh?"

"There's a light on. Someone is in the store!"

All sleepiness left him in an instant. He rolled out of bed and rummaged around in a nearby closet for a crossbow. He pulled the drawstring back and fixed it in a firing position.

"Stay here," he ordered, "and lock the door behind me."

Lillian, face filled with fear, nodded. Pandathaway exited their bedroom and made his way down the nearby stairway.

Eyes adjusted to the darkness, he clearly spotted a bright glow down below. He carefully placed his bare feet one step after another to minimize any sound or creak from the stairs. The further he progressed down the steps, the brighter the glow became. He finally came to the second story landing, the light now so intense, he had to shield his eyes with his free hand.

The crossbow tumbled from his hand to hit the floor with a *clunk*. There, where he had leaned it against the stairwell, stood the Staff of the Test. Bright white light surged from the lodestone.

And every section lit up like a beacon.

CHAPTER 5

W IND WHISTLED BY TAL'S EARS.
Exhilaration always filled him when riding the winged horses. His mount slashed effortlessly through the cold, crisp air, its powerful wings beating a cadence. They flew high enough to make it difficult to be seen by any prying eyes from the ground below.

Below, a vista of green forests and fields sprinkled with azure lakes, ponds, and the occasional lonely farmhouse, spread toward the distant horizon. The long, ribbon of the blue Stollar River meandered in loops and curves. Originating in the distant Blue Teeth Mountains to the north, the river flowed south and toward the even more distant Ocean of Dreams.

The snow-capped peaks of the Three Sisters appeared directly south of them. The extinct volcanoes lifted their rugged cones precipitously into the sky. To the southwest, Tal could make out the beginnings of low foothills which meant their destination neared. The ancient and weathered remains of this once mighty mountain range, stretched hundreds of miles in a line due east and west. Today, only heavily forested hills and glens along with an occasional bald knob of granite, remained. Waldez had been founded and built on one of these rocky outcroppings three hundred years earlier.

Tal's thoughts returned to the plan that his First Advisor and Lord Gravelback, had hammered out the previous day.

"Utmost secrecy must be maintained," Bozar had admonished

Tal again and again. "The Queen's Lord Governor of the Waldez Prefect, Gullbard Stokely, will ask questions about your visit. Your banishment to the least populated province in the Empire, however, will provide the perfect excuse…you're bored."

His *Eldred* cast Tal a wry look. "For once, your hotheaded reputation works in our favor. Harder to explain is why *you* need to escort Artemis Thurgood. Just stick to the simple explanation that since you are returning to the garrison outpost, you will bring my old friend back as a favor to me."

Tal wrenched his thoughts back to the present, and glanced at his escort. Spread out like a formation of geese, they formed a "V" with Tal at the point and ten winged riders on either side. A smile came to his lips at Gravelback's insistence that *his* men form the escort.

The gruff garrison commander had said, "Every one of my men has been blood-sworn to me. I have known most of them since they were babes at their mother's tit. More importantly, they share my vision when it comes to matters of Marlinda's accursed raiders."

"And what is this vision, Lord Gravelback?" Bozar had asked.

"Death to every Veil raider! And because of that, I can vouch for my men's silence. They will do nothing to threaten the possibility to kill even more of the evil vermin."

Tal fingered the lodestone beads in the leather braid tying his long hair back.

I couldn't agree more.

Several hours later, evidence they were drawing closer to Waldez appeared in the form of farms and homesteads dotting the landscape below. The habitations grew more numerous with each passing league, and a summit came to view on the distant horizon. Tal grunted in satisfaction at the sight of the most important military outpost in the Empire.

Dark specks rose from the citadel and moved in their direction. Wheeling into the air, these "specks" surrounded them and resolved into a flying wing of Imperial cavalry.

A voice, transmitted from the communication Artifact worn on Tal's wrist, resounded in his ear. "Identify yourselves immediately!"

"Prince Talmund and escort," Tal replied. "Here to accompany Artemis Thurgood from the gateway back to the garrison outpost."

"And why would the Prince and Heir be engaged in such a menial task?" the voice demanded. "Such things are left to underlings."

Tal quelled the impulse to bark an angry retort. The history of Waldez dripped with the blood of the Empire's soldiers. It took fifty years to construct the mighty fortress, each one marked by repeated savage attacks from Marlinda's sorcerers, melded beasts, and her army of turncoats and traitors. The Dark Queen knew the citadel, once completed, would be impregnable. Waldez's ideal location could prevent incursions and raids along a wide swath of the Veil. While direct assaults on the fortress ended centuries ago, the Dark Queen's spies and saboteurs continued to wreak havoc whenever possible.

Tal decided to ignore the suspicious nature of the cavalry commander.

"Because any chance to get away from staring at a dreary barracks wall is one I would jump at," he answered. "Including a trip to Waldez."

Tal played his role of angry, bored prince to the hilt, and added, "Is this how you greet all members of the royal family?"

Silence followed before the voice returned with a penitent tone. "My apologies...Sire. If you'll follow me we'll accompany you to the citadel. I'm afraid once we arrive you and your men will have to surrender your weapons until we can validate your identity."

The commander barked orders, and his forty riders swooped down to join Tal's escort. Then he moved his mount next to Tal, the wingtips of the flying horses almost brushing against one another. As they made their final approach to Waldez, Tal took the time to study the mighty fortress.

The citadel was perched above a vale sandwiched by heavily forested hills. A stream ran through the valley floor, and flowed past the stronghold. A prosperous city sprouted at the foot of the citadel, and a well-maintained road led to the bastion. One glance reinforced every story Tal ever heard about Waldez.

The fortress was unassailable.

Built atop the summit of a granite pillar thrusting half a league above the weathered hills, Waldez held a commanding position. This gave the citadel a dominant tactical advantage over any force sent against it. Furthermore, the only access from ground level was the vale road which ascended up the granite knob. Hewn from the column of rock, the narrow lane formed switchbacks as it climbed the sheer stone facing. Any invaders intrepid enough to use the road, would find themselves under constant assault from the fortress above. Death would rain down in the form of arrows, javelins, stones, and boiling oil. While struggling up the steep road, the raiders would be unable to return fire with any accuracy.

If an enemy force managed to survive the approach, they would find an iron portcullis guarding entry into Waldez with little room to batter the entrance open. The road formed a sharp right angle as it ended at the gate. On one side was the sheer rock-face of the granite mountain, while the other side presented the gate itself. Only a low wall on the outside of the road protected travelers from a precipitous drop of hundreds of feet.

The battlements atop the fortress bristled with catapults, arrow slits, and the black metal of *scorpions*, ballista capable of releasing a hail of bolts at airborne attackers. Proof against attacks of sorcery, lodestones—kept fully charged with magic—completely encircled the fortress.

Tal nodded in appreciation. *Small wonder the Veil Queen and King tried so hard to stop the construction of Waldez, or why, after its completion, large-scale attacks on the citadel stopped.*

The formation of riders wheeled about and approached the flank of the stone peak. A slot-like opening had been excavated from the rock. The wide flyway, like that for a hive of bees, allowed up to fifty of the flying horses to enter or leave at a time. A brace of the menacing *scorpions* guarded the entrance from unwelcome visitors.

Tal followed the commander and glided into the flyway. Shadow replaced the bright sunlight, and the clatter of hooves echoed in the cavern. Grooms caught the bridles of the horses while the cavalrymen dismounted, and led them to the stables.

Tal's escort surrounded him, hands on their swords as soldiers approached to take their weapons. A powerful voice called out. "No need for that."

A tall official wearing the Empire Crest of a Lord Governor, pushed his way through the soldiers. Hair a steel-gray, he wore a short sword and dagger beside his right hand for quick use. Brown eyes, perched above a beard peppered with gray, apprised Tal.

The Lord Governor greeted him with palm head-to-heart. "Welcome to Waldez, Prince Talmund.

"Now, why are you here?"

CHAPTER 6

ALEX PRESSED TELL'S WARM LIPS AGAINST HERS.

They stood just outside her suite on the sun-drenched terrace. Her back against the stone façade framing the veranda doors, she held the lieutenant tight against her. The musky scent of horses, camp smoke, and resin soap clung to the legionnaire. She kissed him again, and this time, he returned her kiss with a ferocity which caused a kindling of heat within her.

"Long have I dreamed of this," Tell's husky voice whispered in her ear.

"And I as well," Alex murmured.

What started as a discussion about the plans for the day, turned in an instant to their passionate embrace. Having just strolled outside, the light had struck Tell's sun-browned face and highlighted his rugged features. His clear, sea-blue eyes drew Alex into their depths.

Before she could stop herself, she drew him to her and kissed him.

She couldn't explain it. Maybe it was her sense of extreme isolation. Maybe the loneliness within her had grown to the point she could bear it no more. Living on the knife's edge since her arrival on Meredith left her with an understanding of just how short life could be.

I want to be loved once, just once before—

A peripheral movement caught her eye. She whipped her

head around and a pool of shadow quivered beside one of the ornamental trees. She blinked and looked again.

The shadow lay unmoving.

Tell stiffened in her arms. "What? What is it?" He stepped back and drew his sword.

Alex shook her head. "Nothing. I thought I saw something move, but it's only the shade of a tree."

She reached for Tell again…then dropped her hand. The moment had passed. Instead she patted his sword arm. "I'm sorry. I didn't mean to startle you."

Disappointment flashed across his face. "Of course." To her relief, he didn't mention their ardent embrace.

Tell motioned to the door. "Shall we go?"

Alex nodded. *The city will be a delightful distraction.* Later she could try to sort her thoughts and come to a conclusion.

On how I feel about Tell.

Dorothea listened intently.

Duke Alton Duvalier, her husband, lay abed snoring loudly despite the late morning hour. His red hair liberally streaked with grey, his pallid skin gray, the slow poison she slipped into his drink every night continued to milk his vitality. This allowed her abundant time to be about her business.

She sat before a large, gilded vanity, the remains of her breakfast beside her on a silver tray. The mirror in front of her reflected not just her pale beauty, but something else.

A dark shape at her ear.

The shade quivered, jellylike, as sibilant words flowed from it. Legs, arms, head, and torso oozed in and out of shape, disappearing then re-forming.

Dorothea's lips pressed into a thin line. Cold fury burned within her at the shade's muttered report. "Go!" she commanded. "Do not let Alexandria out of your sight." The shade whispered across the bed chamber and flowed under the crack between the door and floor.

She stood, pulled her robes tighter, and hurried to an adjacent room. She shut and bolted the door. Pouring water from a pitcher into a glass bowl, Dorothea mumbled an incantation. The water rippled…then resolved into an image.

Rodric.

He wore his familiar cruel smile.

"My, my, aren't I the popular fellow? Contacted twice before the moons have even completed a cycle. I'd blush if I knew how."

"Shut up!" Dorothea snarled, in no mood for Rodric's barbed quips. "I want you to return immediately to Wheel."

Rodric's mouth dropped. His image leaned closer. "Truly? What happened to your demand I exile myself—"

"Alexandria is falling in love! I knew I couldn't trust her!"

"What? *Who* is she falling in love with?" Rodric demanded.

"The young lieutenant in charge of her guard detail," she spat.

Rodric's face twisted. "Then have him dismissed. Better yet, arrange for him to have an accident."

"You fool!" Dorothea snapped. "If only it was that simple."

Rodric's eyes flashed. "Yes, *death* is an easy and final solution. Pray why, oh wise Dorothea, do you so quickly discard this 'simple' answer to our problem?"

The Duchess sat back, and with great effort, reigned in her temper. "First, Lord Ruffin, the Duke's Military Advisor, recommended the Lieutenant's commission. Second, he comes from a well-respected family which supplies many of the horses for the flying legions. He can't suffer a fatal accident, or be summarily dismissed without good reason. Both would produce an outcry for an investigation."

She leaned forward. "How many times have I explained this? Murder—your favorite method of choice—often causes more problems than it solves."

"Enough of your tedious lectures!" Rodric barked. "Stop wasting my time and explain how my speedy return to Wheel resolves this situation."

Dorothea smoothed her robe and took a deep breath. "You will leave for Wheel straightaway. Once you arrive, arrange a private meeting with the Duke. Tell him of your love for Alexandria, explain you can't bear to be separated from her any longer. Ask for her hand. The old fool has been expecting such a request from you for some time now. I have no doubt he will grant your betrothal to Alexandria.

"But, you *must* get him to agree to a much shorter engagement. Before Alexandria can involve herself in anymore mischief."

Pitching forward, face inches from the bowl, Dorothea hissed, "And *you* will make sure she doesn't interfere with our carefully laid plans. Woo her, *pretend* to be charming, shower her with gifts. Most of all, give her no reason to challenge your marriage proposal."

An amused look appeared on Rodric's face. "Very well. I'll play the part of doting suitor. Just remember our earlier bargain. Once Wheel is ours and Alexandria has whelped a brood for the Dark Queen's purposes, then she is mine."

He rubbed his hands. "Mine to do with as I please."

Alex sat alone on the darkened terrace.

Unable to sleep, the low roar of the falls and the hum of the city far below serenaded her. The clarity of the night sky and its myriad of stars provided a beauty she never tired of.

My favorite place to think.

Her thoughts returned to Tell, the taste of his lips, the press of his hard body against hers. She now realized how close she came to giving herself to him right then and there.

But why? Do I love him, or am I driven by something as simple as lust?

She occupied the body of Alexandria, but her mind and spirit were Mona's...and Mona's experience in matters of the heart wouldn't fill a thimble.

What she *did* know was the way passion exploded like fireworks within her when Tell held her tight. It left her giddy...she never felt so alive.

Frustrated, a tear slid down her cheek. *Why is everything so complicated?*

She stood to return to her bed, and to the restless sleep which awaited her.

***

Alex stood in a field filled with a sea of yellow wildflowers.

Bright sunlight from a cloudless blue sky warmed her skin. An ancient oak, massive and moss-covered, occupied the middle of the meadow. She recognized the scene.

The same one from her earlier dream.

Bare toes dug into the soft loam, and her thin nightgown rippled in the gentle breeze. She searched, not for Tell, but for the one who haunted her dreams, the one who ignited such a fire within her.

There, there he is!

Reclined on one of the oak's lower limbs, his back rested against the hoary trunk, his long legs stretched out before him.

He beckoned to her.

Hand clutched to her breast, Alex's breath came out in explosive gasps. Once again, a molten desire erupted in her.

She picked up her skirt and ran to him.

Breathless, she arrived at the base of the huge tree. Face hidden by a bough of leaves, the young man reached down and, effortlessly, pulled her up. Once on the limb, he positioned Alex so her back was against him. Then he put his arms around her and held her tight. Alex rested her head on his muscular shoulder. She closed her eyes and savored the feel of his warm embrace.

He smelled of earth and sky, of leather and, masculinity. His broad hands caressed her bare arms, and her yearning faded to a dull ache, replaced by something she hadn't felt in such a long, long time.

Peace.

CHAPTER 7

TAL EYED GULLBARD STOKELY AND CONSIDERED HIS REPLY.

"As I explained to your patrol commander, I am here as a favor to Bozar, my *Eldred*, to retrieve his friend, Artemis Thurgood, and provide escort back to the frontier garrison."

The Lord Governor stroked his beard. "You must pardon me for asking, but why would you, a Crown Prince, be engaged in so lowly a task?"

Heat crept into Tal's voice. "I've explained that as well. I'm sure you're aware of my situation and know of my...*posting*. At this point, any excuse to leave the dreary confines of the wilderness barracks is one I would jump at."

A broad smile slowly grew across Gullbard Stokely's face. "I knew your father, Mathias, well. I can see you are much like him."

The cord of anger building in Tal loosened. "A high compliment—though I can scarce hope to ever fill his shoes."

The tension dissolved, and Stokely reached forward to grip Tal's hand. "Welcome, Sire. Since this is your first trip to the Citadel of Waldez, please allow me to take you on a brief tour of the fortress."

Tal nodded eagerly. The Lord Governor signaled for stewards who appeared and led Tal's escort away for food and rest.

Stokely motioned. "This is my son, Brandon."

The leader of the flying wing which intercepted them, stepped forward, and bowed. Tal noticed an immediate resemblance of the younger Stokely to his father. He recalled the blunt challenge issued earlier by Brandon.

The Lord Governor and his son are much alike as well.

The inspection of the citadel occupied the next hour. Already impressed with the exterior defenses, the interior of the fortress left Tal even more so. Rooms and chambers honeycombed the bastion. Billets, food and weapons storage, assembly halls, kitchens, all had been excavated from the stone. Even a cistern had been carved out to capture rainwater. Should Waldez ever be put to siege, the defenders were apt to die of old age before they ran out of food or water.

The last stop was the Gateway. The largest chamber in the citadel, it housed the magical gate which provided transportation to and from Waldez. Unlike the Veil whose portals were twisted creations of dark sorcery, magical gateways existed in natural abundance on Meredith. One particularly large gate existed at Waldez...another reason for the construction of the fortress there.

Stokely led Tal to a pair of large doors at least ten feet high. Thick metal bands girdled the ironwood doors in a crisscross fashion. Embedded in each door was a single, large lodestone. No less than a score of guards stood watch beside the entrance, and Tal's group was immediately challenged when they rounded the corner.

The sentries snapped to attention as Lord Stokely appeared before them. Acknowledging the guards with a nod, he tapped one of the lodestones. With a *click*, the door unlocked and swung open. It revealed a vast cavern.

As the administrative nerve center of the citadel, smaller chambers and offices lined the sides of the cavern. Charts and maps hung from walls, while stacks of official papers were stacked on tables. A beehive of activity, clerks, aides, and military men scurried about carrying out their tasks.

Stokely led them to a room containing a series of elliptical frames secured to the granite wall of the cavern. Each contained a featureless gray background that rippled like a disturbed surface of water. Some displayed men and women conversing with the Waldez officials. Artifacts of magic, the communication consoles connected Waldez with the rest of the Empire. Having seen and used them often enough, they registered only a flicker of notice from Tal.

Of much more interest was the Traveling Gate.

The oval gate hovered in the middle of the chamber unsupported by rope or chain. Tal knew size had no effect on a Traveling Gate's physical boundaries. Rather, these magical portals *stretched* to allow passage. One of the huge, four-masted merchant ships plying the Ocean of Dreams could pass through without difficulty.

Clean-shaven with brown hair clipped short, an officer stepped forward. He saluted palm-to-heart. A head shorter than Stokely, he said, "We are ready to open the gate from Meredith City, Lord Governor."

"Very good," Stokely replied. "Sire, this is Lieutenant Garter Mance, our Chief Magister for transportation. His command is responsible for manipulating the magic of the gateway."

Tal acknowledged the magister with slight bob of his head. Their eyes locked for the briefest of moments. In that fleeting second, Mance's eyes seemed to shift.

Suspicion? Fear? Wariness?

Then, just as quickly, the furtive look disappeared.

Mance bowed. "We are honored by your presence, Prince Tal. The First Advisor's guest will arrive shortly."

Tal's smile froze. Although curious to see the 'expert' Bozar sent for, the shifty look in the Chief Magister's eyes bothered him. *Perhaps I'm imagining things.*

To gain time to gather his wits, he asked, "How does a Traveling Gate function? Their magic fascinates me."

Mance nodded. "Of course, Sire. The gates all operate on the principle of folding time and space. The practical effect of this is to shorten distance. Although a magical gate can bend over the interface of land, sea, or sky, they cannot pass through solid or even liquid substances. They also work best on a straight, line-of-sight passage. Fortunately, magical 'holes' exist in the barriers of land and sea which allow naturally occurring Gates to connect."

The transportation officer's face darkened. "As we are all painfully aware, no such limitations exist for Sonja's orb, and the Dark Queen has used that to her full advantage. Despite centuries of trying, we have been unable to duplicate Sonja's feat."

Mance was interrupted by a disturbance on the surface of the Traveling Gate. More undulations spread, and suddenly, a figure stepped through. Having never met Bozar's friend, Tal expected a small, studious academic. Instead, a large and beefy man emerged.

Untidy, flaming red hair crowned Artemis Thurgood's head. His fiery beard was sprinkled with crumbs from his last meal, while wine stains appeared on his wrinkled robe like leopard spots.

This is the expert Bozar sent for?

Before Tal's incredulous mind could take another turn, a large wooden chest followed the Grand Master out of the Gate and floated inches off the ground behind him.

"Kravitz olendolis!" Thurgood commanded, and four short wooden legs with pawlike feet "grew" from the base of the chest. As Thurgood walked from the Gate toward Tal, the chest waddled after the Grand Master.

"Prince Tal!" he boomed. "I thought I'd never leave Lodestone Castle! You have my sincerest gratitude for this opportunity to study the Veil." Giving Tal a bone-crushing handshake, he asked, "When do we make for the cursed barrier?"

Tal took an immediate liking to the garrulous Grand Master. "If it pleases Lord Stokely, we will leave on the morrow."

Disappointed, Thurgood asked, "You mean we cannot leave tonight?"

Tal chuckled, "It is a full day's journey even on a winged horse. Lord Stokely has been kind enough to extend his hospitality for the night."

Even the Lord Governor smiled at the reaction of Artemis Thurgood. "We shall have your horses saddled and ready at first light, Sire. I hope that is soon enough for the honorable Grand Master."

"Of course, Lord Stokely." Thurgood rubbed his hands together. "Well, lads, since we are to spend the night together, I have an important question to ask."

The Lord Governor frowned. "And what would that be, Grand Master?"

"What do you have to drink here?"

CHAPTER 8

CLATTER OF HOOVES RANG OUT ON THE COBBLESTONE ROAD.
Alex looked up from the stand of leather boots she
had been examining. The cobbler's shop, like most of
the establishments in Wheel, was built close beside the web of
avenues and alleys bisecting the city. A legionnaire dressed in the
Duke's livery galloped up to the shop and leaped off. After a brief
conversation with Tell, he remounted and rode away.

Boots forgotten, Alex hurried over to Tell. "What is it?"

Tell motioned to the guard escort. The two soldiers ran to retrieve the horses. "The Duke has summoned you. We must leave
immediately."

Alex blinked. "What? Why?"

He grabbed the bridle of Alex's horse from the guard and
helped Alex into the saddle.

"It seems you have a visitor."

The urgency of the Duke's request left Alex with no time to
make herself more presentable. She arrived with wind-blown hair
dangling in a mass of curls, and still dressed in her riding attire of
brown pants, knee-high boots and white tunic. A servant showed
Alex to the small audience room the Duke used for informal
occasions.

A fire blazed in the hearth to chase away the early spring

chill. At the end of the room the Duke and another man stood sipping amber drinks from glass snifters. Although the stranger's back was turned to Alex, he seemed familiar. He turned at the sound of her boot heels. A vise gripped her heart.

Rodric Regret.

Terror flooded her mind. She wanted to turn and flee, but her numbed legs wouldn't obey.

"Come, come, Alex," the Duke admonished her. "Is this how you greet our friend and ally, Lord Regret?"

A breath...then two, then three. Alex's stunned mind began to recover, and she forced her deadened limbs to continue the trek forward.

"I'm sorry, fa—father," she stuttered. "Where are my manners? How are you, Lord Regret?"

Rodric flashed a smile. "Oh, *so* much better now that I am graced by your loveliness."

He took both her hands in his. The touch of his cold flesh caused sirens to shriek in Alex's mind. It took every ounce of self-control not to wrench away and sprint from the room.

Rodric spun her around. "I must say, your attire, while unusual, only accentuates your beauty."

She felt like a prime heifer being examined for purchase at a sale barn. "You are too kind, Lord Regret," Alex managed to say.

The Duke beamed. "Lord Regret has concluded matters at his estate." He leaned closer and winked at Alex. "He plans on spending *much* more time here in Wheel."

Rodric released Alex and wiggled a finger at the Duke. "Now, now, Alton. You have given away my secret."

Alton? When did he become on a first name basis with father? Alex didn't think it possible, but her heart sank farther.

"I took the liberty of making dinner arrangements this evening at one of Wheel's finer establishments," Rodric continued.

He turned to Alex, "I hope I am not being too presumptuous to ask you to join me?"

"Nonsense, Rodric," the Duke answered before she could reply. "Alexandria would be glad to join you."

"Delightful!" Rodric replied. "I'll send a coach to pick you up." He bowed and kissed Alex's hand.

Retaining his firm grip on her hand, he pulled Alex closer. "The first of what I hope are *many* happy times we spend together," he whispered.

Rodric spun on his heel and left the room.

Silence, thick and stifling, filled the vacuum left by Rodric's absence. The Duke, tired of Alex's reticence, cleared his throat. "What is wrong with you? You act as if you lost a favorite pet rather than receiving a dinner invitation by the most eligible man in all of Wheel."

"I-I don't feel well," Alex answered. "May I be excused?"

Duke Duvalier studied her. "You have not been the same since your fall from that accursed horse. For the most part, I have welcomed this...this *change* in you. But there are times it wears thin."

He turned and walked to a section of the wall adjacent to the hearth. Raising his right hand, he pressed a blood-red lodestone ring he wore against another similar lodestone inset within the masonry. A *rumble* echoed through the room, and a part of the wall swung open.

"Come," he said with an impatient gesture.

After a moment's hesitation, Alex followed.

A cold, damp draft greeted her as she entered the dark opening. A trace of mold and mildew seasoned the air. Stopping long enough for her eyes to adjust to the dim light, she discovered a series of stone steps hugging the rock wall. As they descended into the murky darkness, bracketed sconces flared to life.

Alex took care to place her feet cautiously on each step. By the time she caught up to her father, he had reached the bottom. The Duke, spent by the exertion, leaned one hand against the wall and wheezed. Air rasped in and out of his lungs like a leaky bellows.

Alex moved to help him but was waved off.

"I-I wanted you to see this," he panted. He hoisted himself upright and raised the lodestone ring. Spears of light exploded from the magical gem, so bright it forced Alex to shield her eyes. When the illumination dimmed, she gingerly moved her hands.

A gasp escaped her lips.

Row after row of sarcophagi lay before them. Upright, the coffins were arranged in precise ranks, and marched away into the dim recesses of the vast chamber.

They stood in the midst of an immense tomb.

"The final resting place of our ancestors," the Duke whispered. "Here lies the evidence of our lineage, an unbroken succession of Duvaliers dating back thousands of years."

He moved to a nearby sarcophagus and stood. Tears fell from his eyes and dripped into his beard. Alex joined him and gasped at the sight. Completely constructed of flawless crystal, the coffin contained a beautiful woman. Dressed in a gem encrusted gown with hands folded in front of her, the woman's flaxen hair was encircled by a thin, gold crown. Her face, reposed in peace, removed any doubt of her identity.

My mother.

Duke Duvalier placed a hand against the crystal. Grief shook him. "Too soon. Taken from me too soon, my love." Alex moved closer and put her arm around the Duke. He clung to her, snuffling.

Curious, with her free hand, she reached out and spread her fingers on the clear, smooth surface of the coffin. A glow, followed by a pleasant tickle, warmed her skin. Startled, she snatched her hand back. To hide her surprise, she asked, "How is it mother looks so alive…like she is only sleeping?"

The old Duke wiped his eyes. "It is the magic of the crystal coffers. It holds the deceased in a suspended animation, proof against the ravages of time and corruption of the flesh."

Alex inspected more of the nearby coffins. Each contained a deceased duke or duchess in lifelike, peaceful tranquility.

Duke Duvalier turned toward Alex. "I have something to tell you, something wonderful which will strengthen the Duchy. Rodric has asked for your hand, and I have agreed to your betrothal. The wedding will be three weeks hence."

Staggered by the announcement, Alex's knees almost gave way. The cold within the tomb felt like desert heat compared to the ice in her blood.

"Wh-what?" she gasped. "No! I won't marry him!"

The Duke's face turned hard. "It has been my lot to bear the burden of responsibility for Wheel in these dark and evil times. I was given no choice in the matter…just as you have no choice. You *will* marry Rodric."

"But-but you don't understand. He isn't who you think he is," Alex blurted. "He is evil, a monster!"

"Your accident has continued to addle your wits. This 'monster' came to my aid when we were sorely pressed by the Dark Queen's army," Duke Duvalier snapped. "Because of Rodric, we survived and won a great battle."

"It's a trick, Father, meant to deceive you. Don't make me marry him," Alex pleaded.

"Then we need more tricks like this!" he barked. The Duke gripped Alex's arms. "Have you no understanding of our position?" he cried. "We have been separated from the Empire for over a thousand years! During that time, constant warfare with

Marlinda's forces has decimated our ranks. Our flying legion-naires, the main strength of Wheel, have been reduced to half its normal compliment. *Half!* We can barely defend our own walls, much less the surrounding countryside."

Alex cried out as his fingers dug into her flesh. "You're hurt-ing me."

The Duke ignored her cry. "Don't you see? Lord Regret's ap-pearance is a godsend. With a marriage to seal this alliance, we can survive and push back against the Veil Queen and King."

Livid, he shook her. "So you'll forgive me if I put the needs of our people over your petty wishes. You *will* marry Rodric! You *will* produce an heir, and continue the Duvalier lineage."

Sobbing, Alex jerked away. "So that's it? I am to be a brood mare to a man I loathe? I hate you!"

Barely able to see through the flood of tears, Alex flew up the stairs.

CHAPTER 9

A FTER A LONG NIGHT OF ALE AND THURGOOD'S BAWDY TALES, dawn came, and as promised, the winged horses were saddled and ready.

Tal's escort was already mounted when he and Artemis Thurgood walked out onto the concourse, the Grand Master gnawing on a fat sausage. Finished, he licked his fingers, belched, and wiped his fingers on his robe where the grease spots joined a patchwork of fresh wine stains.

Tal waited by his horse while Thurgood's trunk waddled up to him. The Grand Master retrieved a pinch of powder from a pouch within his robes, and sprinkled it on the chest. With a *poof*, the trunk shrank to the size of a child's toy, and he dropped it in his pocket.

Lord Stokely was on hand to see them off, and Tal thanked him for his hospitality. With a rattle of hooves, the horses galloped down the flyway. They plunged off the cliff and with a snap of wings, twenty horses soared up into the air. Brandon Stokely and his command wheeled high above Waldez, ready to see Tal and his men safely to the edge of their patrol territory before turning back.

A roar of delight rang out. Artemis Thurgood, robes, beard, and hair streaming behind him, grinned ear-to-ear.

"I had forgotten what a thrill it is to ride a winged horse, Prince Tal!" he shouted. "To soar like a bird, to have freedom from the restraints of ground travel…it's indescribable!" Another whoop of joy followed, and Tal laughed at the Grand Master's giddy excitement.

The day was clear with little turbulence, and they made good time. At the end of the rolling foothills, their Waldez escort turned east to begin their patrol. Tal saluted the younger Stokely, impressed with the commander despite their rocky beginning.

His thoughts were interrupted when Artemis Thurgood began to belt out a song. The bawdy ditty involved the anatomies of a tavern wench, a milkmaid, and a farmer's daughter. Gravelback's soldiers, familiar with the melody, joined in. Soon, the entire cohort was singing. Tal discovered the ditty contained an inexhaustible supply of verses, due to the Grand Master's ability to create new ones.

During a rare lull in the boisterous singing, Tal commented to the Grand Master, "I can imagine your university classes to be anything but routine."

A wide smile split Artemis Thurgood's face. "Levity is a spice to lighten what might ordinarily be a tedious presentation of magic and its principles. But don't be fooled, Prince Tal. I take my position and my students seriously."

He rubbed his chin. "You see, inquiry begins with curiosity, and curiosity leads to learning. I have never met someone with a strong intellect who didn't also have an equal amount of wonder. A relaxed atmosphere removes impediments to learning and allows this inquisitiveness to gallop along."

"So what you mean is there's never a dull moment in one of your classes."

Artemis Thurgood beamed. "Exactly! You are quite discerning for one so young."

Bozar would argue that point. Nonetheless, Tal's appreciation for the Grand Master grew. There was much more to Artemis Thurgood than ale-stained robes.

Soon, the Grand Master started another round of singing with enthusiastic abandon. Within moments, a score of voices added to his.

Tal couldn't help himself...he joined in.

There were still a few hours of daylight left when they arrived at the site of the battle with the Veil raiders. Tal looked in vain for any evidence a battle had been fought and could find none. Gravelback and Tarlbolt had made good use of their time while Tal was gone. Only camp tents dotted the previously blood-drenched field.

As soon as they landed, Bozar, Tarlbolt, and Gravelback hurried toward them. Artemis Thurgood's eyes lit up at the sight of Bozar, his former protégé. He threw his arms around the First Advisor in an energetic hug which left Bozar puffing. When he caught his breath, Bozar made introductions. By their expressions, Tal could see that Gravelback and Tarlbolt didn't know what to make of Artemis Thurgood.

The Grand Master's eyes gleamed. "I came as soon as I received your message. What is this business about the Veil?"

Bozar shook his head. "Time enough for that after we get you settled in. We have arranged a tent—"

"Nonsense! I have my own accommodations."

Gravelback and Tarlbolt looked at each other uneasily. "Ah, pray what accommodations are you referring to?" Gravelback asked. "You appear to have nothing but the clothes on your back."

"What? Oh, forgive me. Here, I'll show you." Thurgood took the miniature trunk from his pocket, placed it on the ground, then retrieved the pouch from his robe. Once again, he sprinkled a bit of powder on the tiny trunk. This time the chest grew to full size.

Stubby legs sprouted from the chest. Agitated, the trunk hopped up and down, the objects it contained rattling and banging. Above this clamor, the chest released a *yip* like a dog.

The Grand Master wagged a finger at the trunk. "You'll have to wait until I have unpacked all of my things." With a whine, the chest settled on its paws.

He reached down and opened a drawer. Rummaging around, he retrieved a toy-sized object in the shape of a tiny pavilion.

"Stand back," Thurgood commanded, and placed the object on the ground a good distance from the small group. He sprinkled more of the dust on it and hurried away. Canvas sprang up and billowed upward and outward before staking itself to the ground. The palatial pavilion dwarfed all the other tents.

A flap opened. Artemis Thurgood motioned with his hand. "Follow me."

Tal, curiosity piqued, hurried after the Grand Master, the others right behind him. His mouth dropped once inside.

Thick rugs carpeted the floor. A huge bed with soft blankets and plush pillows occupied one side of the pavilion. Cushioned easy chairs, arranged around a low table, filled the other side. Wedged next to the chairs was a full-sized bathtub. Directly ahead, a fully-stocked pantry stood the height of a man's head. Beside it, perched on a sturdy bench, sat a huge ale barrel. Next to the spigot, tankards hung from hooks.

The Grand Master made directly for the barrel and filled a mug. Ale sloshing over the rim, he waved the stein at the small group still gaping in disbelief. "Traveling is a thirsty business," he announced, then moved to the pantry and produced the roasted leg of a fowl. Taking a bite, he mumbled around a mouthful of meat, "And one that sharpens the appetite as well."

Thurgood placed the mug on the bench, more of the ale spilling to the floor. "But where are my manners? Please join me."

Silence greeted his invitation.

Artemis Thurgood chuckled. "My pardon. I decided long ago to forego the hardships of travel. Having mastered the magic of reduction as a student-apprentice, I put this knowledge to good use. Handy don't you think?"

Tarlbolt nodded an acknowledgement, still speechless. Bozar took the whole scene in with amusement.

Gravelback found his voice and said, "It would seem you came...*well prepared*, Grand Master."

Before Thurgood could reply, more rattles and clanks came from the chest which had resumed its agitated hopping.

The Grand Master sighed. "I won Daisy from a colleague in a game of *Castles and Towers*. At the time, he didn't seem too disappointed at the loss. I have since learned why. Enchanted chests are demanding. *Very* demanding."

He reached into a bag tied at his waist and removed what appeared to be chips of wood. A pungent odor rose from the kindling. "Daisy is finicky. She'll only eat Burlwood soaked in dragon oil." He tossed the snack to the excited chest.

A hidden drawer popped open to expertly catch the wood chips. A munching sound came from inside the chest, and the trunk stilled. Suddenly, Daisy hiked a stubby leg up.

"Brraap!"

A pleasant odor, a mixture of cedar and cinnamon, filled the air.

Artemis Thurgood apologized. "My pardon, Lords. The Burlwood always troubles Daisy." As if to emphasize this, the trunk waddled off, each step punctuated by another sharp *brraap*.

Gravelback, face turning crimson, turned to Bozar. "Might I have a word, First Advisor?" The two men exited the tent, Tal and Tarlbolt close behind.

The garrison commander shook his head. "Forgive me

Bozar…*but have you lost your mind?* You want *this* man to advise us on the open portal? His talents would be better spent at a roadside alehouse!"

Tarlbolt agreed. "You have been gone from the University many years now. People change over such a long period of time. Perhaps the Grand Master is not the same person you remember."

Chuckling, Bozar said, "Appearances can be deceiving. Trust me when I tell you there is no finer mind concerning the Veil—"

"What…*is that?*" a voice cried.

Artemis Thurgood stood at the entrance of his grand pavilion, his eyes fixed on the swirling wormhole in the Veil. The tankard fell from his hand, followed by the partially consumed leg.

"That, my old friend," Bozar answered, "is why you are here."

CHAPTER 10

A LEX LAY ON HER BED AND STARED AT THE CEILING. FRESH plaster covered a section.

The same place Darcy's Rodric-controlled body bounced off of.

She had cried herself out. With no tears left to consume her, only dark memories remained.

His cruel touch, the reptilian feel of his skin on hers, the oily evil which seemed to ooze from his pores.

Marriage to Rodric would be a horror she couldn't even begin to imagine—made worse because her father desperately wanted this union to produce an heir. The thought of him inside her, his twisted seed—

Alex jumped off the bed and raced to the privy. She vomited until her empty stomach produced nothing but yellow bile. She staggered to her feet and splashed cold water on her face. The water revived her somewhat, and she became aware of a persistent knock on the door of her chambers. She wiped her mouth, and made her way to the door.

Alex steeled herself before putting a hand on the knob. *Father, here to follow up on his command I marry Rodric.* She opened the door. Tell stood outside wearing a worried look.

She launched herself into his arms.

Trembling, she buried her face in his chest. Tell looked around, then half-carried, half-dragged Alex back into her room and kicked the door shut. Picking her up, he sat her on the edge of the bed.

"If I hadn't dismissed the sentries, I can only imagine the number of tales their wagging tongues would voice at the sight we just provided," he admonished her.

"I don't care. I—"

"Not here! The Duke's manor has grown more ears than a cavern of mountain bats."

Finger at his lips, he led them out the balcony doors and to the very edge of the terrace. Only by standing face to face could they speak over the roar of the falls.

"Now, what's wrong?"

Alex told him of the meeting with her father and her forced marriage to Rodric. "The marriage ceremony is to take place in only three weeks. What am I to do, Tell? His very touch sickens me."

Jaw clenched, Tell stood ramrod straight. His eyes seemed fixed on a faraway object. Finally, he stirred and leaned closer to her ear.

"What would you be willing to do to avoid this marriage?"

Alex hesitated. A simple question, but one loaded with so many possibilities.

What *would* I do?

There was only one answer, ironclad and absolute.

"Anything," she said. "Anything at all."

Tell nodded. "I have a plan, but one which will take some time to complete. In the meantime, you must play along, act as if you look forward to this union with Rodric. Give no hint of your reluctance to marry him."

"But what—"

Tell shook his head. "Ask no questions. Its best if you know nothing now. When I'm ready, I'll tell you everything."

He squeezed her hand. "I will take care of this, I swear." With that, he turned and left.

Alone with only the mighty cataracts for company, Alex felt a tiny flame ignite in her heart, one she feared had been lost forever.

Hope.

Ⓜ

The evening with Rodric, although uneventful, left Alex wrung out. The restaurant served grilled trout caught just that morning from the Misty River, along with croissants which melted in her mouth. Dessert was a fruit tart slathered in cinnamon butter.

All tasted like ashes.

When the coach delivered Alex back to the Duke's manor, Rodric walked her to the gate where he pulled her aside. One hand on her shoulder, his other hand slid down to rest on the swell of her buttocks.

"A night I will treasure forever," he said, then kissed her, his lips lingering.

As Mona, she remembered the televised feats of competitors during the Olympics. However, Alex doubted any Olympian could have matched the herculean effort to stifle the reflex to push Rodric from her, and run screaming into the night. Instead, she returned his kiss and murmured, "One I will remember as well."

Later in the tub, she scrubbed herself raw to remove any remnant of Rodric's touch. Her efforts were so vigorous, they captured the attention of her handmaiden, Darcy, who stood nearby, a concerned look on her face. "Did M'Lady take a fall in the stables?" she asked. "Do you need me to add rose oil to your bath?" Alex shook her head.

Afterward, Alex sat at the vanity with Darcy brushing her hair. The handmaiden, brow wrinkled, remarked, "M'Lady looks ill. Shall I fetch the court physician?"

Alex glanced at her reflection in the mirror. Her eyes appeared dark and sunken. She patted Darcy's hand. "No. I'm just tired. I'm going to turn in early."

After the servant girl left, Alex opened one of the large doors to the terrace, and let some fresh air in. The atmosphere of her chambers, despite its enormous size, still seemed too close, and she felt as if she was suffocating. A storm brewed to the north and flashes of lightning stabbed the dark night. A steady wind blew, molding her nightgown against her figure. The light from her chambers reflected her image on the glass panes of the doors. She stared at herself, the cool breeze hardening her nipples to spearpoints, her small waist, flared hips, and proud breasts displayed like an artist's sculpture. She closed her eyes and leaned against the door frame.

A face and figure men on two worlds would fight and possibly die for. Yet it is my life that hangs in the balance.

The irony was not lost on her. She looked up at the storm-tossed sky and shook her fist. "What kind of guardian angel would do this to me?" she screamed. "Didn't my miserable life on earth cause me enough suffering?"

Her reply came in the form of lightning, followed by a long roll of thunder.

Weariness settled on her like a heavy blanket.

She locked the door and went to bed.

Alex awoke with a start.

Lightning flashed continuously and thunder hammered the air. Sheets of rain pelted the windows, the panes rattling like dice shaken in a can.

Alex sat up, shaken by the violence of the storm. While she

considered if it would be worth the attempt to go back to sleep in such a tempest, she noticed a muted glow from the full length mirror beside her vanity. Curious, she rolled out of bed and padded over to the old mirror.

Silvery light came from it. Peering closer, she realized this ghostly illumination came from *within* the mirror.

She touched the antique mirror's frame. The quicksilver glow spread and in an instant, flowery script flowed across the aged wood in a language completely alien to Alex. Gripping the wooden framework with both hands, Alex peered closer, her face within inches of the strange text.

The mirror exploded in eye-searing light.

With a cry, Alex fell backwards to land painfully on her rump. When the spots in her vision cleared, her jaw dropped. Fiery words appeared and burned their way down the mirror's surface like a molten river.

The Mirror of Diana
Serves the pure of heart and soul
A gateway to the Maze
Where secrets will unfold
The magic of the mirror
Will draw upon the One
Making clear the murky threads of time
To foretell what is to come
The Mirror of Diana,
Is the gateway key,
Reserved only for the few,
With courage and will to see

Heart pounding, Alex read and re-read the writing. It reminded her of a children's nursery rhyme, and made no sense.

It's obvious this is the Mirror of Diana, but who is Diana? What gateway does the rhyme refer to? What is this Maze?

Nancy E. Durham

Alex stood and rubbed her sore rump. As she did so, her left hand grazed the mirror's surface...and passed right through it. With a yelp, she snatched her hand back.

For long moments, she stared at the mirror and tried to decide what to do next. Gathering her courage, she reached out and again, her fingers passed through the reflective surface. This time she did not pull back. She could feel cool air caress her skin. Emboldened, she shoved her entire arm through.

Nothing but more chilly air.

Alex retrieved her arm. She pulled a chair up to the magical Artifact and sat contemplating. *Maybe the mirror is the gateway which leads to the maze.*

Steeling herself for the next important test, Alex pressed her face against the mirror's surface. Her head passed through, and she experienced a moment of panic as everything went black... then she realized her eyes were squeezed shut. When she opened them, a stone landing materialized with steps leading down into shadow. Water trickled down the rock walls adjacent to the landing. A torch attached to the masonry flickered. Its weak light revealed nothing beyond the empty space.

Alex pulled her head back and considered. Abruptly, she made her decision. *What have I got to lose? Time to go exploring.*

As she stripped off her nightgown, it occurred to her that she had used this same logic when agreeing to Thaddeus Finkle's proposition to swap her life with another.

And now look at me.

Alex shook her head. If things could get worse—and she didn't think that possible—then they got worse. There could be no turning back now. She pulled on her riding pants and boots, and not bothering with a bodice, slipped on her white blouse. Rummaging around in her apartment-sized closet produced a light jacket. She cast about and spied the lamp beside her bed.

Small enough to carry, it would have to do. She paused, then opened a drawer and pulled out a small dagger Tell had given her. She shoved it in her belt.

She stepped up to the magical mirror, took a deep breath... and then stepped through it.

Unseen by Alex, a dark shadow moved to the foot of the mirror.

And followed after her.

CHAPTER 11

"A HORSE. BRING ME A HORSE!" ARTEMIS THURGOOD demanded.

"Surely this can wait until tomorrow," Bozar offered.

"Blast you, Bozar. Has your hearing left you? FETCH ME A HORSE!" the Grand Master thundered.

The transformation amazed Tal. Gone was the happy, slightly inebriated university professor, replaced by a coldly sober, no-nonsense academic.

Bozar nodded, and Gravelback signaled one of his men. A short time later, the cavalryman trotted up leading a saddled mount. Artemis Thurgood leaped into the saddle with the dexterity of a man half his size.

Robes flying, he galloped toward the open wormhole.

❖

Hours later, Tal sat with Bozar in the large field tent set up as the command center. The moonless night was pitch black, and still the Grand Master had not returned.

Earlier, when Tal watched Artemis Thurgood disappear into the open portal, he had to fight the urge to follow. Now this feeling was replaced with unease.

"It's late. Shouldn't one of us check on the Grand Master?" he asked Bozar.

His *Eldred* shook his head. "Imagine a dog on the hunt following the scent until its prey is treed. *That* is Artemis. He will not rest until he has unraveled this mystery."

"But—"

Tal was interrupted by the sound of hoof beats outside the canvas walls. Thurgood burst into the command pavilion, his wind-blown red hair stretched behind him like flames from a campfire.

Intense green eyes speared Bozar. "Where is the nearest Watch Tower?"

"A few leagues Northwest of here," Bozar replied. "But why—"

"No time for explanations! I need a flying mount. A ground horse is too slow."

The First Advisor stood. "It nears midnight. You have not eaten or slept since leaving Waldez. Why not resume your research at first light?"

"Bollacks and battens! I already have a mother, Bozar, and she is far fairer than you. We have no time to waste. Now, do I get the flying horse from you, or must I find it myself?"

With a sigh, Bozar signaled a sentry. Artemis Thurgood hurried after the soldier.

Tal chuckled. "You are right, my *Eldred*. The quarry has yet to be brought to heel, and the Grand Master is *still* on the hunt."

With a yawn, he left to seek out his bed.

Tal awoke before the hand could shake him. Bozar's face peered down at him. "Artemis has returned. He requests we assemble in his quarters."

Tal took a moment to stretch and yawn, then emerged from

his tent. The sun was barely above the horizon, the morning clear and chilly. The Grand Master's pavilion, easy to spot, dwarfed the smaller campaign tents. Tal made his way and entered the cavernous lodging. Bozar, Gravelback, and Tarlbolt were seated around a large table, steaming mugs of strong tea in their hands.

Artemis Thurgood, a sparkle in his eye, greeted Tal with a wide grin, his infectious humor apparently returned.

The Grand Master handed Tal a cup of the same brew the others sipped. He cautiously tasted the hot liquid and nodded in appreciation. Slightly bitter with a hint of chocolate, it helped dispel any remaining drowsiness and sharpened his senses.

He took his seat with to the others.

The Grand Master waved his hand, and the table before Tal became a map, a miniature version of Meredith. Complete in every detail, clouds scudded above the map, and sunlight glittered off lakes and rivers. Snow-capped mountain peaks thrust into the air, trees swayed in the wind, while flocks of birds took wing. The Veil was as a pale shimmer of gray as it curved across the chart.

A red spot indicated their position, while another represented where the portal opened on the other side of the Veil.

"I have mixed news, some good, some bad," the Grand Master announced. "First the bad...the portal is shrinking in size. Perhaps a large wagon or a pair of mounted soldiers, can now pass through the wormhole."

Tal's throat constricted. *No, no, no,* he choked.

"But the good news is I have stopped this collapse. I believe we can stabilize the gateway and keep it at its current breadth."

Artemis Thurgood cast an apologetic glance at Bozar. "Time *really* was of the essence. If I had not acted when I did, the closing of the portal would have been certain."

Gravelback's features went from apoplectic, to relief, to confusion. "How, why...*explain yourself!*"

"Certainly, Lord Commander," Thurgood replied. "The first step was to secure the Artifact which opened the portal." A wooden box lay on a table next to the Grand Master. He opened the lid and produced a grisly trophy.

The severed hand of the dead raid leader. Completely encased in a clear crystal, it clutched the Artifact.

"We now have no fear of decay or any act of man deactivating the Artifact's magic. It is preserved for perpetuity in its current state.

"Next was my trip to the Watch Tower. Everyone knows this magical system serves dual purposes—to provide warning, and for defense against the Dark Queen's marauders. Few know, however, that while powerful, the magic of the Towers is quickly drained. Once activated, this magic must be recharged. If not replaced, over time the Towers become dormant."

The Grand Master leaned forward. "I took the liberty of bleeding off more of this magic."

Bozar frowned. "Why?" he asked. "If what you say is true, you leave this area defenseless."

"Because it is the Watch Tower's magic causing the portal to decay, just as it is designed to do. I know of no example of a gate opening in the Veil this close to one. There *had* to be a reason. Once I reached the Tower, I discovered the answer. The edifice's lodestones have discharged most of their magic. They need to be recharged."

Giddy, the Grand Master practically danced a jig. "Don't you see? There wasn't enough magic left to close the portal. By removing a bit more, an equilibrium has been reached. *We can keep the gateway open for as long as we want.*"

Stunned silence followed. Then Tal, Gravelback, and Tarlbolt jumped to their feet with roars and shouts of exultation. Only Bozar remained reticent.

"I see you have an elaborate map laid out for us. What is its purpose?" Bozar asked.

The Grand Master's enthusiasm visibly waned. With a sigh, he approached the map and pointed at the red symbol marking the exit through the Veil. "Besides size, the gateway has one other limitation. It is frozen in place. The exit point cannot be manipulated and will remain fixed to where it is now—in a wilderness far to the south, and hundreds of leagues from any population center."

Bozar rubbed his chin and walked around the map studying it. He stopped beside Thurgood. "One more question my old friend. What happens if the Dark Queen learns of this hole in the Veil?"

Artemis Thurgood's face fell. "Uh, well…" His arms dropped to his side. "She would close it. There would be nothing we could do to stop her."

The euphoria of the earlier celebration evaporated.

"Absolutely nothing?" Bozar persisted.

The Grand Master scratched his beard. "I can place magical pillars within the wormhole. These Artifacts will resist and slow the closure. But this only buys time—one turn of the sun at best—to exit. Anyone more than a day's ride from the wormhole would be trapped, unable to escape."

"Then we must make sure Marlinda does not learn of this open portal." The First Advisor stood. "It is time to contact Queen Celestria. Only her closest advisors can know of this glorious discovery."

He turned to Gravelback. "*Now* we plan for invasion."

CHAPTER 12

ALEX EXITED THE MIRROR.

Her room appeared through the ancient Artifact, as if she looked through a window. Her nightgown lay on the bed, her slippers on the floor.

Shivering, Alex clutched her jacket close, glad she thought to wear it. The air carried a cold, close dampness. With the lamp held before her, she studied her surroundings. She stood on a rectangular landing made of rough-hewn rock. A narrow set of stairs led downward from the landing and disappeared into darkness. She took a shaky breath.

Then started down the steps.

Torches, set at intervals, blazed to life as she passed by. The walls, beaded with moisture, reflected the light like thousands of tiny gems. Dust lay in a thick layer everywhere. Even the stone the steps were carved from reeked of antiquity.

The staircase ended at a fan-shaped balcony. A waist-high wall ran the length of the gallery. Alex cautiously approached the partition and looked over it. A gasp escaped her lips. A vast cavern stretched for leagues. Stalactites hung like giant dragon's teeth from the ceiling high above. Far below, a lake shimmered, its dark water rippling. Seven arches of stone led from the veranda and crossed the abyss. Each followed a different path, and each varied in width from broad to narrow.

An eerie green luminescence appeared all around her. Alex peered closer and discovered an algae-like growth upon every surface. With a sharp intake of breath, she realized *this* was the source of light! Alex turned off the lamp, and the entire cavern glowed like a neon sign from top to bottom. The breathtaking scene displayed a rare beauty unlike anything she had ever seen.

With great reluctance she turned away and studied the stone arches. Alex knew little about structural engineering, but it didn't appear possible that the stone pathways could cross such a wide chasm without buttressing. They should have collapsed of their own weight long ago.

Magic. They must be supported by magic.

She puzzled over what to do next. The stairs ended here. *There is nowhere else to go.* The only way to leave was to retrace her steps, or use one of the gravity-defying bridges.

Maze. The rhyme mentioned a maze…and this must be the beginning.

I have to choose a path.

The nexus of each pathway joined at a central point here on the veranda. Alex moved closer to get a better look. Carved from rock, each footpath was smooth with no railing to prevent a precipitous fall to the lake far below. One of the lanes was wide enough to allow several men to walk abreast. Since it represented the safest choice, Alex decided to take it.

She lifted a foot to take the first step…then stopped.

Too easy. It doesn't feel right.

Her head urged her to take this route, but her heart pulled her in another direction. She turned and approached another course. She halted…and knew without a doubt. *This is the one, the one I should choose.*

The narrowest pathway of all.

Barely wide enough for one person to walk upon, the stone bridge also diverged dramatically from the other passages. Arching over the other six bridges, it disappeared into the surreal greenish gloom.

Alex took a step and made the mistake of looking down. Far below, the lake glittered like a many-faceted, black jewel. Fear gripped her.

She scrabbled back to the safety of the landing. Hands clasped to her breast, Alex's heart threatened to erupt. *I can't do this.* Logic told her the crossing was impossible and would lead to certain death. But Alex couldn't shake the feeling she had been led here for a reason. She sensed to turn back now would seal her fate.

A future with Rodric.

With a smooth pivot, she approached the path and with more courage than she felt, stepped on it...and kept going.

The first few paces were the hardest, but the farther she went, the more her confidence grew. Refusing to look down or to the left or right, she kept her eyes locked on the narrow strip before her.

Time passed without reckoning. All that mattered was to place one foot forward, then another.

Crunch. Alex blinked. Her boot scattered some crumbled scree. Her feet rested on a broad terrace—she had crossed the chasm and safely reached the other side.

I made it.

The atmosphere within the maze was as silent and undisturbed as a tomb. Alex picked up a rock among the gravel at her feet and hurled it into the abyss. Long moments passed while she waited for the telltale splash.

It never came.

Alex turned and studied her new surroundings. As with the bridges, seven different trails lay before her, each disappearing into a cramped tunnel. Dismay filled her heart. *Not again.* Forced to choose, she walked back and forth, but there was nothing to distinguish one from another.

She stopped, closed her eyes, and cleared her mind. Alex took a deep breath, then held her hands before her, palms up. Like a blind person, she shuffled slowly along. A gentle pull tugged at her. She halted, eyes still closed, then continued. The feeling faded. Reversing course, the pull on her returned.

She opened her eyes.

Before her lay the third passageway from the right. She took it without hesitation. When she entered the pinched corridor, she discovered her shoulders barely cleared its width. At times, she had to bend to keep her head from hitting the hard rock of the corridor's ceiling. After traveling for several minutes, Alex realized the tunnel had narrowed to the point she couldn't turn around now even if she wanted to. She had no choice but to follow wherever the maze took her.

Alex made steady progress, anxious to leave the claustrophobic tunnel. Without warning, Alex stumbled into an open space. Torches flickered, casting shadows that leaped and danced. Their light revealed a circular chamber. Set in the floor of the room was a hole slightly larger in diameter than a wagon wheel. Dressed stone formed a smooth lip over the round opening. It reminded Alex of a well. She approached the shaft and gingerly looked into its depths.

Black as a starless night.

Further study of the chamber revealed no other exit. The maze ended here…or did it?

Alex, certain she had taken the right path, couldn't believe the maze had led her to a dead-end. If so, only one other avenue remained.

The well.

She slid a sputtering sconce out of its iron bracket, then stepped up to the rim. *Let's see how deep this hole is.* She dropped the torch.

It fell only a few inches, then stopped and drifted like a milk-weed seed caught in the wind.

Amazed, Alex put her hand out over the dark shaft. A pleasant prickling spread across her skin, and her hand "floated" like a cork on the water. She extended her entire arm and made no effort to hold it up. It too hovered, supported by a buoyant force.

Alex stepped back, her mind equal parts trepidation and triumph. *I found the way to the next part of the maze.* But she had tested only a single appendage. What about her entire body?

There was only one way to find out.

Once again, she walked up to the edge of the well. She took a step forward, careful to keep most of her weight on the foot still on solid ground. She edged forward, more and more of her body now perilously over the black and empty maw.

It felt like stepping onto a giant rubber band. It gave, but did not collapse. Emboldened, she took another step and now her entire body floated above the well. A sigh of relief escaped her.

Then she plummeted down the shaft.

CHAPTER 13

BOZAR OBSERVED GRAVELBACK AND TARLBOLT'S MEN FILE through the swirling portal.

The highest honor the Empire could give had been bestowed upon them—the first soldiers to set foot on land thought lost forever. Land torn from their ancestors by the black-hearted sorceress, Marlinda Darkmoor. Now, after a millennium, the chance to take it back, to free citizens on both sides of the Veil from her blood-stained atrocities, drew near.

The First Advisor shook his head. These same soldiers would not see their families again until the campaign against Marlinda, the Veil Queen was concluded.

When the initial meeting with Tal's mother, Queen Celestria, and her closest advisors ended—after the tears, shouts of celebration, and euphoria—they reached a unanimous decision.

The secret of the open portal must be kept at all costs.

This meant any journey through the gateway would be a one-way trip. No chance could be taken on a slip of the tongue. None would be allowed to return until the Veil was destroyed. Although Bozar had no doubt of the outcome—the Empire's military should make quick work of the Dark Queen's forces—all hinged on *if* they could buy enough time to marshal their forces in sufficient number.

A grim smile of satisfaction came to the First Advisor. This time it would not be helpless farmers and villagers Marlinda's cowardly turncoats and melded beasts faced, but hardened campaigners.

Unfortunately, the constricted nature of the portal allowed for only a trickle of soldiers and supplies. It was like threading a thick rope through the eye of a needle one thin strand at a time. Civilian and nonmilitary resources would be needed as well. Someone had to rebuild bridges, repair roads, heal the sick and wounded. The list seemed endless.

And all to be done in absolute secrecy.

It would take months, perhaps years, before a sustained campaign could take back the huge province of Dalfur, and destroy the Veil. Would a large enough force be in place by the time Marlinda realized an imperial army was in her midst? Their invading legions could be concealed for only so long.

Bozar could read the future no better than the next person, but one thing he *was* certain of. Sooner or later the Dark Queen would become aware of the invading army in her midst...and close the portal. Everything hinged on delaying this day of reckoning for as long as possible.

He motioned to Tal. His young charge watched the line of cavalrymen disappear into the gateway like a ravenous man watching a chef prepare a tasty meal. "It is time."

The First Advisor braced himself for what came next. They entered the command tent, deserted now except for the two of them. After the frenetic activity of the past few weeks, the emptiness held a lonely, isolated weight.

Bozar turned to Tal. "Remember to let me do all the talking."

Face lined with tension, Tal nodded.

Bozar retrieved his staff from where it leaned against a camp chair. He pointed the tip, and drew a glowing line in midair. He completed a circle and touched its center. A gray fog filled the ring, then clarified.

Celestria, Queen of the Meredithian Empire, appeared. Honey-colored hair fell in silken tresses about her shoulders. Eyes of intense blue regarded them. In one hand, she held the scepter of office, her gown richly embroidered with tiny lodestones of various colors. Tall, she carried herself with regal grace. Bozar always considered her a rare beauty, but the strain of rule had taken its toll. Forced to ascend the throne upon the death of King Mathias, her eyes no longer sparkled. Rather, they retained a hardness produced by too many decisions upon which life and death rested. Lips formerly quick to smile, now seemed frozen in a tight line.

Bozar shook his head. *More than Mathias perished the day he was slain.*

Beside her stood Malcolm Ashanti, Lord Marshal of the Empire's army. His brown eyes, a shade lighter than his ebony skin, shifted from the First Advisor to Tal.

"My Prince," he boomed. "I understand your quick-thinking is responsible for this glorious event. The Empire owes you a debt that we can never repay."

"Yes, we need to hear more of your exploits," added Celestria. "Perhaps in much greater detail than you've shared to this point. You will return to Meredith City immediately."

Tal's face reddened. "Mother, I—"

"Why don't you wait outside?" Bozar interjected quickly. Tal opened his mouth, and the First Advisor speared him with a hard look.

He turned and stormed out.

Bozar returned his attention to the Queen.

"No!" Celestria barked.

Bozar sighed. "Come, come, Celestria. You haven't even heard me out yet."

"The answer would remain the same. My son, my *only* child,

will not travel with the legions through the Veil. He will remain here with me in Lodestone Castle until we have killed the Dark Queen and King, and removed the abomination of the Veil."

"That is *exactly* why he must go. A Royal, a Prince of the Blood wields powerful magic. It will be needed against the evil sorcery of Marlinda. It may even be the advantage that tips the odds in our favor. We cannot squander this opportunity."

Celestria dismissed the comment with a wave of her hand. "We have many powerful nobles and Grand Masters. They will go in Tal's place."

"None carry the latent power of a Blood Prince." Bozar ground his teeth. "You *know* this."

"Then I will go. My magic is more than a match for Tal's."

Bozar spread his hands. "You are Queen at the most critical period in the Empire's history. You are needed here. Besides, your absence from the throne would be noticed immediately— at a time when complete secrecy is needed. How long before Marlinda's spies learn why? All know of Tal's banishment and the reasons behind his exile. He can slip through the Veil unnoticed. *He is the only Royal who can.*"

Celestria pointed a finger at the First Advisor. "This from my son's *Eldred*, the very one who counseled for his exile? *You* said he is too impulsive, too reckless, too quick to act before thinking. And now you want him to ride straight into the mouth of the dragon? To his certain death? *No*, my answer will always be no!"

The Queen's response did not surprise Bozar. In fact, he expected it. In truth he felt much the same and he feared for the young prince's safety. But the fate of millions, present *and* future, rested on the successful destruction of the Veil.

And as much as he loved Tal, until this was accomplished, *all* were needed in the struggle to come.

"You are both a mother *and* a Queen. One wars against the

other. I love Tal as well…and I understand." Bozar steeled himself for the hard words he knew must come. "But decide if you serve the interests of the many or of one. It is not just Tal's life that hangs in the balance but those of countless others."

Tears welled in Celestria's eyes. "Damn you, Bozar," she sobbed. "Damn you for forcing me to choose between my son and our people."

A commotion came from the entrance of the command pavilion, followed by a voice which rang out, "I will stand by the Prince's side. I will see him safely through the Veil and back."

Startled, Bozar whirled around. Behind him stood a white monk, his *haloub* extended to full length and held before him like a staff. Recognition dawned on the First Advisor.

The white monk, Pulpit.

Tal, next to the monk, wore a sheepish look. "He appeared like a wraith. Before I could stop him, he got by me."

The prince stepped up to Bozar. "Mother, I will take care, I swear," he pleaded. "I will listen to my *Eldred* and give heed to his counsel."

He moved closer. "Father told me something once. Although too young to understand then, I think I do now. He said life isn't a random collection of acts, but events that happen for a reason."

Tal put his hand on Bozar's shoulder. "I know I have seen too few summers, and others are far wiser than I am. But if what Father said is true, then aren't we meant to be here at *this* time, at *this* place? Shouldn't we have the faith to follow this path placed before us?"

The First Advisor's eyes welled with emotion. *Why do I continue to underestimate him? A boy no longer…but a man.*

Reaching forward as if to touch her son across the many leagues, Celestria whispered, "So much like Mathias." She pulled her hand back and wiped her eyes. "Very well."

Voice cracking, she said, "Somewhere, a part of me dwells in you, Tal. Use this when your impulse is to rush in when a careful tread is needed."

She turned to Pulpit. "I hold you to your pledge, Monk. Help rid our land of Marlinda's scourge. Destroy the Veil.

"And bring my son back to me."

CHAPTER 14

A LEX'S SCREAMS FOLLOWED HER DOWN THE SHAFT.

Her descent suddenly braked and she began to drift. Hyperventilating, her heart raced and she felt light-headed. She fought to steady her nerves, and slowly her breathing returned to normal.

Inky darkness surrounded her, so complete it took on a physical aspect, thick and suffocating. High above, the entrance to the well was a mere speck of light, while below, another pinprick of light appeared. As her downward drift continued, the illumination grew.

At last, Alex's boots settled on a smooth stone floor. An arched opening led from the well to yet another chamber. She stumbled out and blinked. An enormous amphitheater lay before her.

Elliptical, it looked like a giant ice cream scoop had been used to excavate and create the amphitheater. A flat, elevated platform like that used in a stage production, lay at the foot of the amphitheater. A short flight of stairs led onto the rostrum. Alex took the steps and stood on the dais where a single chair rested on its surface. Turned away from her, the chair faced seven large panels. Spaced evenly apart, they reminded Alex of giant flat screen monitors on earth. Easily ten feet in height and half as wide, they hung suspended in midair.

Alex walked in front and behind the panels. They were made of white marble, however, not a single cable, cord, or rope supported the heavy slabs.

Amazed, Alex returned her attention to the only other object on the platform.

The chair.

Upon closer inspection, it resembled a throne. Intricate scrollwork etched the sides, back, and even the seat. The script carried a familiarity to Alex. *The same writing on the magic mirror.* The throne's fan-shaped backrest stretched upward six feet or more, the armrests ending in burls chased in silver. But the most interesting aspect of the throne lay on the seat.

A circlet of gold.

Alex picked up the crown. Turning it over in her hands, she inspected it. The smooth metal was cool in her hands. No symbols or inscriptions marred its surface. On impulse, she placed it on her head.

A perfect fit.

A whisper, like the rustle of blowing leaves came to her ears. She strained to locate the source, the murmur growing louder. A muttered word was repeated over and over. A chill ran up her spine. No, not a word but a name. *Her* name.

Alexandria.

A mist rose from the floor before her. The ghostly fog thickened and swirled. Faster and faster it spun with a tornado-like intensity. The whisper became a roar, rising higher until it exploded with a brilliant incandescence. Particles of light skipped and skittered across the floor like sparklers from a fireworks display.

Where the mist once churned, a woman stood.

She wore a pale blue gown. Her hair, silver-gold, fell to her waist. Eyes the color of rain-washed sky settled on Alex.

Alex leaped up. The sudden motion caused the crown to fall from her head, and she prepared to bolt from the amphitheater. Before she could take a step, the women spoke in a tone both melodious yet with the ring of authority.

"Welcome, daughter. Long have I waited for you."

No malice existed in her words. Alex hesitated, torn between whether to stay or flee.

"You unraveled the mystery of the maze and discovered the Windows of Time. Over the long ages, only you have managed this feat. Your magic is *strong,* daughter, as it must be to reveal to you this secret place."

What magic is she talking about? I have no magic.

Alex studied the woman. Her face, although beautiful, seemed far older than it appeared. In fact, she carried an aura which reminded Alex of a recent experience.

The crystal sarcophagi and the dead they contained.

A cold chill traveled up her spine. "Who...*what* are you?"

"I was once called Diana, a Healer who lived among the people of Dalfur. Now," she ran her hands down her gown, "I exist as an *Afterimage.*"

"Afterimage? I-I don't know what that is."

A ripple of laughter issued from Diana. "One who once walked on this plane of existence in mortal flesh. I endure as thoughts, memories, deeds done and undone, the pieces of the life I once lived intertwined with the magic gifted to me by the Creator."

Her answer left Alex puzzled. None of it made any sense.

Diana glided toward her and stopped at the foot of the throne. "A better question for you to ask, is *why* are you here?"

Alex nodded. "Okay. Why *am* I here?"

The Afterimage waved a hand, and the amphitheater disappeared. Only the seven panels remained, and beyond them, the universe with its stars in their millions and billions appeared. Pinwheel galaxies slowly turned, flares from supernovas winked bright, and purple, blue, and red gases of newly birthed stars formed a pastel.

Gossamer filaments shot from Diana's hands, weaving in and out to form intricate geometric patterns as they raced toward each distant star. When finished, the countless strands formed a network much like a spider's web.

Diana spoke. "You see the threads of time, possibilities, potential hopes and dreams, the promise of what may come. All lead in different directions, random in every way save one."

Fascinated, Alex asked, "And what is that?"

"They are all connected to *you.*"

Alex's mouth went dry. "Wh-what do you mean?"

Instead of answering, Diana pointed. "You must select seven strands, but prepare yourself. For what you are about to see may be terrible, even horrific. Your courage will be tested."

The Afterimage leaned closer. "Choose well."

Diana motioned for Alex to approach the web. Not sure what to do, she cautiously reached out and touched one of the silvery strands. The thread quivered like a guitar string, and a musical note, high and piercing, rang out. The first panel on the left glowed brightly, then coalesced into a lifelike scene.

She and Tell were on a grassy knoll beside a small lake. The soft lap of waves washing ashore serenaded them. Tell threw a blanket on the dew-covered ground, while Alex carried a basket and placed it beside them.

Alex smiled. *A picnic.*

They sat on the blanket, laughing and talking. Tell put his arms around her and they lay back on the blanket intertwined with one another, a picture of bliss. Startled, Alex discovered she could taste Tell's kisses, *feel* the warmth of his breath.

The panel faded, leaving her disappointed. *Was this to be her life? One shared with Tell? Could it actually happen, and if so, how?*

Diana left her no time to ponder on it further. "Again," she commanded.

Alex touched another filament. Again, a musical note resonated, but this one of a different, higher pitch. The next panel flared to display another sight.

Alex walked along a forested trail. Soon she was joined by a stranger. Tall and lithe, he appeared quite young—probably not much older than Alex—with emerald-green eyes and long, copper-colored hair. However, the rest of his features were clouded, unfocused. Try as she might, most of his face remained hidden from her.

He moved with the ease and stealth of a mountain cat down the dappled footpath. They walked side-by-side until they came upon a meadow carpeted with a riot of yellow wildflowers. An ancient and massive oak grew from a hillock in the middle of the field. The young man looked about searching for something. His long stride parted the golden blossoms, and he plucked a lavender orchid from the midst of the yellow sea. He tucked it in her hair behind her ear.

Alex's breath quickened. *The meadow. The gigantic oak tree. The young stranger.* The one who filled her heart with such passion. Her previous dreams and the future thread.

They were one and the same.

CHAPTER 15

TAL SOARED HIGH ABOVE THE BAGGAGE TRAIN BELOW.

Men, horses, and wagons laden with supplies, stretched in a line for leagues. Three days out from the Veil, and the only signs of life were creatures who walked on four legs, not two. No evidence of the former inhabitants was found. The entire land had a deserted feel about it, like a virgin wilderness never touched by civilization.

"Where did they all go?" he mused.

"This area of Dalfur, even before the creation of the accursed Veil, was sparsely populated," Bozar reminded him. "No doubt the Dark Queen's minions captured and enslaved those who didn't manage to escape."

"Fortuitous, Prince Tal, since our movements must remain cloaked from the sorceress."

Tal glanced to his right where the White Monk, Pulpit, flew next to his First Advisor. Since his pledge to Queen Celestria, the monk never strayed far from his side.

"One would have to be deaf and blind not to see or hear our legions, Pulpit."

"All the more reason to celebrate the site of the invasion, my prince. There is a purpose to everything we receive from the Creator," Pulpit said with a grin. "We must have the faith to accept that which we do not understand."

Tal gave a wry nod. He now understood how the monk came by his nickname. He often sounded much like Bozar...perhaps the reason why the two got along so famously.

"We'll bivouac soon to allow our forces and supplies to catch up," Bozar said. "We are making progress, slow to be sure, but progress nonetheless. At this pace, we should arrive at the gates of Markingham within a fortnight."

"If we don't awaken the entire countryside before then," Tal groused.

Bozar sighed. "You know the plan, Tal. It is impossible to completely cloak the movements of an invading army. That's *why* we chose this route. It keeps us off roads and away from villages."

The First Advisor scanned the horizon. "From what I've seen so far, I'm not sure we should have bothered. The hand of man has not touched this area in many years."

Below, the baggage train stopped by a meadow fed by a small stream. Wagons were aligned in an orderly fashion, teams unhitched, then led to the stream to be watered. Apparently, Gravelback had decided to halt for the day.

Tal looked at the sun. *At least three hours of daylight left.*

"I'm going to scout ahead," he announced.

"I'll accompany you, my prince," Pulpit said.

"Don't take offense, good monk, but I would rather make the journey in silence despite the benefit of your pearls of wisdom. Bozar has already filled me with a lifetime of sage advice upon which to ponder."

"Most of which you have ignored!" Bozar quipped.

"All the more reason quietude is needed so I might better absorb your sagacious lessons."

Pulpit chuckled. "I *did* pledge to see to your safety."

Tal pursed his lips. "I ride a storm mount of unsurpassed strength and endurance. I have my sword, bow, and most importantly, my wits. If need be, I can call upon my magic."

"Magic which you are not to use unless all else fails," Bozar reminded him. "A Royal using magic on *this* side of the Veil would announce our presence far and wide."

Tal's patience grew thin. "I attended the war council, my *Eldred*. I know the plan! It included no mention that prevents me from scouting. We need to know what lies ahead, and there are none whose *farsight* surpasses mine."

Bozar and Pulpit exchanged looks. "Very well," the First Advisor said. "Carry out your reconnaissance, but return before sundown."

With a *whoop*, wings beating the air, Tal peeled away. Bozar and Pulpit soon disappeared from sight.

An hour later, Tal prepared to turn back. His sharp eyesight detected nothing of note. Other than eagles wheeling in the sky, deer, and other wildlife, he'd seen no sign of human habitation, only an endless panorama of forested wilderness.

He tugged on the reins to turn the storm mount, when a flash of sunlight from the ground below caught his attention. He circled the area.

There! There it is again!

Tal zeroed in on the location and swooped down to take a look. A small clearing came into view. A cabin sat tucked into a corner of the glade. As Tal drew nearer, he sensed magic, ancient but powerful. He landed on the grass-covered dell, and loosed his sword in its sheath. Dismounting, he left the storm horse's reins dangling over the saddle horn in case he needed to make a quick escape.

Tal discovered the entire area to be suffused with magic. He sniffed the air, tasting the ancient charm.

A preservation spell…and one of great power. No wonder the clearing isn't overgrown.

He approached the cabin with great caution. A covered porch fronted the structure, and held several rocking chairs spaced evenly apart on the threshold. A wooden door with a metal handle, sturdy but otherwise unremarkable, was flanked by a pair of curtain-covered windows.

He pulled his sword and reached for the knob.

With a *bang*, the door rebounded against the wall with the force of Tal's shove. No missiles tore through the opening in response, and Tal peeked around the corner of the doorframe. Nothing moved. He gathered his legs under him and dived into the cabin. He rolled to his feet, dagger in one hand, sword in the other.

Silence greeted him.

Then the door slammed shut, and light flared to life. Tal leaped to the side and slashed with his blade. He crouched, eyes searching every corner. No adversary appeared. Senses on high alert, he scanned the cabin's interior only to discover he was alone.

A chuckle escaped his lips. *The magic of the spell. It lies dormant until a guest appears.*

He re-sheathed his sword and dagger and inspected the cottage. Above his head, the source of light—a wagon wheel festooned with light crystals—hung by a chain from the ceiling. A hearth of mortared fieldstone lay near the back of the wall, a black iron pot on a swivel arm beside it. Dragon Stones rested beneath the metal grate on the floor of the hearth. Used in place of wood, the magic-infused stones could produce heat for the cabin and for cooking.

A kitchen and pantry lined the wall to the left of the fireplace. A wooden counter held a stone sink with a curved metal tap arching over the basin. Tal placed his hand under the spigot and water gurgled out. He wiped his hands on his tunic and opened the pantry doors. Sacks of flour and meal rested on a lower shelf, while jars of spices, pickled meat, and a variety of vegetables filled the upper shelves. All appeared as fresh as the day they were placed in the pantry.

Two rooms and a privy occupied the right side of the cottage. A cursory inspection revealed a bed in each room, a tiny wardrobe, and a rough-hewn dresser. The privy held basic amenities, including a sink and a small mirror mounted on the wall. A brass tub rested on four clawed feet, and took up the rest of the space. Above the bath, a wooden shelf held neatly folded towels.

Tal shrugged. There could be no doubt as to the purpose of this isolated refuge.

A hunting cabin.

While interesting an ancient and powerful charm still gripped the building, it held no strategic value Tal could see. Nor did it provide a clue to what happened to the former inhabitants of the region.

After a final look, he left the cabin. Foot in the stirrup, before he could swing himself into the saddle, a voice cried out in his mind.

Help me.

CHAPTER 16

T HE SAME YOUNG MAN OCCUPIED THIS POSSIBLE FUTURE *AND* HER recurring dream…with the same result.

Drawn to him like moth to flame, Alex's arms encircled his neck.

He pulled her close and placed a smoldering kiss on her lips. Warmth spread through her body like molten lava. Alex gasped, the heat within her unbearable.

The image disappeared.

"No! Bring him back," Alex pleaded.

I've never felt such a connection to someone.

Breathless, Alex held one hand to her wildly beating heart, while her other hand crept to the hollow of her abdomen. *Why does he cause such a reaction in me?*

"The power of the heart is an irresistible force…and a pure heart always rings true," Diana said.

Alex blinked. "I don't understand. Is he the one I am to…be with?"

"Yes—no—perhaps. The future is not set," Diana replied. "Choose again."

Alex selected a different silken strand. This one produced another melodic refrain, a tenor note softer than the others.

She stood in a baby's nursery drenched in sunshine streaming from a pair of nearby windows. A crib, rocking chair, changing table, and a small dresser completed the room's ensemble. Her hands were folded across her swollen abdomen, evidence of an advanced pregnancy. She knew without a doubt the one who haunted her dreams with such passion was the father. A sense of contentment filled her at the prospect of the impending birth. *I will be the mother I never had.*

The vison ended too soon, leaving her confused and unfulfilled. Hormones raced through her blood and she fought the urge to burst out crying. Alex's hands searched her body, her belly flat and smooth.

"It's so real," she whispered. "I could feel the baby moving inside of me."

"Of course. *All* possibilities are real." Diana gestured for Alex to make her next choice. Gathering her tattered emotions, she took a deep breath, and touched another of the web's strings. A bass note echoed, harsh and severe.

Dorothea and Rodric appeared with chalices of wine held in their hands. The Duchess touched her glass against Rodric's. "Congratulations on your marriage to Alexandria. We can now put in place the last piece of Marlinda's plan for the fall of Wheel."

"Ah, the sweet smell of success," Rodric snickered. "I wonder if the little slut has any idea of what is going to happen to her?"

Dorothea waved her hand. "Who cares? All you need to worry about is getting Alexandria with child as soon as possible. With an heir to the Duchy, we can finally rid ourselves of the Duke. He is so weak from my poison, a final dose is all that's needed to kill the old fool. To think I'll no longer have to endure the touch of his wrinkled flesh!"

The Duchess pulled a stoppered vial from her dress. A clear liquid swirled within. "Mix this with anything Alexandria drinks. Once it touches her lips, she will become as fertile as a gnome's garden. A child will be born less than a year from your wedding night."

"Mores the pity," Rodric smirked. "I was so looking

forward to the practice. Oh well, I can always amuse myself with Alexandria afterward."

"Entertain yourself any way you see fit, but not until *after* Alexandria has produced an heir. After the birth, the Duke will die and we will establish a regency—with you and me as regents. Your men will infiltrate the Ducal militia, and we will summon the Veil host to attack Wheel. The city will fall like a rotten fruit, with the defenders not knowing the enemy is already within their midst."

The scene faded.

Horror filled Alex. The pleasant thoughts and feelings from the previous threads evaporated. *A future with Rodric? Used like a game piece to kill her father and ensure the fall of Wheel?*

Suddenly another view appeared, this one with Alex sitting in a chair. Enormously pregnant, her distended belly stretched against the formless dress that she wore. She carried a vacant expression, and a thin line of drool trailed from the side of her mouth. It dripped off her face to join food stains on the gown's fabric.

Rodric stood nearby, an insolent grin on his face. "I must say you look in fine form today, Alexandria. Motherhood *does* become you."

Alex struggled to her feet and staggered out to the terrace. Rodric followed and stopped at the door lintel. He leaned against the frame and watched her progress with amusement. "Do be careful, my dear. I wouldn't want you to trip and fall."

Alexandria waddled to a table and pulled out a chair. She dragged it behind her to the edge of the terrace. Using it like a ladder, she placed one foot on the chair and stepped up onto the balustrade. She turned around to face Rodric, the roar of the falls a throbbing backdrop.

"You are cursed, your seed is cursed...and I am cursed."

She fell backwards and disappeared from sight.

Alex couldn't believe her eyes. *"No,"* she whispered. *"No!"*

"Again!" Diana demanded before she could dwell on the dreaded possibilities.

With great reluctance, she plucked another of the silvery strings. A boom, a deep note resonated against the walls of the amphitheater. When the echo faded, another scene presented itself.

An immense cavern stretched before her for leagues. The floor of the vast grotto was black with rank after rank of melded creatures prepared for war. Tusks, hooves, fangs, and claws gleamed from the fires illuminating the underground hollow.

A black turret thrust above the mass. Two figures stood on the tower's parapet, a man and woman. As one they pointed at the creatures.

Grunts, howls, shrieks, and screeches rose from countless throats. The roar rose to an ear-splitting crescendo. The creatures turned and ran.

The view shifted and displayed the foot of a mountain. Like ants, an endless number of the Dark Queen's army disgorged from numerous hidden exits. They spilled out to spread across the countryside, cries of bloodlust shaking the night.

The cold terror produced by the sight left Alex shivering. The next scene, however, made it seem like a warm summer breeze.

Bodies—by the tens of thousands—formed a twisted landscape of blood and death. Stabbed, hacked, and impaled, the dead had been killed by every means possible. Severed arms, legs, and heads lay where they had been cleaved from once-living flesh. Disemboweled coils of intestines glistened like grotesque worms in the pale sunlight. Swarms of carrion birds picked at the slaughter, so gorged with the flesh of the slain, many could only hop, not fly. Above it all, the smell of death permeated everything. The scene, the sight and smell, filled every pore of Alex's body.

She screamed.

She screamed until she had neither the breath nor the energy to continue a second longer.

Diana drifted toward her. "Why…why have you shown me all of this?" Alex croaked. *"Why am I even here?"*

"Because you are the key. You have within you the power to correct an ancient wrong and prevent this future."

"What power? How?" Alex sobbed. "I'm so scared I may never close my eyes again."

"What lies within you far exceeds what lies without. You and only you must discover this, daughter. But let this be a clue." Diana reached out and touched Alex's chest. Instantly, her fears and worries evaporated. She felt invigorated, renewed.

"Ask yourself: *What drives each of the futures you have seen?* Because therein lies your true power. So as it was with me, so too will it be with you.

"I must leave you now, daughter, but before I do—"

Diana reached out and snatched something not far from where they stood. She held up a puddle of shadow. It struggled, twisting in her grasp. Anger lined the Afterimage's face.

Alex pointed a trembling finger. "What…what is it?"

"The Enemy, spawn created by dark sorcery. It followed you through the maze." Diana closed her fist. A shriek came from the shade, then it shattered, pieces falling like broken glass to the floor. Oily smoke rose from the residue, black and noxious. Soon no evidence of the shade remained.

Diana's image began to waver. It became transparent and Alex could see through her. Soon only a wisp remained…and then disappeared.

Alex blinked. A mirror, the twin to the one in her bedroom, occupied the space where the Afterimage once stood. Rather than her reflection, however, the mirror displayed her personal chambers. Anxious to leave the now cold and lonely amphitheater, Alex stepped through.

The storm still raged as Alex undressed, put on her nightgown and returned to bed. She didn't know which was more likely to keep her sleepless; the malignant pool of ooze Diana shattered, or the possible futures she presented. But it was the Afterimage's final comment she returned to again and again. *What drives each possibility?*

A smile came to her lips at the picnic scene with Tell. But then she recalled the image of the meadow, the orchid tucked in her hair, the stranger's arms around her, the feel of his lips on hers.

And she knew. Despite having never met him, she knew.

This future could only be produced by one thing.

Love.

CHAPTER 17

HELP ME.

Tal dropped the reins and fell into a crouch. He searched for the source of the voice.

Help me.

Tal's hands flew to his head, fingers rubbing his temple. The words came not from the cabin or woods.

They came from within his mind!

"Who speaks?" he asked the air.

One who will die without your help.

Tal noticed a definite female inflection within the voice. Wary of a trap, he asked, "What is it you need?"

A trail leads from the clearing into the forest. Follow it until you come to a brook. Track upstream and you will find me. I sense your caution, but you have nothing to fear from me, Prince Tal.

The shock of a voice appearing in his mind registered as a mild tremor compared to the quake which shook him.

She knows my identity.

All the carefully laid plans to keep their invasion hidden crashed about his ears. The scale of this disaster could end the efforts to kill the Dark Queen and King and destroy the Veil... before it even started.

The desperate voice left him no choice. "I'm coming."

He found the game trail and entered the forest. The bright sunlight, swallowed up by the canopy, reduced the interior to dim shadows. Tal's sharp vision, unaffected by the faint light, easily compensated. At the burbling brook, he turned and followed it upstream.

Alert for an ambush, he made no sound and flitted through the underbrush, as much a part of the woodland as the native vegetation. Soon, he came to a fallen evergreen, a true titan of the forest. Like a giant sword, the colossal tree had slashed an opening through the thick canopy when it fell. Tal's breath caught in his throat at what lay on the ground beside the tree.

A Cyclops.

The blue-skinned creature lay with eye closed, her breath coming in ragged gasps of pain. A bulging belly paired with engorged and ponderous breasts pressed against a fur tunic, revealed her as pregnant and close to term. Sharp tusks protruded from the Cyclops' lower palate and past thick lips. An ivory horn grew from the center of her forehead, a single eye positioned below. If she stood, Tal estimated her height to be at least nine feet.

The reason for the Cyclops' dilemma was immediately evident. Looped like a snare, a thick, gnarled root had caught the creature's ankle. Wound tight against her swollen flesh, the Cyclops' thick fingers could find no purchase to wrench herself free. With her advanced pregnancy, the only comfortable position was to lie supine.

A heavy club whose length matched Tal's height, rested close beside the Cyclops. Her anvil-sized hand, composed of three fingers and a thumb, lay within easy reach of the bludgeon. Tal circled closer, eyes on the weapon.

I will not harm you, Prince Tal.

Wary, Tal didn't respond and instead, squatted and studied the root which entangled the Cyclops' ankle. A small gap existed between her trapped ankle and where the tough root protruded from the ground. He stood, drew his sword, and chopped once, then twice, with the blade. The woody matter parted easily.

Freed, the Cyclops struggled to a sitting position and rubbed her injured ankle.

Tal retreated to a safe distance the sword still in his hand. "How is it a Forest Mother speaks in my mind? How do you know me?"

The Cyclops grasped the club and used it like a crutch to push herself into a standing position. She limped to the fallen tree and rested against its massive bole.

Ah, the name your kind have given a female of my species. She placed a spade-sized hand on her distended abdomen. *You saved two lives this day. I am in your debt.*

"Then consider the debt paid by answering my questions."

A rumble akin to a growl erupted from the Cyclops. Tal tightened his grip on the sword, then realized the Forest Mother was chuckling.

You view me like any other woodland animal, mindless and driven by instinct. But as you can see, I am anything but. Tell me, what do you know of my kind?

Tal recalled the woodlore drilled into him at an early age by Fern Fernleaf. The forest gnome proved an apt teacher. His lessons always began and ended in the same location—the wilds.

"Cyclops are by nature reclusive, shunning even each other," he recited. "Long-lived, with one exception they usually pose no threat to others."

The Forest Mother smiled, revealing more saber-like teeth. *And what is this exception?*

"Once every century, females come into season. The hormones they release can be detected by males a hundred leagues away. It drives them into a mating frenzy, but since a Forest Mother can mate only once, the competition is fierce and brutal. The males will kill anything, including each other, for the opportunity to couple with a female. During the rut, a Forest Mother must be given a wide berth to avoid the crazed males."

Very good young prince. The Cyclops caressed her belly. *This will be my tenth, and last, birthing.*

Tal's eyes widened at this information. "That—that would mean…" His words trailed off at the implication.

"You are over a thousand years old," he managed to finish. "You were alive before the creation of the Veil."

The Cyclops' face darkened. *Aye. An abomination exceeded only by the foul wickedness of those responsible for this handiwork.*

A rumbling sigh bubbled from the Forest Mother. *Since the day of my own birthing, I have been different. I hear the thoughts of others, feel their emotions. Down through the long years, I often slipped close to the camps of men and listened to their thoughts. I learned much of your kind, Prince Tal. Whereas animals are driven by the simple needs of their nature, the mind of man is often determined by emotion. Such an environment breeds unpredictability. Hate, love, fear, joy. Who can say which will spring forth?*

She shook her head. *Alone among the creatures of the forest, only man kills for sport, and inflicts needless pain. Yet man can produce a love and compassion to give life extraordinary meaning. Your kind are two sides of the same coin, Prince Tal. Both a blessing and a curse.*

The Forest Mother shifted more of her weight to the other foot. A hiss of relief escaped her lips. *One day when young in my life, voices appeared in my mind. Curious, I followed them to the very abode you came from. I discovered two humans, a man and woman. Although I knew little of magic then, theirs was of such power the very air crackled with it.*

They were a mated pair though different in every way save one— the bond of love they shared. The male, tall and dark-haired, possessed magic like an iron-forged blade, sharp and unyielding. The woman, pale of skin and hair, held a magic of warmth and light.

She knew of my presence immediately—the only one in my long life who could read my thoughts as easily as I read others. Rather than respond with fear or surprise, she bade me welcome and said I was expected. Then she told me one day another voice would speak to me. When this happened, I was to make my way back to this same dwelling.

The Cyclops paused. *I have made this region of the forest my home ever since.*

Tal sheathed his blade and nodded. "Now I understand how you know me. My thoughts have revealed who I am."

The lengthening shadows cast by the treefall reminded him of his promise to Bozar. "I must return soon or a search party will be sent to look for me." He turned back to the Cyclops. "Good fortune to you, Forest Mother. You may repay me by keeping all knowledge of our meeting to yourself."

The growl he recognized as laughter again erupted from the Cyclops. *Your secret is safe with me, Prince Tal. It is impossible for me to tell another.*

Tal frowned. "Why"

For the same reason I knew you were the one whose path I was fated to cross. My gift to read minds is a trail which leads in only one direction. I can hear but cannot share my own thoughts. Only the noblewoman—the one called Diana—have I ever been able to mind-speak with. But today I heard a voice, another I could exchange thoughts with.

You, Prince Tal. The voice belongs to you.

CHAPTER 18

THE DUKE'S MANOR BUZZED WITH FRANTIC ACTIVITY.

Alex stood on the balcony and watched a long line of carriages pull up and disgorge their passengers. Evening had fallen and the estate, lit up like a small city, glowed with a thousand lights.

Tonight, a formal ball to announce her engagement and marriage to Rodric would be held. Her father spared no expense, and the guest list numbered in the hundreds. Wine would flow, food consumed, and music played to celebrate this union. A joyous occasion for all save one.

Only I know the truth.

She had seen the threads of time. Her husband-to-be along with her stepmother, Dorothea, were in league with the Dark Queen, the evil sorceress who created the Veil. Proving it, however, was another matter.

No one will believe me.

All her hopes now rested on Tell's shoulders. The young lieutenant, cryptic when she asked, would only say that he was working on a *plan*. However, as each day drew her marriage date nearer, her desperation increased. She long ago reached the point it didn't matter what Tell suggested. *Anything* was better than Rodric.

Possibilities. The Future is not set.

Alex clung to the Afterimage's comment like a shipwreck victim to flotsam. She *could* change her future. She didn't have to marry Rodric. *But how?* Diana provided her with no clues.

She forced back the bile in her throat at the thought of Rodric's touch. While she continued to play the part of eager fiancée, this meant she had to suffer his hands roaming over her body. He grew bolder each time they were alone together. She now wore a stiff corset, thick bodice, an extra petticoat, and gowns which buttoned up to her neck. Uncomfortable and hot, they were a small price to pay to forestall his lecherous gropes.

Tonight, however, she had no choice in attire. The Duke commissioned a gown for her to wear at the betrothal proclamation. Seed pearls lined the shimmering gold material of the dress. Stiff thread in royal blue formed intricate patterns on the floor-length hem. A delicate chain of pure gold girdled the fabric at her small waist. A scalloped neckline ended at a bejeweled bodice which pushed her breasts into a crevice of tight cleavage. The gown left her slim arms exposed, and a necklace of glittering diamonds draped from her neck.

When Darcy helped her dress for the event, the maid had piled her hair high on her head and arranged it in layers of curls. Delicate strands of silver chain interwoven with tiny gemstones formed a web holding her golden tresses in place. Standing before a mirror, Alex drew a sharp breath, awestruck at her image.

"M'Lady will be the most beautiful woman at the ball tonight," Darcy commented.

The gown was absolutely stunning. When combined with her hair and jewelry, Alex glowed with a beauty she found hard to believe.

Is this really me?

At times, Alex still found it difficult to separate herself completely from her past as plain and homely Mona. *Maybe it will always be this way no matter how long I live in someone else's skin.*

Alex closed her eyes and envisioned the young man from the meadow. "Why can't *he* see me like this? Why must it be Rodric?"

she whispered…then felt immediate guilt as she knew it *should* be Tell foremost in her thoughts.

With a heavy sigh, she returned her mind to the present. The guests were arriving, and her father expected her to greet them. At least their public presence and the large crowd should force Rodric to keep his manners formal.

And his hands off her.

⬛

Dorothea dismissed her maid and eyed herself critically in the mirror.

Her alabaster skin contrasted with the dark blue gown she wore. Rubies cascaded from a necklace nestling like drops of blood between the swell of her breasts. Pale yellow hair, arranged in elaborate loops and whorls, framed her face and slender neck.

"You look ravishing," Rodric said. "Alas, if only I weren't about to wed. You tempt me sorely."

The Duchess, lip curled, turned to face Rodric. "Your flattery is wasted on me. I'd as soon bed a viper than you. Save your charm for where it's needed—for Alexandria."

Rodric leered at Dorothea. "Just as well. I *should* save myself for my wedding night."

Dorothea waved her hand. "Your indulgences are none of my concern." She stood and smoothed her gown. "However, when it comes to Alexandria, that *is* my concern. For example, the shade has not reported to me these past three days. I'm sure you have an explanation for this."

Rodric's smug expression evaporated. "That's not possible."

"I assure you it is. Perhaps your magical skills are slipping, your sorcery not as potent—"

"My proficiency is more than a match for yours!" Rodric

snarled. "More likely it's your *own* incompetence which has cost you the shade's service."

Dorothea's lips formed a thin line. "I do so enjoy our conversations. Might I ask then, what do *you* think, Lord Regret, is the reason behind *your* shade's disappearance?"

Rodric paced back and forth, fuming. Then he stopped, his face pale. "The shade should have reported. There is only one reason why it wouldn't. But it makes no sense. Alexandria has no power." He pointed at Dorothea.

"You told me yourself the shade revealed she couldn't ignite even a spark when she grasped the Staff of the Test."

The Duchess frowned. "What does this have to do with the shade?"

"*Something* caused its dissolution. Something possessed of powerful magic."

Alex stood next to her father as the invited guests waited to be formally announced. The line stretched from the great hall into the ballroom. Inexplicably, neither Rodric or Dorothea had appeared yet, forcing everyone to wait.

A side door opened and the Duchess and Rodric hurried toward them. Both wore harried expressions. Rodric greeted the Duke, then took Alex's hand and kissed it. "Hello, my love. Please forgive my tardiness."

He squeezed her hand so tightly she bit back a cry. He released her and turned to Duke Duvalier. "Shall we greet our guests?"

Although smiling, something lurked behind the façade that chilled Alex's blood. He reeked of cold anger which he disguised quite well for all except one...Alex.

She knew his true nature.

She suppressed a shiver. *It must have been Dorothea or Rodric who sent the shade to follow me. Nobody else makes sense. By now they must know something has happened to it. But they can't connect the shade's disappearance to me...can they?* The seneschal announced the first guests and soon she was too busy to give it more thought.

An hour later, the last of the dignitaries passed by and Alex sagged with relief. The crowded ballroom bustled with servants scurrying to fill glasses, serve delicacies, and carry off empty flagons of wine and dishes. Rodric took the opportunity to grab a wine bottle and glass. Filling the glass, he emptied it then filled it again. Drinking steadily, he showed no signs of slowing down, and left Alex to disappear into the crowd.

Alex heaved a sigh of relief. With the press of numerous guests, the ballroom felt hot and confining. She needed fresh air and a chance to escape the crush of so many bodies. The balcony doors beckoned, and she made her way to them.

Her progress took much longer than she expected. She was forced to a stop every few feet. Everybody wanted to greet her, tell her how fortunate she was to marry Rodric, and wish the happy couple good tidings. Frozen smile in place, she managed to extricate herself and move a small distance before the process repeated itself.

She reached the sanctuary of the balcony. Finally alone, the music and chatter of voices dulled to a muted cacophony and she took a deep breath of the cool night air. Hands on the balustrade, she surveyed the city far below. Like a many-faceted diamond, Wheel glittered with tens of thousands of lights.

So beautiful.

"Ah, there you are my sweetness."

Startled, Alex turned. Rodric, empty wine glass in hand, staggered drunkenly toward her.

Reaching her, he tossed the glass over the railing and pulled her roughly to him. He kissed her, and Alex gagged at the sweet-stale odor of wine on his breath.

"Why wait till our wedding night? How about a taste right now?" He bunched the hem of her gown, pulled it up, and groped up her thigh before reaching between her legs.

Throat constricted, her heart pounding, Alex said, "No, please don't. We must wait."

"Waiting is for fools. I take what I want *when* I want." His other hand tore at her bodice.

Alex struggled to escape his grip. "Stop it!" she screamed.

A figure darted from the ballroom and a blade pricked Rodric's neck. "Remove your hands...or you will not draw another breath."

Tell stood beside Rodric, a dagger at his jugular. Rodric released Alex and she stumbled away. "You dare threaten me?" he hissed.

"You mistake me, Lord Regret," Tell said through bared teeth. "A threat implies *possible* action, while what I intend is a certainty...to gut you like a suckling pig."

"I think that is quite enough, Lieutenant!" The tall form of Alabaster John stood at the balcony doors. With a quick flick of his wrist, the dagger wrenched itself from Tell and flew into the Court Magister's hand.

He moved between the two men. "And you, Lord Regret, have guests wondering where you have disappeared to. I suggest you attend them."

Rodric smoothed his tunic. "Of course, you are right, Grand Master. I'll just take Alexandria—"

"I think this is an excellent opportunity for me to offer my congratulations to Lady Alexandria," Alabaster John said. "*If* you don't mind," he added.

"Very well." Rodric paused, his black eyes locked on Tell. "I'm sure our paths will cross again, Lieutenant. Very soon." He spun around and left them.

"Grand Master, I was—" Tell began to explain before Alabaster John cut him off.

"I know what you were doing!" He handed the knife back, hilt first. Leaning closer, he spoke harshly in Tell's ear. "I warned you not to wear your feelings for Alexandria so openly. Please leave us."

Tell bowed stiffly. "As you wish." He gazed at Alex for a moment, then disappeared into the ballroom.

"You don't understand. He was just trying to help me," Alex stammered.

"But I do understand." Alabaster held up his palm when Alex tried to speak again. "Others, however, will not."

He grasped her hand, his touch cool and soothing. "You may always come to me if you have need. Try to remember your friends number more than just the young lieutenant...and you may have need of them in the days to come."

The Court Magister smoothed his robe. "Now I think it time for you rejoin your guests. Take a moment and compose yourself." He squeezed her hand and left.

Alone, Alex blinked back the tears which threatened to overwhelm her. Then anger rose within her at how Rodric so openly violated her. She clenched her fists, fingernails digging into her palm. *I will not cry.*

I'll never let him make me cry.

CHAPTER 19

TAL SAT IN ARTEMIS THURGOOD'S PALATIAL PAVILION WITH BOZAR, Pulpit, and the Grand Master.

Thurgood swallowed a huge mouthful of ale and slammed the tankard down onto the table they were arranged around. "A Forest Mother which can mind-speak, eh? An enchanted cabin? I expected melded man-beasts and other dark sorcery, but not this."

"She knew you would be there?" Pulpit asked.

Tal nodded. "The Cyclops told me she heard my thoughts. The noblewoman she mind-spoke with those long years ago, told her that one day the Forest Mother would discover another to share thoughts with."

Bozar listened with keen interest. "No one could have predicted your whereabouts—much less from a meeting which took place before the creation of the accursed Veil." The First Advisor tapped his lips. "It is a coincidence, nothing more."

Pulpit shook his head. "A way through the Veil is finally found, then days after we move through the open portal, the young prince happens upon a charmed cabin and an intelligent Cyclops...one which just happens to be able to communicate via her mind. I fear I must correct you, First Advisor. This represents not *a* coincidence, but a *series* of ordained events."

"Surely you don't believe these occurrences are related?" Artemis Thurgood harrumphed.

Pulpit smiled. "I am a Monk of the White Order. *Of course* I believe it."

Bozar chuckled. "The good monk has a point. Nevertheless, we have more immediate concerns. The narrow gateway through the Veil has proven to be more of a chokepoint than we imagined. The legions trickle through with the haste of a snail. At this pace, we will reach Markingham with less than half the compliment of soldiers and supplies we expected. We must concentrate on what comes next—not be distracted by speculation linked to past events."

The others murmured their approval.

Although Tal agreed with his *Eldred*, he couldn't bring himself to believe the encounter with the Forest Mother to be a lucky happenstance. A prickle, like static electricity before a storm, traveled up his spine.

Something was coming. Something was going to happen.

And soon.

Alex walked through the stables. After the noise and bustle of the ballroom, the occasional nicker of horses and jingle of tack soothed her tattered nerves. The *crunch* of her slippers on the dry hay was magnified like the crack of dry wood among the quiet stalls.

No one's here but me. Even the groomsmen have gone to their bunks for the night.

The impulse to leap on a horse and ride away gripped her with such strength, she found herself reaching for a saddle.

I could leave. Just ride out through the gates and keep going.

"I knew I'd find you here."

Alex whirled and stifled a scream. Tell stood a few feet from her.

Hand pressed against her wildly beating heart, she gasped, "What are you doing here?"

Instead of his uniform, he wore a brown tunic, pants, and scuffed leather boots...the clothing of a civilian.

He took a step toward her. "I know you come here sometimes to think. When you don't want to return to your chambers."

She brushed a strand of hay off his tunic. "I should have known. You know me better than anyone." Both stood quietly, neither speaking. Finally, Alex asked, "Why aren't you in uniform?"

Eyes downcast, Tell kicked at the dirt and straw. With a sigh, he looked up. "After the incident with Lord Regret, I was confined to the barracks. Worse, Lord Ruffin relieved me from command of your guard detail."

A wane smile appeared. "Alabaster John was right. I didn't conceal my feelings for you nearly well enough...which meant to continue my military career, I wouldn't see you anymore. Given this choice, I did the only thing my heart would allow me to do.

"I resigned my commission."

Alex's hands flew to her mouth. "That's not fair! I'll get father to reinstate you and have Lord Ruffin—"

"No, Alex. What's done is done. I have no regrets. Rodric had his filthy hands on you and if given the chance I'd do it again... except the next time I wouldn't stay my blade."

He squeezed her arm. "That part of my life is over. *You* are all that matters now."

Tell looked around then leaned closer. "I can get us flying horses. Between our two mounts, we can carry enough supplies to see us through the first few weeks."

Alex's heart leaped. *We can leave Rodric and Dorothea—all of this—far behind.*

"Then let's go." She put her hand on Tell's chest. "Can we leave tonight?"

A troubled look crossed his face.

"What? What is it?" Alex asked.

"There's a problem. Where would we go? We can't go to my

parent's estate. It would be the first place the Duke would look. And I know of no other place left in Dalfur not under the dominion of the Dark Queen. We can't just hide in the wilderness the rest of our lives."

"Why can't we?"

Tell shook his head. "You deserve better. Far better. Besides, you have no idea how difficult it is to survive in the wild. I could be leading both of us to our deaths."

With, hopes shattered, Alex tried to pick up the pieces. *Think. Don't give up.* "We still have time. There must be a place somewhere. I have books with maps of Dalfur, and now that you are free of military service, you can look as well."

Tell chewed his lip. He nodded. "Okay. The marriage ceremony is in two weeks. Maybe we can find a place of sanctuary before then. In the meantime, gather the necessities you will need. Take only riding clothes, and make sure you find a safe place to hide what you've packed."

He gripped her shoulders. "Don't try to contact me. Give no clue to what we have planned. To anyone! Thanks to my foolish act with Rodric, we will be watched more closely now. I'll find a way to contact you when I'm ready."

"Oh, Tell. You *saved* me from him. There's no telling what he might have done. I'm so lucky to have you for a friend."

Tell swallowed. "Is that what we are, Alex?" he asked. "Friends?"

She stroked his arm, the flesh warm beneath her fingers. Her hands traveled upward and cupped his face. She kissed him and held his lips against hers, reluctant to release him. "No. You are so much more to me," she whispered.

He put his arms around her and they stumbled backwards in their rush to embrace one another.

Alex's back slid up against a stall. Breathless, she moaned as his lips found the sensitive nape of her neck. She gripped his hips and pulled him against her. Passion boiled inside her like an over-heated kettle. Pushing him away, she fumbled with the stays on her bodice.

"N-no," Tell gasped. Face red, his breath came in explosive gasps. He pointed at the dung heaps littering the hay. "How would you explain *those* stains on your gown?"

"I'll tell them I fell." She continued to loosen her bodice.

"Alex!" He held her hands stopping her. "Don't you under-stand? The Duke and Rodric are already suspicious. We can't afford to do anything which heightens these suspicions. They'll double the guard on you, or worse, confine you to your chambers until the wedding. Then it won't matter if we find a place to flee to."

Alex stomped her foot, hot tears of frustration leaking from her eyes. "My life is not my own, even when we're alone together. *I want to leave this place!*" she cried, an edge of desperation in her voice.

Clutching his tunic, the fabric twisted in her fingers, she pulled him roughly to her. "I'm going with you, and I don't care where we go as long as we're together."

Anger replaced the tears, and a steely determination erupted within her like a wellspring.

"No more! I want my life back." She turned to him. "Have the flying horses and our supplies ready.

"I don't know how, but I'm going to find us a place...one far away from here."

CHAPTER 20

WHEN ALEX RETURNED TO HER CHAMBERS SHE NOTED WITH dismay the *four* sentries now standing watch at her door instead of the usual two.

Tell's prediction had already come true.

With great effort, Alex kept her anger in check and warmly greeted the guards. Once inside her chambers, she sprinted to her closets, threw open the doors, and began to choose clothes and boots to pack. When finished, her selections piled on the bed, she was surprised at how small the accumulation was. Despite her enormous wardrobe, the few practical articles of clothing she owned were the ones she'd had the court seamstress make.

Next, she picked through her underclothes and stifled the urge to curse. Her only choices were silken underwear, corsets, and bodices with complicated laces, hooks, and hasps. *My kingdom for just one normal bra!*

In the end she selected the sturdiest—and sure to be the most uncomfortable—underclothes she could find. More rummaging around produced a large leather satchel. She stuffed her collection inside the bag and looked for a place to hide it. Her eyes fell on the enchanted mirror.

Perfect.

Alex carried the satchel to the mirror…then stepped through the magical Artifact. Once again, she stood on the stone landing, the weak light from sputtering torches illuminating the area. Footprints lay in the thick dust and led down the steps. Other than this evidence of her previous journey, nothing had changed. She placed the bag on the floor and exited the mirror back into her room.

Smug, she crossed her arms. *Try to find that.*

Pleased with herself, she patted the top of the charmed mirror. The act caused a slight shift in the ancient Artifact's position. In an instant, the scene changed.

Alex's jaw dropped at the sight of Alabaster John seated at a desk in his chamber scribbling on a parchment. She gasped and dove behind the nearby vanity. Heart pounding, she peeked over the top of her dressing table.

The court magister continued writing, oblivious to her presence.

Alex sat back against the vanity, her thoughts racing. *He doesn't see me.*

She recalled the mirror left when Diana's Afterimage faded. She used it to return to her room. *Could there be other magical mirrors scattered throughout Wheel?* If so, maybe Alabaster John had one too.

An idea came to her and she scrambled from behind the vanity and stood beside the Artifact. Small lodestones were embedded in the rim of the frame. She ran her fingers over them and the panorama changed to stark blackness. She moved her fingers again and the scene remained blank. Frustrated, she tapped one of the lodestones hard. A room with an eclectic collection of items from dusty furniture to various tools materialized. The dim light displayed a polished wooden bar in the background with stacks of glasses. The sight produced a spark of recognition, and a gasp left Alex's mouth.

Pandathaway Pandergast's store!

Fingering the lodestones on the enchanted Artifact produced the same effect as using a remote. Instead of changing a channel, however, it changed to the location of another mirror.

Alex sat on her bed and rubbed her eyes. *Where did all of these enchanted mirrors come from? Were there more at one time? Had the passage of time assured only a few would survive?*

Idly, she wondered at the odds of how one managed to remain undamaged through the long years...and end up in her chambers.

How fortuitous.

She recalled the gnome's vast collection of diverse items, some of it clothing. *Maybe I can find something useful to wear.*

She stood up and walked to the mirror, took a deep breath... then stepped through into the store. Alex let her eyes adjust to the darkened shop. As she suspected, another mirror, identical to the Artifact in her room, stood beside her.

Alex started her search, the *tick-tock* of the store's many clocks forming a choral serenade. Although she walked with as light a tread as possible, the *creak* of old floorboards followed every step. She came to a chest and fumbled with the latch in the darkness. She managed to free it, then pushed the lid up. Clothing was folded neatly to one side, several pairs of boots on the other side. She picked up a pair and examined them. *They just might fit.*

Kicking off her slippers, Alex was just about to slip on a boot when a bright light blinded her.

"Don't move or I'll skewer you like a roasted goose!"

Clunk. The boots fell to the floor. Hands raised to shade her eyes, Alex's heart threatened to leave her chest.

Pandathaway Pandergast stood a short distance away, a cranked and loaded crossbow aimed at her. In his other hand, he held a light crystal.

The gnome squinted in disbelief. "La-Lady Alexandria?"

Alex burst into tears.

With Pandergast on one side and his wife on the other, Alex sobbed uncontrollably. Lillian held her tightly and tried to comfort her.

"Insensitive oaf!" she scolded her husband. "See what you've done!"

"But-but—"

"Buffoon! Go make some tea before I box your ears!" Pandathaway scurried off.

"I-I'm s-sorry," Alex hiccupped, "I-I'm n-not a thief. I c-can pay—" Unable to finish, she dissolved into another round of tears.

"Shush, child. We know you're not a common thief."

All the bravado Alex felt earlier with Tell left her in a rush. In its place, shame competed with a sense of helplessness. Different world, different identity, same result.

Nothing changes.

The store owner returned with a pot of tea he set on a nearby table. Together, the diminutive gnome and his wife helped Alex into a chair. He poured tea for everyone and handed a steaming mug to Alex. "Drink this," he urged her. "It will help calm you."

Alex cupped the mug in her hands, the heat soothing her chilled fingers. She sipped the tea, and the delightful taste of chocolate, cinnamon, and cloves tickled her tongue. She drained half the cup and fortified, took a shuddering breath.

"Th-thank you. You are both so kind," she managed to say.

Pandathaway stretched his arm across the table and took her hand in his. "Nonsense. You are more than welcome here... though most usually visit our shop during the day and *when* we are open."

Alex dropped her head. "I know," she whispered.

The gnome patted her hand gently. "Lady Alexandria, this is where you tell us *why* the nocturnal visit."

Alex took another sip and tried to pull her tattered emotions together. *Tell said to do nothing which might tip off others about our plans.*

Like sediment, Alex's secrets continued to be deposited one layer atop the next. The weight of this stratification paralyzed her. *Who to trust, who not to trust?* But the kindly faces of the gnomish couple across from her contained nothing but concern.

The dam broke.

"I'm leaving Wheel with Tell," she blurted. "I can't marry Rodric. All I own are useless gowns, and I need sturdier clothing. I thought you might have what I needed."

Once started, Alex couldn't stop, and the rush of words poured from her mouth in a torrent. She told them about Rodric possessing Darcy's body and attacking her, his confrontation with Tell at the betrothal celebration, about the enchanted mirror, the maze, and finally, meeting Diana. She described the futures the Afterimage presented her, particularly the one which revealed Dorothea and Rodric's betrayal of the Duke. Once finished, it felt as if a pus-filled boil had been lanced, and an enormous burden lifted off her shoulders.

"Dorothea is slowly poisoning Father and I don't know what to do about it. I can't prove it and no one will believe me," she added bitterly.

She expected shock and disbelief to be reflected in the gnomes' eyes. Instead, Pandathaway and Lillian shared a grim look.

"It is far worse than we feared," the shop owner said.

Astonished, Alex stared at the gnomish couple. "Wh-what? You mean you know?"

Pandathaway nodded. "We have long suspected the new Duchess and Lord Regret are in league with the Dark Queen. The Duke's first wife died not long after Dorothea appeared in Wheel.

I strongly believed foul evil to be responsible for this, but much like you, had no convincing evidence."

The gnome stood and walked around the table. With Alex seated, he matched her height and fixed her with a determined look. "Now, I must ask *you* something." He leaned closer until mere inches separated them. "And I need the truth." Alex sucked in a breath and nodded.

"What happened to you? The Alexandria I knew is as different from you as the night is from the day."

Alex froze. *Reveal another secret?* This one she didn't dare divulge—nor could she bring herself to lie to Pandathaway. He and Lillian had shown her nothing but kindness. In the end, she decided a partial truth was better than none at all.

"When I woke after the fall from my horse, all the details of my life were lost to me. I didn't even know my name. From that day to this, everything has been different, everything is new." She turned the now empty cup in her hands. "It's like I started a fresh life with a new beginning."

For long moments, the gnome remained still, his eyes searching hers. A smile appeared. "I must say I like the new Alexandria much better than the old."

Relief washed over Alex. Curious, she asked, "How did you know about Rodric and Dorothea?"

A sadness spread across Pandathway's face. "I was once the Duke's Weapons Master. My responsibilities included training new recruits, and keeping our arms inventory up to date."

Alex frowned. "Why don't you still hold that position? Did you retire?"

The gnome's face twisted. "When the Duchess—your mother—died, Alton Duvalier became a shell of a man. He retreated so far into himself, we feared he would die of a broken heart. Then Dorothea appeared. How she got her talons into him, none of us know, but within a short period of time, he announced his attention to remarry—to her."

"Gnomes are very sensitive to magic, particularly sorcery," Pandathaway explained. "I sensed this about Dorothea immediately...doubly so when Rodric appeared in Wheel. I expressed my concerns to Alabaster John, and although he shared my fears, he urged me to keep them to myself until we could prove it."

Pandathaway shook his head. "I should have listened. Instead, I went to the Duke and told him what I suspected. He flew into a rage and forcibly removed me from his presence. The next day I was dismissed."

The gnome's information painted a clear picture for Alex. Somehow, Dorothea bewitched the Duke. This triggered the appearance of Rodric, and in turn, set up the final piece.

Alex's marriage to him.

The table thumped with the force of the gnome's fist striking it. "They want you for something, Lady Alexandria," he said grimly. "Sabotage is one thing, producing an heir, quite another. Why? Is it something in your bloodlines—"

Pandathaway stopped, his face drained of color. "The Staff of the Test!"

Alex recalled her initial visit and holding the Artifact. "But nothing happened."

"Something *did* happen...but long after you had left."

Alex frowned. "I don't understand. What are you talking about?"

Pandathaway looked at his wife. Lillian nodded and he continued, "I discovered the Staff later that night lit up from base to tip, every lodestone brimming with powerful, vibrant magic. What's more, the magic it exuded is unlike any I ever experienced before. Only one person held the Staff that day."

He pointed. "You, Lady Alexandria."

Nancy E. Durham

Alex's breath froze in her throat. "M-me?" she finally stuttered. "Th-that's impossible."

"Not only is it possible, but now it makes sense why you are part of Dorothea and Rodric's plans. Magic resides in you that the Veil Queen must want badly."

Pandathaway turned. "Normally, I would advise you to stay in the city and against fleeing. Dangers abound outside the walls of Wheel." He gave a grim shake of his head. "But far worse awaits if you stay. You cannot fall into the Duchess and Lord Regret's hands."

The gnome bowed. "We are at your service. Whatever you need, Lady Alexandria, you have but to ask. When can you and the Lieutenant be prepared to leave?"

Alex's face fell. "That's the problem. We don't know any safe place to go."

"Hmm. I see." Pandathaway rubbed his chin, deep in thought. He stopped suddenly and snapped his fingers. "I know of a place, one far from here and still not conquered by Marlinda."

He ran to a cabinet and talked as he rummaged through it. "I met an old gnome years ago who claimed to be from a city which, like Wheel, remained free of the Dark Queen's clutches. Ah, here it is."

He threw a map down on the table and unrolled it. "This is it. You can go here." His finger speared a point on the map.

"Markingham."

CHAPTER 21

T HE CARAVAN OF WAGONS ROLLED BY ONE AFTER ANOTHER, RAISING clouds of dust as their drivers urged their teams of horses forward.

A long line of trudging soldiers, horses, and supply wagons stretched ahead and behind. Above the snaking column, flying mounts soared in lazy circles. A cacophony of creaks and rattling of wheels accompanied the caravan.

Tal shook his head as the procession slowly wound past him. For the hundredth time he worried how easily the invasion could be revealed to anyone with eyes or ears.

"We have seen no sign of man or gnome the entire journey. You concern yourself needlessly, Tal."

Tal glanced to his left. Bozar sat astride a flying mount, studying him.

"Aye. This entire region is deserted. The few dwellings we have come across were abandoned long ago," Gravelback added. He waved at the countryside. "The population has either fallen into Marlinda's merciless clutches, or gone into hiding."

"What can we expect once we reach Markingham?" Tal asked the garrison commander.

Gravelback shook his head. "I would give much to know *that* answer. It all depends whether they remain free from the Dark Queen. If not, we must conquer the city, and make sure none escape to warn the black-hearted bitch. We must prepare for either."

He snorted. "Given our slow pace and the trickle of our army through the Veil, it might take months to marshal our forces in sufficient size to defeat any force defending the city."

Nervous energy coursed through Tal and he fingered his sword hilt, unhappy with Gravelback's response. Since meeting the Cyclops and mind-speaking with her, his nights were restless, his sleep fitful. The premonition he felt days earlier not only remained with him, but had grown stronger. To combat boredom and as a release for the pressure inside him, he now scouted non-stop. Often he would leave early after breakfast, soar into the sky on the storm mount, and not return until early evening.

Bozar seemed to sense his turmoil, and other than the usual warnings, allowed Tal to scout as often and as long as he pleased.

Pulpit was another matter.

The white monk took his vow to his mother, Queen Celestria, seriously. He insisted on accompanying Tal every place but the privy. Tal learned to sneak away on his scouting missions before Pulpit could find a flying horse.

He now sat in a horse-drawn wagon next to Artemis Thurgood. Oblivious to the choking dust and deep, teeth-rattling ruts, the two were engaged in a lively conversation. Tal smiled. In the Grand Master, Pulpit had met his match. The pair could talk the paint off a brick wall.

Bozar moved his horse closer to Tal's storm mount. Observing the spirited back and forth between the Thurgood and Pulpit, he said, "Now would be a good time to make your getaway."

Tal grinned and urged the storm horse into a trot. Powerful wings beat the air and within seconds, they were airborne. He circled once far above, then left the caravan far behind.

Alex continued to visit the gnomish couple via the magical mirror.

Lillian found sturdy boots, pants, and tunics for Alex, and although actually men's clothing, with her height they fit her well. Nothing could be done about her underclothes, and with great reluctance, she kept her original meager selection.

Using discrete inquiries of his numerous friends and business acquaintances scattered throughout Wheel, Pandathaway located Tell at a nearby inn. Over tankards of ale, the gnome slipped Tell a note from Alex which detailed her meeting with Pandathaway. The note carried one other important instruction.

They would make their escape the next night.

The new day glowed with the first faint light, and Alex, too restless to sleep, was up to see it. Time crawled by with agonizing slowness. Alex forced herself to go through her normal routine, but found it impossible to keep her thoughts from leaping ahead.

Tonight we leave Wheel.

So far, everything had gone according to plan. It seemed too easy and Alex worried that something would go wrong and ruin everything. Her biggest fear concerned Rodric.

What if he calls on me? What if he wants to take me to dinner?

Chill bumps covered her skin at the prospect of being with Rodric. If he so wantonly pawed her in full view of hundreds of guests, what would he be capable of when they were alone?

She kept Tell's small dagger hidden on her at all times now. She had never hurt anyone...but if he tried to force himself on her again, she would gladly use it.

Mercifully, Rodric never made an appearance other than to have a servant deliver to her a basket of fresh flowers—which she immediately tossed over the terrace railing and into the roiling water below. Dinner with the Duke and Duchess came and went without incident, complete with Dorothea's usual suspicious glances. Soon darkness fell, and Alex told the handmaiden she planned to go to bed early.

To complete the subterfuge, Alex undressed, put on her nightgown, and crawled under the covers before dismissing Darcy. She lay wide awake, the seconds seeming like minutes, the minutes like hours. Excitement grew inside her to the point, she threw off the covers and sat in a chair beside the cold fireplace. Her thoughts drifted to a conversation with Lillian as they searched for suitable clothing.

"The young lieutenant's love for you must be deep indeed to resign his commission and leave Wheel with you," she said. "Your love for him must be equally strong."

Spoken more as a statement than a question, Alex simply nodded. But when Lillian mentioned "love" the image of the young man in her dreams swam into her mind—not Tell.

Annoyed with herself, Alex stood and paced. "Tell is who I love," she said through clenched teeth, "not some face from a vision or the thread of a future shown to me by a ghost."

But with each step, the memory of the young stranger's touch, the taste of his warm lips, grew stronger. She stopped, arms hugged to her chest. Eyes closed, the tingle within her grew to a roaring, irresistible flame.

"You are the one meant for me," she whispered, the words slipping from her lips.

Alex dug fingernails into her palms, angry tears falling from her eyes. "No! Tell has my heart. No one else!"

Fuming, she sat in the darkened room. Hours later, the chime from the clock signaled midnight. She threw off her nightgown and dressed. Reaching through the enchanted mirror, she retrieved her satchel, then adjusted the charmed mirror until the gnome's store appeared.

Alex turned and took a last look around. If anything on this world represented a safe harbor, it was her chambers. It also embodied a life she desperately wanted to leave behind. Her hope lay someplace else.

She stepped through the magical mirror.

CHAPTER 22

EMERGING INTO THE GNOME'S STORE, ALEX BLINKED. In front of her stood Pandathaway and Lillian. Close by and pacing back and forth was Tell. She dropped her satchel and ran to him. He caught her in his arms and they held each other for so long, the gnomish shopkeeper was forced to clear his throat.

"My pardon, but you must be off. According to the Lieutenant, the patrols which fly watch over Wheel are due for a rotation change. The window of opportunity is now."

With a reluctant sigh, Tell released Alex. "He's right. I saw the duty schedule myself—"

His face flushed. "Be-before I resigned. There is always a delay while one patrol is relieved by another. We can use this time to slip away unnoticed."

Tell handed Alex a warm cloak. "Here, wrap this around you. The night air will be much colder than you realize."

Alex draped the mantle over her shoulders. She grabbed her satchel and followed Tell to the back of the store. He opened a door into an alley behind the shop. Two flying horses waited for them, their saddle bags filled with supplies. They raised their heads at their approach. The sight of Tell caused the animals to nicker and shake their wings. He spoke softly to them and stroked their necks. He motioned to Alex, and she joined him beside a tan mare with dappled sides.

"This is Della. You will be riding her. She is a strong flyer but very gentle." Alex reached out and Della nuzzled her hand.

Pandathaway and Lillian watched from nearby and Alex hurried toward them. Kneeling, she hugged each in turn. "I will never forget your kindness."

"Nonsense," Pandathaway said. "After what you have been through, it is the least we can do."

"Yes, "Lillian agreed dabbing her eyes with a dainty kerchief produced from a pocket, "forget what has happened and look forward to happier times."

At Tell's puzzled look, Alex realized much of what she shared with the gnomish couple she had kept from him. She hadn't even told him about what she suspected about Rodric.

She stood, brushed the dirt off her knees, then took Tell's hand. "We have a long journey and much to talk about. Be patient."

Her heart clenched at the hurt in Tell's eyes. He recovered quickly and squeezed her hand. "Good!"

They moved to Alex's horse and he helped her into the saddle. A leather strap dangled from the saddle. Tell pulled it across her waist like a belt, and fastened it to the other side.

"This will keep you seated and from falling off Della," he explained. "It may be uncomfortable at first, but you will get used to it." He pointed at his own mount, a bay stallion. "Della will follow us. Just hang on and your horse will do the rest. It sounds odd, but riding a ground-based horse is *not* the same as on a flying one. Until you become more proficient, just let Della have her head."

Alex nodded, her fingers already grasping the pommel.

Tell walked back to the gnomes and thanked them. Returning to his horse, he leaped into the saddle and waved goodbye. He urged his horse into a trot which quickly transitioned into a gallop. Moments later, he soared into the night sky.

Della followed the sudden motion almost jerking Alex's

hands from her grip on the saddle. She stifled a scream when the ground fell away and they became airborne. The air rushed by carrying her hair like streamers. She turned her head and saw the rapidly diminishing forms of Pandathaway and Lillian below. They waved and soon were lost in the dark night.

An ache pulsed within her. Though she only knew them for a short time, it was clear their hearts were far larger than their small stature.

I already miss them.

The lights of Wheel faded to pinpricks as they continued to climb. With each beat of Della's wings the distance grew, the city shrank until it was nothing but a flicker of light. Soon, even that disappeared.

The three moons of Meredith were in partial phase, their pale light creating ethereal shadows on the ground far below. Ahead, Tell's mount beat a steady cadence, Della matching each wing-stroke. Other than the rushing wind, a quiet lay upon the land and air. No pursuit followed, and they were already far away from Wheel. The fear of discovery which gripped Alex loosened. She took a deep breath. *We did it.*

We escaped Wheel.

Tal scowled. "We have been traveling for a week. Am I the only one who thinks it strange that we have seen no evidence of the former citizens of this region?"

"I must agree with the Prince," Artemis Thurgood admitted. "No matter how sparsely populated this area was before the Veil, such a rich land should still have a few hardy souls living here."

All of the leaders of the expedition were gathered in Artemis Thurgood's opulent pavilion. Amassed round a table drinking ale from tankards, they discussed the daily progress and reviewed the next day's plan. Gravelback—the Queen's appointed military leader—led the deliberations, although Bozar's final approval was needed on every decision.

The First Advisor, fingers steepled in front of him, shook his head. "Do not underestimate the Dark Queen's reach. She's had centuries to consolidate her power. Those who managed to slip through her cruel fingers would have gone into hiding. We must assume they will view us not as liberators, but with fear that we are part of her evil dominion. And why wouldn't they? The Empire's soldiers have not been seen here in over a thousand years."

Gravelback gulped a mouthful of ale and belched. "Aye. This is my greatest fear. When we reach Markingham, it's likely we will have to fight our own brothers. They won't believe we have come to deliver them from Marlinda's clutches."

Tal sat forward. "Then let me scout ahead...far ahead," he said eagerly. "I can be in sight of Markingham's gates within a week. I'll sneak in and mingle with the populace. The information will help us better prepare for the day our army arrives at the city's gates."

Pulpit shook his head. "It is too dangerous. But, if we agreed to this, I must accompany the prince."

"A white monk in Markingham?" Tal asked in disbelief. "You would stick out like a thistle in a field of poppies. I might as well stand on the city's tallest building and shout *we have arrived*."

Under normal circumstances, Bozar would have rejected Tal's request out of hand. But since Tal's experience with the Forest Mother, Bozar found he agreed with Pulpit on one thing. Too many coincidences had dovetailed together with precision-like timing...and all involved Tal. With each passing day, his sense of larger events converging to some unknown end grew.

He tapped his lips. "Perhaps."

Every head swung toward the First Advisor. "You are not *seriously* considering this?" Gravelback asked.

"Tal's woodcraft is second to none. He rides the most powerful flyer among our steeds, and none can match his magic. Under normal circumstances, he would be the logical choice."

"Yes, but these are not normal times nor are they normal circumstances," Artemis Thurgood reminded Bozar.

Pulpit stood, his jaw set. "I *will* accompany Prince Tal wherever he goes."

Bozar smiled. "Forgive me, good monk, but *you* were the one who pointed out the events involving Tal were more than just happenstance. Perhaps you've changed your mind?"

Pulpit opened his mouth—then closed it. With a heavy sigh, he sat. "The Queen chose wisely when you became Prince Tal's *Eldred*...and no, I have not changed my mind."

Tal couldn't believe his ears. He leaped to his feet. "I'll leave in the morning." Bozar fixed Tal with a steely gaze.

"Make sure I don't come to regret this decision."

CHAPTER 23

"**H**OW LONG HAVE THEY BEEN GONE?"

Dorothea spat the question at Lord Ruffin who stood uncomfortably within the Duke's private ante-chamber. Ashen-faced, the Duke listened to Ruffin's report.

"Sometime last night" he replied. "When Alexandria's hand-maiden arrived at her room this morning, she was nowhere to be found. We searched the castle and found nothing. When questioned, the handmaiden said she last saw Lady Alexandria yesterday evening. Lieutenant Tollet is also missing. They're almost certainly together, and while it's possible they could be hiding somewhere in Wheel, we don't think they remained in the city."

"Why?" Duke Duvalier asked in a tremulous voice.

"Because two flying horses are missing. We assume Lieutenant Tollet took them." Ruffin cleared his throat. "Past that, all we can do is speculate."

"What of Alexandria's guards?" Dorothea demanded. "How could she slip past them without detection? They must be in league with Alexandria and Tollett! Interrogate them at once!"

Lord Ruffin shook his head. "No. They were just as surprised to discover her gone. In fact, each one volunteered to search for Lady Alexandria."

"How very convenient!" Dorothea sneered. "What is their explanation on how she managed to slip by under their very noses?"

"There were *four* guards on watch, Duchess," Ruffin

reminded her. "The one thing I *am* certain of is Lady Alexandria did not leave through her doors but by some other means."

The Duke stirred. "What of the search?" he asked.

"We are in the midst of a massive ground and air search. Every available soldier and rider not involved in patrol is searching for Alexandria."

"I have known you for many years, Randolph," the Duke said in a voice thick with resignation. "I can tell from your tone you do not hold out much hope."

Ruffin hesitated. "Alton, they have a full day's lead. They could have gone in any direction. The Lieutenant is an expert with horses, and he picked two of the most capable flying mounts in the stable." He put his hand on the Duke's shoulder. "I'm sorry. They're many leagues from here, and it is unlikely we will find them unless they want to be found."

"Someone had to know they were leaving!" Dorothea insisted. "The servant girl, Darcy. She must know something."

Ruffin shook his head. "Possible but unlikely. She broke down in tears when we told her. She became so distraught, we were forced to give her a sleeping draught to halt her hysterical weeping."

"The gnome then! She's been to his shop and he could have helped her. I have never trusted him." Dorothea snapped.

"Pandathaway? The former weapons master?" Ruffin spread his hands. "Duchess, this is highly unlikely. Alexandria visited his store only once. We have, however, begun to question the vendors Lady Alexandria favored. So far, they deny any involvement."

"All lies!" Dorothea shouted.

Dorothea turned her angry invective on Duke Duvalier. "And you! How can you sit there sniveling while your daughter has run off with that philandering Lieutenant?"

"It's my fault," the Duke whispered miserably. "If I had

listened to her and not insisted on a marriage she wanted no part of, she would not have left."

"You fool!" Dorothea spun on her heel and stalked out.

Dorothea hurried to her suite curtly ignoring the formal bows of the servants she passed. Arriving, she slammed the door behind her. Once alone, fear gripped her with such intensity, that she leaned against the door for support. When she lifted her head, the sight of Rodric reclined on a couch and drinking wine, greeted her.

He held the tumbler up into the light and swirled the blood-red liquid. "A good year I think."

"Alexandria is missing and all you can think to do is critique wine? You have truly lost your mind!"

Dorothea pushed away from the door and wrung her hands. "The Dark Queen will blame *me*. If we don't find her and return her to Wheel, she will kill me in the most horrific way possible."

Rodric smiled thinly at Dorothea. "Oh, I think my mind is just fine." He drained the wine in one swallow. "And I am the only one in Wheel who can locate Alexandria."

Dorothea whirled. "What? Stop talking in riddles! Where is she?"

Rodric stood and faced Dorothea. "Oh, but you ask the wrong question. A better query would be, *where* is the Lieutenant? After our altercation at the Duke's betrothal celebration, he became a person of interest to me. I had him followed."

Rodric cast about. "Ah, there you are." He picked up the wine bottle and refilled his glass. "Did you know we are all creatures of habit?" he asked Dorothea. "For example, one man butters his toast, while another spreads only jam. And then there are favored items like a particular pair of shoes, a tunic...even a saddle."

Dorothea exploded. "Enough! Explain yourself."

Rodric pulled an object from his pocket, and held up a

ceramic disk the size and shape of a large coin. Embedded in the middle was a lodestone. "Now let's see. You want to know where oh where is our sweet Alexandria? I had an Artifact like this one sewn into the leather of Tollet's favored saddle…a saddle which is missing along with the Lieutenant."

Dorothea snatched the Artifact from Rodric's hand and examined it. "What does it do?" she demanded.

Rodric smirked. "Only one thing. It exudes a very distinctive form of magic. Like the aroma of freshly baked bread, we just follow the scent. Earlier, I took the liberty of procuring a flying mount, and after being in the air for just a short time, I found the magic's spoor. The trail is obvious enough even the greenest Dark Brother or Sister could follow it. They are headed due south."

Dorothea handed the Artifact back. "How do we get Alexandria back?"

Rodric's eyes glinted. "I have already contacted my brother, Stefan. If they continue south, their path takes them close to an eyrie of gargoyles. Stefan stands ready to dispatch a flock of the creatures to intercept our wayfarers."

Dorothea carefully considered Rodric's plan. Stefan, second son of the Veil King and Queen, was by all accounts a more cunning and crueler version of Rodric. She only hoped his self-control was better as well.

"What are their instructions?" she asked.

"The gargoyles are to kill Tollet, capture Alexandria, and take her to Stefan."

"What happens when Alexandria is returned? Once she sees the creatures which captured her, she'll tell everyone, including the Duke. Then *we* will be exposed as agents of the Veil."

Rodric wore a smug look. "I have already thought of that. It occurred to me that Alexandria has already suffered from one bout of memory loss. Who's to say she won't suffer another? I'm sure with your expertise in potions, you'll have no difficulty concocting a potion to cause part of Alexandria's memory to leave her. One, say, that removes her reminiscence of fleeing Wheel and all which happened after. Perhaps you might also plant some desire or affection in her for me while you're at it. It would *so* make our marriage bed easier."

Dorothea considered Rodric's proposal and nodded grudgingly. "It's a good plan. I'll get started on the potion immediately." She added, "I cannot make her love you, however. Lust perhaps, but not love."

Rodric laughed. "I never mentioned *love*, Dorothea. For what I have planned with Alexandria, *lust* will be all I need."

He stepped close to Dorothea, his breath warm on her skin. "Speaking of lust, I think a reward, a token of your appreciation is in order. Imagine what would have happened to you had Alexandria successfully escaped." He reached for her bodice and toyed with the laces.

With dizzying speed, a dagger appeared in Dorothea's hand, the sharp tip held beneath Rodric's chin. She whispered in his ear, "What did you have in mind?"

A smile spread across Rodric's face. "Oh, just a humble request—one viper to another—to bed you."

Ignoring the prick of the blade, Rodric slowly loosened Dorothea's bodice exposing more and more of her pale cleavage. She caught his hand in an iron grip…then led him to her sleeping chambers. Undressing, she threw back the thick coverlet, but before sliding into the bed, she retrieved Rodric's partially emptied wine bottle and a goblet.

She would need every drop by the time this was finished.

CHAPTER 24

A GENTLE SHAKE AWAKENED ALEX.

She rubbed her eyes to find Tell standing above her. "Time to leave," he said.

The horses, saddled and ready, cropped grass near the bower of pine trees they had slept under during the day. The sun, already low in the horizon, would set soon.

Alex sat up and Tell handed her a flat biscuit of field bread. Crunchy with a sweet taste, she munched on the biscuit while trying to remove the pine needles stuck to her head. She jerked one particularly stubborn pine needle glued to her scalp, and in the process, removed some of her hair.

Annoyed, Alex scratched her head. While she finished the hard bread, she reviewed the progress they had made. To avoid discovery, they flew only at night and slept during the day. After several nights of steadily traveling south with no sign of pursuit, the knot of fear within her gradually loosened. With fair weather and the partially full moons to help speed their way, Alex finally allowed herself to believe the impossible.

We escaped Wheel.

Groaning, she stood and stretched, her joints and muscles protesting. After days of sleeping on the cold, hard ground, she ached everywhere. Taking a long drink from the canteen Tell offered her, she went into the woods and relieved herself. When Alex returned, the remnant of their camp was packed and stored.

Tell handed Della's reins to Alex. "Are you ready?"

With a nod, Alex stifled a groan as she crawled into the saddle. "How much longer must we travel in the dead of night?"

"Tonight should be our last," Tell replied. "We have long since passed the last of any villages and farm holdings, but I don't want to take any chances."

Alex sighed, resigned to another round of traveling in the darkness. A short time later, the last rays of the sun disappeared, and they took to the air.

Soon they resumed a familiar routine—Della following Tell's stallion, and Alex simply hanging on for the ride. Although Tell procured communication Artifacts for both of them—leather bracelets with a lodestone mounted in the center—he gave strict instructions not to talk unless an emergency presented itself. The magical device was a common Artifact used by the flying legions, so Tell forbid all talking unless an emergency arose.

This left Alex with plenty of time to herself.

She observed the landscape below and the scattered lights of homesteads and farms. As they traveled farther away from Wheel, these habitations became fewer and fewer, and the past night's travel revealed not a single point of light. At times, she gazed upward to the heavens. Breathtaking in beauty, no light pollution marred the view, the stars in their multitudes forming brushstrokes of patterns and constellations. Twice, she saw shooting stars, a slash of brilliance across the dark sky.

She tried to imagine their life ahead in Markingham. *What will it hold for us?* A thousand other questions appeared in her mind, but strangely, she wasn't the least bit intimidated by any of them. Normalcy, the chance to live without fear, was all that mattered. Everything else was mundane in comparison.

At other times her mind turned to her former home back on earth, and the life she once lived as Mona. *Had it only been a few short months?* It felt like centuries, her former life like dusty pages in a history book. She thought of her brother, Joe, and Mr. Finkle's promise that he would have a happy, successful life ahead of him. She clung to this with a fierce determination. *Promises made must be promises kept*, she told herself. After Rodric and Dorothea, the things she had seen and experienced in Wheel made the cruel bullying she suffered in school appear as an annoyance, nothing more.

Wherever her thoughts led her during each long night, however, they always ended in the same place.

On *him*.

She replayed each dream with the stranger, the future threads shown to her by Diana, over and over again. If anything, time had sharpened, not dulled, their intensity. She could feel his breath on her skin, the firm play of his muscles beneath his tunic. When he embraced her, she could count each beat of his heart. What she could *not* do, was focus on his face. No matter how hard she tried, it remained a murky image in her mind. Then, inevitably, guilt would return, her sense of betrayal toward Tell, a bitter taste she couldn't wash from her mouth.

The hours passed, lost in the mix of rushing air, the stars above, and the dark countryside below. When the first faint glow of dawn appeared, Tell urged his horse lower to look for a suitable place to camp and spend the day. Alex studied the lay of the land dimly illuminated by the coming dawn. It seemed more rugged and heavily wooded than any place they'd traveled to so far.

Tell found a suitable location, and they swooped in a low circle over a small meadow. As they descended into the clearing, Alex spotted a pond adjacent to the meadow. A mound of partially submerged branches rose from a brook that had been dammed to form the tiny lake. *A beaver?* If not, some creature closely akin to a beaver must have formed the pool of water. After having no opportunity to do anything except wash her face and hands since leaving Wheel, the sight excited her. *Maybe I can finally bathe.*

They alighted on the grassy area, and Tell immediately set up camp. He sent Alex to fetch some water while he took the saddles off the horses and rubbed them down. The nearer Alex drew to the pond, the greater her excitement grew over the prospects of taking a *real* bath. She reached the water's edge and set the canteens down. With hands on hips, she surveyed the little lake. A furry head poked through the water's surface with small branches clutched between its teeth. As the creature swam for the dam of mud and sticks, she decided it was indeed a beaver.

The water looked clear and cold. Alex sat in the grass, pulled off one of her boots, and stuck her toes in the water. She yelped and jerked her foot back.

Yes. Definitely cold.

However, with the day already growing warm, and Alex caked with days' worth of sweat, horse scent, and dirt, even a frigid bath was better than none at all. She quickly filled the canteens with water and hurried back to the camp. Rummaging inside one of the saddle bags produced a hard bar of soap. Tell looked on curiously as she made her way purposefully back to the beaver pond.

Alex reached the pool again, and quickly stripped off everything except the thin shift she wore over her underclothes. Soap in hand, she took a deep breath and plunged into the water. She came up gasping, the shock of the cold water pricking her skin like thousands of needles. Before she lost her nerve, she plunged under again. Eventually, she became acclimated enough to stay in the pond without her teeth chattering. The frigid water felt delicious, and she took the bar of soap and began to scrub vigorously, then washed her hair.

Next she took her clothes from the bank where she had laid

them, and rinsed them the best she could. Placing them on top of some nearby bushes to dry, she returned to the pond.

Curious, she swam to the beaver dam, and tread water while she inspected it. She heard a *splash* behind her. She whipped around and Tell's head emerged from the water. He spluttered and gasped.

"How do you stand it?" he said through clattering teeth. "I've lost feeling in my toes!"

"You'll get used to it," Alex laughed.

They spent the next hour cavorting in the water. They climbed on top of the dam and took turns diving into the pond. Then they would swim to the bottom to see who could hold their breath the longest. When finally they emerged, dripping and laughing, they were tired and clean. They flopped onto the ground and lay side-by side on the grass, Alex in her undergown, and Tell with only a pair of shorts. The sun, now well into the morning sky, joined a warm breeze to dry them. Soon, both dozed off.

Alex woke hours later. She yawned, sat up, and discovered Tell squatted next to her. He leaned over and kissed her.

"I have decided," he said softly.

She raised an eyebrow. "Decided what?"

"That there is no woman in all of Dalfur whose beauty can match yours."

He pulled a strand of hair from her face and pushed it behind her ear. Then he lowered his head and kissed her again. Fingers trailing over her flat stomach, they traveled to her breasts and teased her nipples. The sensation caused Alex to gasp. Tell leaned closer pushing Alex back onto the grass. His kisses became more insistent. Alex found it hard to breathe with his entire weight now upon her. Rather than kindle her own desire, however, she felt detached as if watching the entire scene from afar. Shame warmed her cheeks when she realized why.

The one I long for is not here.

"Tell," she whispered in his ear. Oblivious, he continued, his mouth working its way down her neck. "Tell," she said, louder this time. He paused but only briefly, his lips now at her bare shoulders.

"Tell!"

At her shout, he blinked and stopped. "What...what is it?" His young face a ruddy red, carried a mixture of disappointment and confusion.

"We—we have to stop. Please. This has...has already gone too far."

"But I thought—"

He caught himself, and after a moment's hesitation, pushed himself off her. He sat up and turned away, hurt evident on his face. Alex's heart broke at the sight. Tell stood and made his way to the nearby where bush their clothes had been laid upon to dry. Dressing, he collected her clothes and carried them to her.

She caught his hand. "I was just nervous, that's all. Look, I'm okay now." She tried to pull off her undergown, but Tell forced her arms down.

"Get dressed, Alexandria." He turned and made his way back to their camp.

Watching his retreating back, a sense of loss struck Alex, a cut deeper than the sharpest knife could deliver.

What have I done?

She threw on her clothes and hurried after Tell. He stood beside the small campfire and stared at the bright embers. When she tried to approach him, he held up his hand.

"Forgive me for taking advantage of you, " he said, his eyes never straying from the fire. "You were lying there asleep, your hair spread about you like a golden sheet. You were so peaceful, so... lovely. I couldn't help myself. I had to kiss you and once started, I couldn't stop. I shouldn't have forced myself on you."

He turned and faced her. "It won't happen again."

Alex tried to approach him again, but he firmly pushed her away. She threw her arms up. "You didn't *force* anything! We just need some time. That's all. Tomorrow, the next day, what does it matter?"

She took a step back. "I love you. There, that settles it! Must I say it over and over again?"

"Love between a man and a woman...or love which exists between friends?"

"Between a man and woman," she rushed to reply.

Tell squatted by the fire. He took a long stick and stirred the embers. "When you first woke, still enmeshed in your dreams, I saw it, a brief glimpse to be sure, but nonetheless telling."

Alex shook her head. "I don't understand. What did you see?"

"Disappointment. Disappointment my face appeared instead of another."

Alex's heart skipped a beat. "Not true. You know that's not true."

Tell flashed her a sad smile. "You have a purity about you, Alex. It's fresh and it's clean—like the spring air after a rain shower. It is one of the things I love most about you.

"It also makes you a poor liar."

The rest of the day was spent in strained silence.

CHAPTER 25

TAL SOARED HIGH ABOVE THE GROUND, HIS EYES SEARCHING.
Having left early that morning while still dark, he managed to sneak away before Pulpit became aware of it. The monk took his vow to his mother seriously, and Pulpit shadowed Tal wherever he went. While he appreciated the monk's sincerity, the last thing Tal wanted was another Bozar watching his every move.

The sun's rays were low in the horizon when his quest finally revealed what he had been looking for.

The enchanted cabin.

The clearing appeared like an oasis in the otherwise unrelieved sea of green. His fine-tuned sense of direction, enhanced by the powerful magic innate to a Blood Prince, led him unerringly to the same place where he'd first made contact with the Forest Mother. After circling one more time, he landed.

Unsaddling the storm mount, he carried the saddle to the porch, and removed the few necessities he needed for the night at the cottage. He took a piece of jerky from his pack and chewed it while taking a circuitous stroll around the glade.

Why am I here?

Although in the general direction he needed to travel to reach Markingham, the detour to the cabin did force him to travel somewhat out of his way. Curiosity, of course, still burned within him at the strange set of events which led him to the Cyclops, but something else also drove him to divert the storm horse.

Anticipation.

He couldn't put a finger on it, but this feeling grew with each passing league. The itch became so insistent, he could resist it no more.

And now, here he was once again. With a sigh, he returned to the porch and took a seat in one of the sturdy chairs.

And waited.

❖

Alex and Tell slept the remainder of the day, then traveled part of the night.

They camped next in a large dell with lush grass for their horses. Because the chance of their being discovered was now nearly impossible, Tell unpacked stakes with light crystals fixed to them so they could better see to make their camp for the night. The entire process went efficiently…and with little or no conversation. Every time Alex tried to engage Tell in conversation, *if* he answered her at all, his replies were clipped and reserved. She tried everything, from shameless flirtation to angry demands that he talk to her. Tell remained close-mouthed through it all.

Her long and quiet nights now resembled the days.

They rose late the next morning, and after eating a cold breakfast, Tell made ready to break camp. He whistled for the horses cropping grass in the meadow. Their ears pricked up at the sound and they immediately trotted toward Tell. As Tell prepared to saddle his flying horse, he stopped to look at something on the stallion's flank. Dropping the saddle, he moved in for a closer inspection. He motioned to Alex, and she joined him.

"Look at this." Tell pointed at the stallion's flank where a small area had been rubbed raw.

"It looks like a wound of some kind," Alex said.

147

Tell nodded. "It's a saddle sore and it shouldn't be there. My saddles *always* fit properly. I haven't caused a blister on a horse I've ridden since I was a small boy!"

Tell, brow furrowed, picked up his saddle, and inspected it closely. He turned it over, scrutinizing every square inch. He had almost finished his examination when he stiffened.

"What is it?" Alex asked.

"Feel this," Tell said, and directed her hand to the lining of the saddle.

Alex's fingers brushed over a lump beneath the leather. The stitching had come loose next to the bulge, and Alex found she could move it with her fingers.

With his dagger, Tell cut the seam then pushed and prodded until an object within the lining fell out. He picked it up off the ground.

"*This* caused it!" He held up a coin-sized disk. A green lodestone occupied the center of the object.

"What is it?" Alex asked.

Tell shook his head. "I don't know." He turned the Artifact over in his hand. "I don't understand how it ended up in *my* saddle. Someone had to put it there."

"Can I look at it?" Alex asked. Tell handed her the disk.

The size and shape of a coin, she could find no discernable markings on either side. As she held the slate-gray disk, a strange sensation came over her. In her mind, a mental gate cracked open to allow searing light to pour out. A familiar disorientation followed. *Rodric!* She experienced the same feeling when he attacked her with his Darcy-controlled body. The Artifact grew warm in her hand. Hissing, she dropped it to the ground.

"Rodric!" she cried. "It stinks of his magic. *He* placed it in your saddle!"

"What? How do you know?" Tell demanded.

Heart pounding, Alex grabbed Tell's arm. "Does it matter? It's his charm!"

Tell snatched the Artifact off the ground. "What kind of charm? What's its purpose?" "I...I don't know," Alex confessed.

"You claim to know this is a thing of magic created by Rodric, but you don't know its function?" Red-faced, Tell, voice rising, cried, "What else have you not shared with me, Alex? You must not trust—"

Tell stopped, a look of dread on his face. "Oh no," he breathed.

He placed the Artifact on a stone protruding from the rocky soil. He dug another fist-sized stone from the ground and struck the disk repeatedly. It shattered emitting a brief but bright flash of energy as it was destroyed. Tell grabbed Alex roughly by the arm and propelled her toward Della.

"Get your saddle and put it on Della. Hurry!"

"What's wrong?" Alex asked, dread gripping her.

"It's a tracking device," he said over his shoulder as he cinched his saddle onto the stallion. He shook his head bitterly. "I should have recognized it from the beginning. We use similar Artifacts on young flying horses so we don't lose them."

Tell hurried to Della and helped secure Alex's saddle. "We must be on our way before they discover us." Sprinting around the camp, he collected their gear and stowed it.

"Get on your horse. We need to leave *now*."

Heart knotted in cold fear, Alex asked, "Who...who is tracking us?"

Tell paused long enough to give Alex a grim look. "You should know. The same person who placed the tracking device in my saddle. *Lord Regret.*"

He thundered into the open glade. Soon, both mounts were in the air. Tell urged his flying horse to full speed and they rocketed away from the campsite. For an entire hour, they kept up the grueling pace before Tell allowed the lathered stallion to glide.

Della, struggling to stay up with Tell's stronger mount, nickered at the slower pace, and Alex patted her neck.

Tell's voice appeared in her ear. "To our right and due west is the southern mountain range." Alex glanced over her shoulder. In the far horizon, the dark shape of peaks rose into the sky.

Tell continued. "We need to find a place with grass and water for the horses. I pushed them to the limit to put distance between us and whoever or whatever Rodric sent to follow us. Once they are rested, we'll resume traveling again, only at—"

Tell stiffened and he snatched a binocular device Alex recognized as a far-seeing Artifact. He lifted it to his eyes and scanned the horizon. Alex followed his line-of-sight and spied a cloud of black specks blocking their path.

Abruptly, Tell turned his mount and headed for the distant mountains. Once again, he urged more speed from his tired mount. Della snorted, and surged after the stallion.

The dread Alex felt before morphed into full-blown panic. "Who are they?"

"Not who, but *what*." Tell's taunt voice replied, "Gargoyles riding squarks, a filthy carrion bird. Squarks cannot match our flying mounts for speed, but they have greater endurance. If we can make it to the mountains, however, we can land and have a chance to lose them. The foul birds are all but useless on the ground, and even more so on rough terrain. The gargoyles will have to abandon them."

Alex swallowed. "Why don't we just outrun them?"

Silence followed. When Tell answered, it was in a tone thick with resignation. "Our horses are tired, Alex. They can't keep this up, and without rest, they will begin to falter."

He added in a bitter voice, "It's my fault. I didn't need to push our mounts so hard, and I could have chosen another direction instead of one which led us straight to our pursuers. It's just...I was so *angry* with you, and I made one mistake after another. I'm sorry for failing you."

"You have *never* failed me, Tell," Alex said. "And you couldn't have known which route our pursuit would come from."

Alex peeked over her shoulder. Her blood chilled. *The dark specks were now larger.* She turned to view the distant peaks. "Can we make it to the mountains?"

"I think so," Tell answered, "but it is by no means certain."

They jettisoned all their extra weight, keeping only weapons, and a little food and water. The discarded items plummeted to the treetops far below. Lighter now, their flying horses began to pull slowly away from the gargoyle-mounted squarks.

Then the real chase began.

CHAPTER 26

N HOUR LATER, AND ALEX KNEW THEY WERE IN REAL TROUBLE. Ragged snorts burst from Della, and up ahead, Tell's horse dipped and rose as he struggled to stay aloft. The mountains were close...tantalizingly close. Forested slopes stretched up to rocky crags, some still mantled in snow.

Nearer still were the gargoyles.

They had closed the distance to half and drew nearer with each wingbeat of the squarks. For the first time, their pursuers were close enough for Alex to make out details. The squarks, giant birds the size of their own flying mounts, were covered with a greasy, black plumage. Rather than tailfeathers, they sported fleshy tails like rats. Featherless gray necks led to a heads consisting of red, mottled skin, and curved, cruel beaks extended from below beady, black eyes.

The gargoyles had leathery skin black as coal, and bat-like wings folded on their backs. Sharp incisors for ripping flesh gleamed white in the sunlight. Two vertical slits passed for nostrils, while above, eyes with yellow, cat-like pupils followed every move of their flying horses. Wide, pointed ears flanked brutal faces to complete the picture.

Their leader, a huge gargoyle, pointed at them and shouted in a guttural language. Arrows began to fly by.

"Tell!" Alex cried.

"I know!" he answered. "They can't possibly hit anything at this range, but they might make a lucky shot." In a voice sharpened by desperation, he added, "We *have* to find a place to land."

Alex searched, her eyes sweeping the ground below. No openings in the green canopy appeared.

"There!" Tell pointed. "Up ahead!"

Alex followed his finger to where a large clearing materialized. Another harsh shout came from behind. The gargoyle leader spotted the same meadow and the hail of arrows increased.

Urging their faltering horses on, wings beat the air and it became a sprint to the opening. Tell swooped down, Alex close behind. Trees formed a hedge around the perimeter of the meadow, but a cavity between a pair of enormous oaks appeared straight in front of them. Like a fissure, it formed a breach in the leafy wall. Tell made straight for it.

The air around Tell became thick with shafts. None appeared near Alex, and with a sinking feeling, she realized why. *Rodric needs me alive...but not Tell.*

Tell's stallion shrieked when several arrows struck its flank. Struggling to keep his wounded mount in a controlled glide, Tell aimed for the open space between the trees. More arrows found their mark, and the dying horse faltered and dropped. It collided with the ground and somersaulted end-over-end. Tell leaped from the saddle before he was crushed. Rolling to his feet, he sprinted for the safety of the trees. Several bolts struck him, and he fell heavily, only to rise and continue on unsteady legs.

"No!" Alex screamed. Della glided onto the grassy dell, and Alex directed her at full gallop toward Tell. She pulled up beside him and jumped off.

He looked up, blood seeping from his mouth. "Go. Save yourself," he wheezed.

"Get on Della!" Alex cried. "They dare not shoot at me."

When Tell didn't respond, she grabbed him by the shoulders. "Don't you understand? *They want me alive!*"

Not waiting for him to answer, she lifted his boot and put it in the stirrup, then helped him into the saddle. She climbed in front of Tell. "Hang on to me."

She grabbed the reins, and with his arms around her, urged Della forward. Within moments they were into the gap at the tree line and under the protective canopy.

Alex pushed her exhausted mount forward until the brush and thickening vegetation slowed them down. She hopped off and helped Tell down. She brushed her fingers against his tunic and they came away wet with his blood. He stood beside her swaying from side-to-side.

Hands to her mouth, she breathed, "Oh, no." Of the three arrows protruding from Tel, two were in his lower back and one in his ribcage. She reached for one of the feathered bolts, but he pushed her away.

"The gargoyles use barbed shafts. Pulling them out would only hasten my death."

"What? No! We can save you. Just let me—"

Tell firmly forced Alex's arms to her side. "I'm mortally wounded. There's nothing you can do for me." He pulled his sword, then staggering, was forced to place the blade in the ground to steady himself. "I can still do something for you, however. I'll try to buy you as much time as possible...but you must go *now.*"

Her tears blurred Tell's image. "I'm not leaving you. I'm *never* going to leave you."

Tell brushed his hand against Alex's cheek. He smiled. "When I first saw you at the Duke's banquet, it took only a single glance to be smitten. Imagine my surprise when I discovered the beauty inside you far surpassed that on the outside."

He stepped back and pulled the blade from the ground. With sword held in front of him, he saluted Alex. "Allow me the honor of guarding your way...one last time."

Sobbing, Alex let Tell help her back onto Della. She felt numb, her limbs boneless. *This can't be happening. It's all a bad dream.* He slapped Della on the rump and she trotted away. Alex twisted in the saddle, her eyes never leaving Tell.

Finally, he disappeared, swallowed up in the forest gloom.

***

Krall watched the figures of the man and woman flee into the safety of the trees.

The gargoyle Chieftain growled with displeasure at the sight. The long chase would be prolonged, another night spent away from the comforts of his eyrie. *If only the dark lord hadn't ordered the female to be left unharmed.* Death followed those who disobeyed Lord Stefan, however, and he dare not allow a hair on the female's head to be damaged.

He barked orders and his flock settled in the clearing. He hopped off the squark and stretched, his wings flapping. At almost seven feet, he towered over the smaller gargoyles of his eyrie. Three diagonal scars marred his left cheek, designating him as a Third Circle Chieftain. Each scar represented a battle to the death within the Circle. Only Chieftains emerged from a Third Circle battle, and Krall had killed his own sire to become leader of the eyrie.

He sniffed the air. *Blood.* He followed the scent to a trail leading into the trees. Krall smiled. Wounded, the soft human soldier shouldn't pose much of a threat. After they killed him, capturing the female would be easy.

He signaled with his hand and his sub-Chieftain, Drak, trotted over. Two scars marked Drak a Second Circle survivor. "What is your command," he asked.

"Finish off the human and find the female. Then bring her to me. And Drak?"

"Yes, my Chieftain?"

"Make sure *no* harm comes to her."

Drak growled and seven gargoyles ran from the clearing and into the woods.

Krall squatted on his haunches and waited.

Tell crouched behind a tree. He wiped blood from his mouth and tried to control his coughing. The crashing in the underbrush signaled the gargoyles arrival, but he waited until they were almost on top of him.

Then he attacked.

With a firm, two-handed grip on his sword, he spun from his hiding place and took the first creature's head off at the shoulders with one swing. The second skidded to a stop, long enough for Tell to skewer it. With a yank, he pulled the blade free along with a rope of entrails. The third gargoyle howled and chopped wildly at Tell with a stone axe. He parried the blow, and his return swing opened the creature up from groin to ribs. Another quick thrust stilled the gargoyle's thrashing.

Spots swam in his vision, and he fell to his knees. *Got to hang on. Got to give Alex more time to escape.*

Tell staggered to his feet and studied the dead creatures. One had a quiver and bow strapped to its back. He grabbed both and retreated farther into the undergrowth. He nocked an arrow, then took several more and jammed them into the ground beside him.

He waited.

His patience was rewarded when footsteps, more stealthy this time, reached his ears. He slowly rose and pushed aside a leafy branch. A wolfish smile appeared. Four gargoyles, spread out in a skirmish line, moved cautiously in his direction. Able to hit a bounding deer with an arrow from the time he was a small boy, the targets in front of Tell were child's play.

With a smooth motion, he stood and released a missile then snatched another. *Twang, twang, twang, twang*, the bowstring sang in rapid succession.

Four gargoyles lay dead.

A coughing fit gripped Tell and fresh blood spewed from his mouth. He staggered to the trunk of a nearby tree and slid to the ground. The bow slipped from his hand. *So tired.*

A cold numbness traveled from his legs and up to his arms. He closed his eyes and recalled his favorite memory of Alex— when she unexpectantly embraced him on the terrace and kissed him. A sense of contentment filled him.

His head fell forward, his last thoughts of her.

CHAPTER 27

K RALL ROARED HIS DISPLEASURE.

"Seven dead? At the hands of the wounded human? Why are you still alive?"

Drak stood shaking before the Third Circle gargoyle wondering if his next breath would be his last. "My Chieftain, the soldier was already dead when I found him."

Krall's hands twitched as if eager to squeeze the life from Drak for the unwelcome news. "What of the female?" he growled through clenched teeth.

Drak's trembling increased. "Escaped into the forest."

Krall snatched an obsidian dagger from his waist. He held the tip poised at Drak's throat. "Release the dark lord's beast to track the female down, and bring her back to me," he hissed.

Drak swallowed. "Ye-yes, my Chieftain." He turned and barked orders, amazed to still be alive.

A pair of gargoyles unstrapped a cage secured to the back of a squark, and carried it to Drak. He opened the barred door and stepped back warily. A melded creature emerged. Legs, paws, fur, and torso matched that of a dog.

The other appendages were anything but canine.

Mandibles clacked where jaws should have existed, and instead of normal pupils, the creature possessed a spider's black, compound eyes. Oddest of all was the carapace forming a scorpion's stinger. Instead of a tail, the stinger arched over the scorpion-dog's back.

Drak threw some female clothing on the ground obtained from a pack on the dead horse. The scorpion-dog snuffled it, then bayed with a deep bass howl. It trotted off into the woods following the scent.

Drak and a score of gargoyles trailed after the creature.

※

Lost in her despair, Alex paid no attention to her surroundings or where Della was taking her.

Tell is dead...he sacrificed himself for me.

The ache in her heart far exceeded any physical pain she ever experienced. At times she found it hard to breathe.

He loved me, and I didn't return his love.

Suffocating guilt weighed on her. She allowed selfish desire for someone who didn't even exist to trump her feelings for Tell. "I'm sorry, Tell," she sobbed. "I'm so sorry."

A bass cry, like a dog's howl, intruded into her misery. Della's ears pricked up, and although lathered and tired, she broke into a trot. The baying drew closer and closer. In full-blown panic, Della thundered through the thick underbrush. Branches and leaves whipped across Alex's face with stinging impact. Suddenly, the ground fell away, and they were sliding down a steep embankment. A stout limb caught Alex at the waist. With a *whoosh*, the breath left her lungs and she was catapulted off the saddle.

Landing hard on the forest floor, Alex rolled down the ridge and lay stunned. Strangled gasps came from her throat as she fought to breathe. Able to finally take a breath, she pushed up to her hands and knees. The pleasant murmur of water came from nearby. A stream flowed by her feet. She crawled to the brook and splashed water on her face. Somewhat fortified, she staggered to her feet.

Della stood nearby, one wing canted at an odd angle. As Alex struggled up the slope to reach her, more howling split the air. The mare shook her head. Grabbing the pommel, Alex steadied herself while removing a crossbow from the saddle.

Aroooo!

At the top of the embankment, mandibles snapping, stood a nightmare creature. Eyes rolling in terror, Della reared and took off in a frenzied gallop. Alex threw herself to the side to avoid being trampled, and slid again to the bottom of the ridge. Somehow, she managed to hang on to the crossbow. Getting to her feet, the sight of the scorpion-dog picking its way down the slope greeted her.

Fear galvanized Alex. She ran, splashing, into the stream to cross it. Although it was shallow, she repeatedly slipped on moss-slickened rocks. When she emerged onto the other side, she was drenched and shivering. A large elm grew at the water's edge, and Alex backed up to it.

The scorpion-dog reached the brook. It scurried back and forth baying, stinger pointed at her. In the background, the snap and crunch of underbrush signaled the approach of Alex's pursuers.

Alex turned the crossbow in her hands and tried to remember Tell's directions during their brief practice sessions. "Point, aim, and fire." Simple instructions but with her hands shaking in fear and cold from the frigid water, she was as apt to hit herself as the creature at the water's edge.

The scorpion-dog waded across the stream.

Realizing she hadn't cranked the crossbow, Alex desperately turned the mechanism to draw the bowstring back. Her grip kept slipping, but she managed to get the drawstring locked in place. Prying a bolt from the crossbow's undercarriage, her numb fingers promptly dropped it.

The scorpion-dog neared her growling ominously.

Alex ripped another quarrel free and tried to place it into the loading groove. It wouldn't fit! She pounded on it before realizing she had loaded the bolt backwards. Quickly, she turned it around and the missile slid into place.

The creature crept forward on stiff legs, now just ten feet away. She held the crossbow in front of her and mumbled Tell's instructions like a mantra, "Point, aim, and fire."

Try as she might, she couldn't hold a stable aim on the creature. The shivers racking her from cold and fear kept her hands unsteady. From the sounds coming off the ridge, her trackers were only minutes away. Desperate, a plan hatched in her mind. In order to make sure she hit the scorpion-dog, she would have to draw it closer—much closer.

She edged away from the bole of the tree, and stumbled up the slope. The creature waved its menacing stinger and followed. *It worked.* The scorpion-dog advanced to cut off her escape. She took another step. The creature growled and moved nearer.

Thwack.

The quarrel flew true…and buried itself in the creature's chest.

The scorpion-dog yelped in mortal agony and writhed in the grip of its death throes. As the creature convulsed on the ground, its agonized flopping brought it closer and closer. Before she could leap away from its frenzied thrashing, the stinger whipped outward and buried itself below her ribs.

It felt as though liquid fire had been poured into her side.

She screamed and ripped the stinger out. Staggering backwards, Alex clamped her hand to her side, the poison spreading rapidly into her bloodstream.

Teeth gritted, the pain boiled to an unbearable white-hot agony. A familiar prickle in her mind heralded the unlocking of a mental gate. Another spasm struck Alex, and she screamed again. Her eyes rolled back in her head.

Suddenly, a huge cone of brilliant radiance burst from her. Her body shook as it transformed into a conduit for the release of powerful magic. Flooding from her like a burst dam, the searing white light exploded in all directions.

Then, abruptly, it ended.

Alex, with only dim awareness of the magic's release, slumped to the ground.

Darkness beckoned and she fell unconscious.

CHAPTER 28

TAL STOOD OUTSIDE THE CABIN AS THE SUN ROSE ABOVE THE forest canopy.

He took a last sip tea and tossed the remnants on the ground. He retreated to the cabin's interior, packed his few belongings, and prepared to leave. Before he closed the door, he turned and examined the interior one last time.

Everything in its place.

Since he arrived the day before, his acute sense of anticipation had dulled and he now felt foolish for the waste of time this diversion cost him. Another search of the enchanted cottage revealed nothing new, and other than the powerful and ancient magic that held sway over the structure, the cabin itself remained unremarkable.

With time on his hands, he had even returned to the place in the wilderness where he rescued the Forest Mother. No trace of her remained, and no voice appeared in his mind.

Eyebrows pinched, he shut the door, and whistled for his horse. Moments later, they took to the air. Tal circled once to get his bearings, then resumed the course for Markingham.

The storm horse had taken only a few wing beats, when a powerful surge of magic washed over Tal like a giant wave. Disoriented by the intense flood of power, he gripped the pommel and shook his head. The spots cleared from his vision, and he searched the immediate area above and below him. When no obvious evidence of what caused the mysterious eruption presented itself, he closed his eyes and let the storm horse soar in a loop.

Tal expanded his magical senses. Like a bloodhound, he traced the potent source to the northwest. The magic "tasted" unlike any enchantment he had ever known. At first, he immediately suspected it to be the foul sorcery of the Veil, but it had a clean, warm feel to it.

He turned the storm horse, and they shot northwest.

Krall was thrown off his feet by the powerful blast of magic.

Stunned and temporarily blinded by the intense white light, he rubbed his eyes until his vision cleared.

What happened?

Members of his eyrie bolted past him in mindless terror. Some even attempted to mount their *squarks* who hopped and screeched in panic.

"Stop, you fools!" he roared. Most complied with his order but one of his flock continued a mad dash to his *squark*. Snatching the obsidian dagger from his belt, the eyrie Chieftain threw it in one liquid motion. The blade buried itself to the hilt in the gargoyle's back. He raced to the fallen gargoyle, ripped the dagger free, then cut his throat.

Krall wiped the blade clean on the dead gargoyle's tunic. He bellowed, "Are there any others who would run?" When none answered, he snorted in disgust.

Krall counted the surviving members of his eyrie. Of the original flock he left the Eyrie with, only twenty remained.

What happened to the squad I sent to capture the female?

He hadn't a clue. But it was time to find out.

Krall picked six of his remaining flock to accompany him.

The rest he ordered to stay behind on guard. The human female had already cost him dearly. There would be nothing left to chance this time.

He would find her.

🔲

Tal found the powerful trail of magic straightforward and easy to follow.

The potency of the magic grew as he neared the source. Tal closed his eyes and drew upon his power. When he opened them, they glowed an otherworldly blue and his vision increased tenfold.

A strange sight greeted him.

A path of destruction emanated from the forest below. The trees and foliage had been flattened as if trampled underfoot by some giant creature. Many of the trees had been snapped off at the base, and lay in jumbled piles. The devastation formed a perfect cone-shaped pattern that started from a central point and expanded outward.

A figure lay prone on the ground at the precise point the wreckage began. With a start, Tal realized the slim figure to be that of a woman. *She* must be the source of the magic he tracked.

Tal scanned the area around the woman. He hissed when a group of gargoyles emerged from an undamaged area of the forest. He searched over a broader area, and discovered an open meadow a short distance away...and more gargoyles with their grotesque mounts within it. He counted the number of the creatures and calculated the odds. He bared his teeth.

Time for the Veil filth to face the power and wrath of a Blood Prince.

He removed his bow from its waterproof case and turned

the storm mount toward the meadow. Bozar's last admonishment—*not* to use his magic and risk discovery a Royal had slipped through the Veil—shouldn't be a problem.

Because there won't be any survivors left to tell the tale.

⬚

Krall eyed the destruction in amazement.

The thick scent of sap from the destroyed forest infused the air. Pushed over like twigs, massive trunks lay side-by-side well into the distance. Picking his way through the downed trees, his foot *crunched* on something. Beneath his heel was the misshapen head of a gargoyle.

One mystery solved—the squad he sent after the female was crushed under the fallen trees.

Krall spread his bat-like wings. Only eyrie Chieftains were allowed to grow their wings to full size, while those of lesser gargoyles remained stunted and smaller. He leaped into the air, tiring of the ground-based search. From his aerial view he followed the path of destruction. His keen sight spotted the motionless figure of the female.

She did this?

No wonder the Dark Lord wants her. A woman of such power would be of incalculable worth. Cold fear stabbed his heart at the realization she might be injured, or worse, dead. Lord Stefan wouldn't care why. His implicit instructions were to bring the female back to him unharmed. As Chieftain, blame would fall on only one.

Krall.

He barked at the gargoyles below to join him once they finished a last sweep of the nearby woodlands. He streaked through the air toward the fallen female.

Tal came in low with the sun at his back.

The storm horse kept a stable glide which allowed Tal to sight and aim. He pulled an arrow from the quiver, targeted a gargoyle, and released. The creature groped at the shaft which skewered its throat and fell choking in a geyser of blood.

Two more gargoyles sprouted shafts before the alarm was raised and pandemonium erupted. Tal circled for another pass, and in a blur of motion, pulled the bow to release arrow after arrow. Feathered shafts streaked with unerring accuracy until half the gargoyles lay dead or dying on the grass. He alighted in the meadow, the storm mount's hooves barely touching soil before Tal leaped from the saddle. He jerked his sword from the scabbard and sprinted toward the remaining gargoyles.

A few recovered enough nerve to turn and shoot their own bolts at Tal. He motioned with his hand and a wave of magic deflected the arrows harmlessly into the air.

Then he was in their midst.

His blade rang like a hammer on anvil as he slashed and parried. Although savage creatures, they were disorganized and one after another fell in a spray of purple blood. The survivors broke and ran, some for the gap within the trees and the safety of the forest, while others tried to reach their *squarks* and escape. Tal retrieved his bow and shot one after another before they could mount the giant birds.

A lone gargoyle managed to leap on a squark. Flapping, the bird rose and took flight. Tal reached for another arrow...and snatched air. He had no shafts left.

I can't let any escape!

Tal calmed himself. With deep, even breaths, he held both hands before him, palms up. Blue sparks jumped and grew into sizzling balls of fire. He hurled one, then the other. Streaking like comets, they pursued the fleeing gargoyle. With the squark sandwiched in between, they met in a midair explosion of feathers and blue fire.

The smoking remains of bird and rider fell to the ground.

Tal turned his attention to the gargoyles who fled into the forest. He held the empty quiver before him and cried, "Return!" Bodies jerked as arrows ripped themselves free, and dripping with gore, flew into the quiver. Within seconds, his full complement of shafts was restored.

Tal reached the opening in the forest and stopped. With a grim smile, he pulled his sword and disappeared into the dappled greenery.

A predator on the hunt.

CHAPTER 29

K RALL ALIGHTED NEXT TO THE FEMALE AND REGARDED HER WITH undisguised curiosity.

Careful of a trap, he looked around and fingered the handle of the obsidian sword strapped between his wings. Transformed by the magic of the eyrie shaman to the hardness of iron, the night-black blade always kept a sharp edge. Krall had never lost a battle with the mighty weapon.

Satisfied no immediate threat existed, he returned his attention to the prone figure.

She was motionless, but the slow rise and fall of her chest indicated her continued existence among the living. He folded his leathery wings and surveyed the surrounding area. The contrast to the front and rear of the woman was stark. Behind the female the forest appeared untouched, a thick profusion of vegetation. In front lay a spreading path of destruction marked by splintered and fallen trees.

Krall stepped over the dead scorpion-dog, a quarrel in its chest, and knelt beside his quarry. Puzzled, he moved the pale hand clamped to her right side. It revealed a dark stain of blood and venom. He stood and a snarl burst from his lips.

She'd been stung by the beast!

The blood drained from Krall's face. His worst fears materialized. Only moments ago he thought things couldn't possibly get worse. He was wrong.

They were much worse.

The venom of the scorpion-dog was potent. *How is the female still alive?* She would surely die, and on a task the Dark Lord had specifically sent Krall to undertake! The wrath of Lord Stefan would be as swift as it would be cruel. His only option was to get the female back to the eyrie, and hope the dark magic of Lord Stefan could save her.

He knelt to pick up the woman, but stopped when two of his flock burst from the undamaged section of woods and sped away.

Idiots! What foolishness is this?

Sounds of battle came from the forest as the gargoyles vaulted over fallen trees and raced toward him. Senses on high alert, the female forgotten, Krall snatched the obsidian sword from the sheath strapped between his wings.

The gargoyles skidded to a stop before him. Fear masked their expressions and both tried to talk at once. Losing patience, Krall backhanded one, then the other.

"Speak!" he demanded. "What has happened?"

"Something in the forest stalks us, Chieftain," one of the gargoyles managed to say.

"What? Who—"

Krall stopped as a tall human emerged from the forest and darted toward them. He raised a bow and released a shaft. In an instant, Krall grabbed the nearest gargoyle and held him up before him. Arrows thudded into his living shield, the body quivering with each impact. Krall hurled the corpse away, then grabbed the surviving member of his flock. The archer hurdled over more downed trees and managed to send two more arrows at Krall. Again, they struck Krall's buffer of flesh. He tossed the twitching body away.

With a roar, Krall gripped his sword and leaped to meet the attack.

※

Tal reached firm footing on ground free of broken and shattered trees.

He drew his sword a scant second before the giant gargoyle could land a savage overhand blow to his head. Only Tal's preternatural quickness allowed him to parry the strike before it split his skull open. With a snarl, the gargoyle tried to close again on Tal. The creature's blade, a blur of motion, forced Tal to backtrack. He sidestepped a stroke while drawing his dagger from his belt. The huge creature's forward momentum caused him to lunge past Tal, and he slashed one of the exposed wings with the dagger. The sharp blade sliced a jagged line through the flesh of the wing. The leathery skin separated and flapped, purple blood flowing from the wound.

A primal scream of pain and fury shook the air. The gargoyle took one look at its ruined wing, and driven by insane rage, resumed the attack. The clash of swords echoed like thunderclaps, each strike more savage than the last. The desperate battle went back and forth as the Chieftain tried to overcome Tal's defenses through sheer brute strength. Finally, sides heaving, the gargoyle broke away.

The two regarded each other warily during the momentary respite.

Tal, his own breath a succession of ragged gasps, studied the huge gargoyle. He noted the three ritual scars on the creature's cheek. Sifting through his knowledge of gargoyles, he recognized the marks as those of a Third Circle Chieftain—a formidable opponent.

The gargoyle smiled to expose flesh-rending teeth. "I am Krall, Chieftain of my eyrie. You are a worthy foe, much harder to kill than any soft human I have ever faced. But in the end, it won't matter. Your skull will *still* join the collection in my nest."

He launched another vicious attack at Tal. Sparks of magic

flew, their blades meeting again and again. Krall's snarls rose to ear-splitting intensity over his failure to break through Tal's defenses. The eyrie Chieftain delivered one ferocious blow after another. Finally, he broke away, wheezing. His face radiated disbelief over the inability to kill or even put a scratch upon Tal.

Tal allowed himself a grim smile. *Time to go on offense.*

He attacked the eyrie Chieftain, his sword weaving a deadly dance. Darting in and out, his blade struck like a snake, the constant clash of steel and obsidian carrying on without pause. Krall stumbled backwards, his disbelief replaced by flickers of fear and doubt.

Tal sensed fatigue in his opponent. Third Circle battles among gargoyles were short, brutal affairs, and Krall probably never had a fight last over an extended period of time.

He pressed his attack.

The battle raged, the onslaught now all Tal with the gargoyle defending itself from blow after blow. He began to find small openings in the eyrie Chieftain's defense. The nicks and cuts his blade scored proved more harmful to the gargoyle's pride than to the creature physically. Tal suspected Krall's new level of desperation would lead to an equally desperate attack.

It came seconds later.

The eyrie Chieftain, stamina flagging, threw himself into a final desperate assault. Tal parried one frenzied stroke after another as the gargoyle hammered away. Their blades met in a stupendous violent clash—and the magic of his sword proved to be stronger than the tribal magic of Krall's eyrie. Tal's steel sheared through the obsidian sword, and it shattered. Krall threw the remnant at Tal, pulled a dagger from his belt, and leaped at Tal before he could make a return swing. The gargoyle managed to pin Tal's sword arm, then aimed a savage strike at his heart. Tal caught the gargoyle's hand by the wrist and struggled to hold it, the dagger mere inches from his chest.

The eyrie Chieftain smiled in triumph, his fetid breath hot against Tal's face. "Now you shall *die!*"

The muscles in Krall's massive shoulders and arms gathered in sharp relief with the effort to skewer Tal's heart. Tendon's bulged like cords of rope in Tal's neck as he strained to hold the dagger at bay. The sharp tip inched closer while they grappled with one another in desperation.

Then the blade's movement stopped.

Slowly, the dagger turned. The gargoyle's eyes widened. Despite its size and strength, the blade was being forced away from the soft human's heart—and toward his own!

"Who are you?" the eyrie Chieftain hissed through gritted teeth.

Tal, close-mouthed, increased the pressure on the dagger. The point now jutted at Krall. Grunting with effort, the gargoyle couldn't stop the blade's progress. The sharp tip stopped beneath the Chieftain's chin.

"My lore masters have told me gargoyles can see their deaths moments before they occur. Can you see yours?" Tal whispered into the Chieftain's ear.

With a sudden wrench of his wrist, Tal propelled the dagger upward. With a *crunch*, the blade plunged through the gargoyle's lower chin and palate, into the upper roof of its mouth, then punched through to pierce the braincase. Krall's eyes rolled back into his head, and his body went slack. The gargoyle slumped to the ground.

On hands on knees, Tal struggled to catch his breath. He managed to stand and turned his attention to the prone figure of the woman on the ground—and knew his search was over.

The magic he followed led straight to her.

CHAPTER 30

ALTHOUGH MUCH WEAKER, THE MAGIC STILL PULSED FROM HER. A bloody, discolored blotch stained the side of her tunic. Tal lifted her shirt, and brown fluid leaked from a puncture wound. He dipped his finger in it and placed a tiny amount on his tongue. He immediately spat.

Poison…and a particularly potent venom at that.

He stood and studied the beast lying a few feet away. Having slain a number of Marlinda's melded monstrosities, he'd seen more than his fair share of her twisted creations. This one, however, was unlike any he had ever come across.

Tal carefully grasped its stinger and squeezed. More of the brown poison dripped from it. The bolt in the dead creature's chest told the rest of the story. The woman shot the beast, but not before it managed to sting her.

He felt her pulse. Weak and intermittent. He counted it a miracle she still lived…but not for much longer unless he could find an antidote.

For the first time, he noticed her beauty. Even unconscious, hair tangled and her body lying in the mud, she was breathtaking. He squatted next to her and considered his options. He knew nothing about the woman. She could be friend or foe—although if pursued by gargoyles he strongly suspected the former. Her magic, as powerful as it was unusual, might make her a welcome ally.

If she lived.

A plan formed in his mind. Bozar wouldn't approve, but Tal couldn't leave her here. His sharp whistle pierced the air. The storm mount appeared a short time later and landed a few feet away. The stallion snorted at the sight of the dead gargoyles and the scent of blood.

Tal stooped to pick up the woman but stopped when when a *whinny* came from the nearby forest. A dun flying horse trotted out from the trees, crossed the brook, and pranced nervously a short distance from Tal. He approached the mare and stroked her neck.

This must be her horse.

The mare nuzzled Tal, grateful for the reassuring touch. He recalled the flying horse lying dead in the meadow and the young man he also found dead a short distance into the trees. More of this mystery unfolded. The two must have traveled together, but pursued and overtaken by the gargoyles, were forced to land.

But why? The gargoyles are far from their mountain eyrie. And how did this woman manage to level a whole section of forest?

Only one person could answer these questions...and she lay at his feet near death.

He returned his attention to the mare. One wing was canted at an unnatural angle. Tal moved closer, and discovered the massive joint where the wing attached to the shoulder was swollen from some kind of blow. He crooned soothing words while his fingers gently probed the flesh. He realized that it was dislocated.

Taking a firm hold of the bridle to hold the horse steady, he used his other hand to give the wing a quick shove. The wing popped back into place. The mare jumped and nickered, but Tal continued to whisper softly while he re-examined the joint. Still swollen, but the wing could now function properly—or at least he hoped it would. If the unconscious woman recovered, they would need to rejoin the invasion force—a long journey.

And they would each need a flying horse.

Before he bent to pick up the woman, Tal hesitated and glanced at the tree line. *One more task before we leave.* He threaded his way through the debris and entered the forest gloom. Retracing his steps, he followed a trail of gargoyle bodies to the woman's dead companion.

Tal blinked and took a step back.

Despite the trio of arrows protruding from the young man, he had managed to slay a number of gargoyles before death took him. Tal lifted the body over his shoulder to carry it back to the clearing. He would not dishonor the sacrifice made by the woman's companion and leave him to scavengers.

Strapping the body securely to the mare's back, Tal hoisted the woman's limp body onto his mount and joined her in the saddle. With one arm wrapped around her, he urged the stallion forward. A short time later, they were in the air and winging away from the destroyed forest.

The mare followed, and Tal watched her closely. She didn't appear to favor the wing and had no trouble keeping up. He sighed in relief. His own mount carried the weight of two easily enough, and he allowed the stallion to keep a steady pace. They had a long trip ahead.

Back to the enchanted cottage.

Tal's sharp eyes located the clearing with the charmed cabin in the fading light.

He urged his mount downward, and the storm horse glided in to land in the glade. Tal dismounted, the unconscious woman in his arms. Her head lolled back and forth as he hurried to the cabin and opened the door. Light crystals flared to life, and blinking, Tal looked around.

Everything still in its place.

Tal walked to the wall bunks and lowered the woman onto one. In the grip of fever, heat radiated in waves from her body. Tal hurried to the privy and the stone tub within. Water poured from the tap, and when it filled to halfway, he stopped the water's flow. Next, he concentrated, the magic building within him. He blew on the water, his breath a frosty, billowing, cloud. After several breaths, a thin rime of ice covered the water. He thrust a hand through the skim of frost.

The feel of excruciatingly cold water chilled his flesh.

He ran back to the main room and placed a hand upon the woman's forehead. The heat practically scalded his hand. *I need to get the fever down before she cooks in her own blood, then find an antidote.*

Tal peeled off the sweat-soaked and muddy clothing, then carried her naked body to the tub and plunged it into the water. He kept only her nose and mouth above the water. Forced to switch hands frequently in the numbing cold, he lost track of time as he fought to bring the fever down. When her teeth began to chatter, he carried her dripping body back to the bunkbed. When her flesh heated again, he returned her to the tub and submerged her into the icy water. Back and forth, the chills and fever came and went.

Hours later, Tal believed he had finally stabilized the woman. Exhausted, he placed his palm on her head and cheek. They remained cool to his touch. He moved her off the bed fouled with fever sweat and water, and to another bunk with fresh blankets.

After settling her on the bed, he paused. Unable to help himself, Tal couldn't tear his eyes from her. *She is…breathtaking.* Locks of damp hair strayed across her face, her full lips parted. He gently brushed the stray hair aside. A tug, powerful and unexpected, gripped his heart. He swallowed and forced himself to look away. He wrapped blankets around her, then pulled a chair beside the bed. After a moment's hesitation, he reached for her hand and held it.

"Fight for your life," he whispered. "I'll do what I can, but you have to fight."

Tal jerked his head back when her hand squeezed his.

Just an involuntary reflex, he told himself. Nevertheless, he stood and paced, wracking his brain on what to do next.

Restless, he left the cabin hoping the fresh air would help clear his mind. The two flying horses cropped grass from the clearing, the body of the young man lay still strapped to the mare's back. Guilt wracked Tal, and he untied the corpse, then laid it gently on the porch. He needed to bury the woman's companion properly, but for now the living had to be his priority, not the dead.

He removed the horses' saddles but decided to rub them down later. More pressing matters were at hand. Tal carried his pack into the cabin and removed a leather sack. He rummaged around within the satchel, his arm at times going up past the elbow in the small bag. The satchel, an Artifact called a *Deep Pocket,* allowed for the storage of many useful items.

Tal found the object he wanted and pulled it out. Wafer-thin squares of metal dangled from a brass ring. Tiny lodestones were mounted in each thumbnail-sized square, and were covered with miniscule script so small, Tal had to squint to read it. He flipped through each one, then stopped and removed one of the metal tags. He touched the lodestone to activate its magic, and the tiny metal disk rose from his hand to hover motionless before him. It flipped open and doubled in size, then repeated the process again and again until it transformed into a large book, complete with binding and pages. Stenciled in large letters on the cover were the words, *Medicine & Healing.*

"Venom," Tal spoke aloud. The pages fluttered to a chapter labeled *Poisons & Venoms*.

Tal quickly scanned the section, ordering the book to flip pages until he finished reading. The closest match he found, *Venom of Melded Creatures,* caused his heart to sink. The only known way to counteract the poison was to remove it from the bloodstream using a blood truffle. Venoms and poisons contained properties which a blood truffle found irresistible, and the treatment called for the fungus to be placed upon the point of entry of the venom. It then acted like a filter to remove the poison from the bloodstream.

Tal closed his eyes in despair. These truffles were extremely rare. Short of a fully stocked apothecary, the chance of finding one in the wilderness was nonexistent. He slammed his fist into the palm of his hand. He didn't fight and slay the eyrie Chieftain just to bring the young woman here to die.

No! There has to be something I can do!

Tal paced muttering to himself. He stopped in his tracks when a voice suddenly sounded in his head.

I hear your thoughts, young prince. I know why you are so distressed.

The Forest Mother had returned.

179

CHAPTER 31

"I NEED YOUR HELP!" THE WORDS BURST FROM HIS MOUTH.

The young woman with you. She lies near death.

"Yes, I need to find—"

Something only the forest can provide. I have seen this in your mind.

"Then you know why I need it. Can you help me?"

I owe you a life debt. Follow me, young prince.

It took a moment, but Tal realized the Cyclops must have known of his presence and predicament since he arrived at the enchanted cabin hours ago—perhaps even when he first arrived the day before.

He rushed out the door. The Forest Mother stood at the edge of the meadow. By the glow of the triple moons, her surreal image appeared even larger than before. One shovel-sized hand rested on her swollen belly, the other gestured to him. Then she turned and disappeared into the forest.

Tal raced after her.

For such a large creature, the Cyclops moved through the dense foliage with ease. Even though Tal's night vision was excellent, roots and brush pulled at his feet, and he struggled to keep up. He eventually burst into a small clearing which contained an enormous, lightning-struck tree. The Forest Mother stood by the dead evergreen, its gray, skeletal limbs bare of needles.

She pointed to the ground at the base of the pine. "There is what you seek."

Tal dropped to his knees and began to dig with his bare hands. He excavated the soft loam with ease, and after digging down about a foot, his fingers closed on something hard and leathery. He pulled it out and examined it in the light of the moons.

Thin, black, and tough, the blood truffle resembled an uncured piece of leather left out in the elements to dry and shrivel. He stuffed the fungus into a pouch tied at his belt.

Tal stood. "Thank you, Forest Mother."

When most of your kind would have passed me by or even killed me, you saved my life. Now I give you the means to save the female you care about. My debt is paid.

Tal felt the heat rise in his cheeks. "I've never met this woman before...I don't know who she is." He brushed the pine straw off his knees. "And I thought I made clear you owed me no debt."

The rumble he recognized as a chuckle came from the Cyclops. *Your thoughts concerning the female betray you. They are the steps to your heart.*

She pointed North. *One last thing I give you...a warning. You are not safe here and must be gone by the fourth rising of the sun. Others seek the young female and follow her scent.*

Tal frowned. "How do you know this? And what 'scent' do you speak of?"

The Forest Mother shrugged her massive shoulders. *You ask questions, young prince, you already know the answers to.*

Of course. She had known when he would appear at the enchanted cabin, just like she knew he would come again—this time with the injured woman. This "scent" the Cyclops spoke of was the powerful magic whose residue still clung to her.

Any novice practitioner could follow her trail of magic just as he had. Who *they* were remained a mystery, but if gargoyles were involved, then it would certainly be agents of the Dark Queen.

He turned to speak again, but other than the dead tree, he

was alone. While enmeshed in his thoughts, the Cyclops slipped away in silence, back to her forest home. He lost no time retracing his steps back to the charmed cottage.

Tal reached the clearing and raced to the door. He opened it and removed the blood truffle from his pouch. In the bright light, it looked even more like a piece of old shoe leather. He rinsed the dirt off its cracked and shriveled surface and knelt beside the bed. Pulling the blankets away, he exposed the young woman's ribs where she had been stung. With his dagger, he sliced an "X" through the tough surface of the fungi. Then he pressed the incision directly on the site of the puncture wound.

Long moments passed while Tal held the fungus in place. Then a *sucking* noise came from the truffle. It expanded and grew warm. He removed his hand, the truffle already swollen with blood. Dark veins formed a network as hyphae spread into the woman's flesh.

Tal pumped his fist. "Yes!" *It worked.* The fungi was already filtering the poison from her bloodstream. He rocked back on his heels.

Nothing to do now but wait.

***

The morning sun peeked above the trees as Tal shoveled the last of the soil into the grave. Even though exhausted from little sleep, he didn't want to put off any longer burying the woman's companion. He had chosen a site at the edge of the glade with a slight rise. It allowed for a spectacular view of the wilderness beauty which spread in an unending panorama.

Somehow it seemed appropriate for one who had made the ultimate sacrifice.

Tal whispered a prayer. As he turned to leave, the mound of

soil rippled and boiled. Wildflowers in blues, golds, reds, and purples erupted in a profusion to cover every inch of the grave. The riot of color rippled in the gentle breeze.

Tal's initial shock transformed into a warm contentment. The cabin's ancient enchantment had embraced the deceased young man.

He trudged back to the cottage and checked again on his patient. Some color had returned to her face, and the slow rise and fall of her chest indicated she no longer struggled to breathe. More importantly, she suffered no more bouts of chills and fever.

The blood truffle, ballooned to three times its original size, was unrecognizable. Thick veins crisscrossed its swollen exterior, while the web of hyphae formed fingerlike extensions embedded in the woman's flesh. Hope rose in Tal's chest.

She might survive after all.

With a sigh, he retrieved the communication rings he had placed on the table, and steeled himself for Bozar's reaction when he reported in.

His *Eldred* would not be happy.

With a flip of his wrist, he tossed the rings in the air. They hovered and spun faster and faster until they blurred and resolved into an image.

Bozar's.

In the background, Artemis Thurgood and Pulpit stood, each with concerned expressions.

"Why didn't you report in at the agreed time?" Bozar demanded. He looked past Tal at the cabin's interior. "And where are you?"

"I made a detour." Tal recounted how a wave of magic engulfed him and how he followed its trail, discovered the gargoyle flock, and killed the eyrie Chieftain. He reserved the tale of the unconscious woman for last.

"I brought her here to save her life."

Bozar's nut-brown complexion flushed crimson. "You were supposed to fly to Markingham, scout it out, and return with a report! Simple instructions even a child could follow. Yet here you are back at this charmed cabin *with a woman you know nothing about!*"

A vein bulged on Bozar's forehead. "You were not to employ your magic under *any* circumstance short of saving your own life. Yet you used it to kill gargoyles—and may have halted our invasion before it scarcely started!"

"May I speak?" Tal asked through gritted teeth.

"No! You are to return at once!"

"She has magic!" Tal blurted. "Strong magic like I've never felt before. It *masks* everything including my own magic. And since I left no gargoyles alive, our secret is safe."

Artemis Thurgood pushed past Bozar. "Describe this magic."

Tal grimaced. "It defies description. But it is powerful, so powerful it almost knocked me off my storm horse. It feels..." Tal searched for words, "pure, uncorrupted."

Pulpit joined the Grand Master. "Where is she?"

Tal positioned the ring to display the unconscious woman, the blood truffle attached to her side like a melon-sized bladder.

Bozar shook his head. "Only you could find one so fair in the middle of a wilderness."

Tal felt the blood rush to his cheeks. "Her comeliness had nothing to do with rescuing her!"

Bozar folded his arms. "What do you plan to do if and when she recovers?"

"Take her back with me. We can question her at length and perhaps learn valuable information."

"You realize she could be an agent of the Dark Queen and King," the First Advisor warned.

Tal shook his head. "No. Gargoyles pursued her, and her magic holds no taint of sorcery. It tasted…" again Tal paused, "clean."

Pulpit's face took on a heightened interest at Tal's words. "Her knowledge may prove to be valuable," he advised Bozar.

Bozar released a frustrated sigh. "So be it." He pointed at Tal. "When she has recovered sufficient strength, bring her and rejoin us…with no more *detours!*"

The image faded and the rings dropped in Tal's hand. Before he could place them back on the table, a *plop* came from behind him. He turned. At the sight, a charge of triumph blazed through him.

Swollen and distended, the blood truffle lay on the floor.

CHAPTER 32

ALEX DREAMED.

In her fevered visions, faces swam. Some came from her past life on earth. Her brother Joe, their foster parents, the Bakers, even Lady Anne, the cruel and beautiful bully who had driven her to consider suicide. All floated by as if caught in a gentle current. Some came from her present; Duke Duvalier, Dorothea, Rodric and, with a catch in her heart, Tell. She reached for him, only to see Tell drift away, just out of reach.

One came from her future.

Her dream stranger gazed at her with eyes the color of clover. He extended his hand and she grasped it. His lips moved, but try as she might, only one word resonated in her mind.

Fight.

With a soft groan, Alex opened her eyes.

Her blurry sight refused to cooperate, but after blinking several times, her eyesight slowly resolved into clarity. Sunlight streamed through dusty windows. A table lay before her in a room constructed of rough-hewn planks and logs. A fireplace, chairs, and a kitchen and pantry completed the furnishings.

A young man walked in carrying a large basin of water and a towel. Bare to the waist, he moved with a fluid grace. He placed the washbasin on the table, cupped water, and splashed it on his face. Using a smaller cloth, he began to scrub himself.

The play of his muscles rippled like waves across a pebbled beach. A trim waist swelled to a broad chest and shoulders, his stomach a ridged washboard of toned flesh. Tall, Alex guessed his height to be well over six and half feet. The young man paused as if feeling her gaze. He turned his head and their eyes met.

She recognized him instantly.

Though still groggy and weak, her heart flip-flopped. Only one person had such intense green eyes.

Her stranger.

He threw the towel on the table and rushed to her bedside. "It's about time you rejoined the living. How do you feel?"

"Th-thirsty," Alex croaked.

He poured water from a ceramic pitcher into a wooden cup. With one arm around Alex, he brought her to a sitting position. Everything began to spin, and she pitched forward. He caught her and held her tight. Her head rested on his chest, her cheek nestled against his warm skin. His musky scent filled her nostrils.

"Are you okay?" he asked.

"Just…hold me up until the dizziness passes." Alex never felt so weak. Her limbs acted as though filled with sand instead of bone, tendons, and muscle.

Eventually, the lightheadedness faded, and her raging thirst returned. "I-I'd like a drink now."

Her body propped firmly against his, the young man raised the cup to her lips. The water dribbled into her mouth, and she swallowed greedily. Alex reached to hold the cup herself, and when she did her blanket fell.

And left her naked to the waist.

She coughed and spewed part of the water out. As fast as her leaden arms would allow, she pulled the blanket back up to her chin.

"What is your name?" Alex asked to cover her embarrassment.

"Tal," the young man answered with an amused expression. "And don't worry. You didn't reveal anything I haven't already seen—many times."

"Wh-what do you mean?"

"How do you think you were bathed? Or taken to the privy? Surely you don't believe that occurred with your clothes on?"

Alex face grew hot. "N-No." Thankfully the discussion ended and he raised the cup to her lips again. Alex emptied it. "My name is Alexandria, although most call me Alex." She pushed the cup back to Tal. "Can I have some more water?"

"No more for now," Tal said. "You've had nothing to eat or drink for almost two days, and you'll get sick if you put too much in your stomach."

He laid her gently back onto the bed. "Go back to sleep. When you wake up, I'll bring you some more water."

Alex didn't protest, her eyelids already heavy. Within moments, she fell asleep.

When she woke, the light through the windows cast long shadows. She had slept most of the day away. More of her strength returned and she struggled into a sitting position. She spied a small pot bubbling over the fireplace. The savory smell of soup caused her stomach to rumble.

The door opened and Tal entered the room. He grinned at the sight of her sitting up. "Your color is much better. Are you hungry?"

She nodded and he spooned some of the soup into a wooden bowel. He placed it aside to cool and filled a cup with water. He sat in the chair beside her bed and handed it to her.

"Remember," he warned, "drink slowly."

With one hand holding the blanket tight, she took the cup and sipped. "Do...do you have anything I can wear?"

Tal nodded and left the room. When he returned, he handed her a tunic. "I found clothes in your saddle pack, but until your strength fully returns, it's probably best you wear something light and easy to get into and out of."

Alex took the shirt and Tal turned around while she put it on. The tunic fell to her knees, and the length told her it belonged to him. Exhausted by the effort, she sat heavily back onto the bed.

Tal brought her the broth and held the bowl while she slurped the hot soup. The combination of water and warm broth left her satisfied and drowsy. She lay down on the bed and curled under the blanket. Tal's masculine scent clung to his tunic, the fragrance a comforting distraction.

She gazed at Tal who remained beside her. He leaned forward and squeezed her hand.

"I'm here. You have nothing to fear."

His words followed her into a deep slumber.

CHAPTER 33

Lord Stefan Darkmoor surveyed the scene before him, lips tight with fury.

Stacked like cordwood in the meadow were the bodies of every dead gargoyle including Krall's. The only exceptions were those crushed and buried beneath the mounds of downed trees. Even though some were already ravaged by scavengers, Stefan inspected each body to ascertain the cause of death. So far, their deaths came in the form of arrows and sword thrusts, with one burned to ashes.

He saved Krall for last.

The eyrie Chieftain's own dagger protruded beneath his chin. Stefan signaled, and a large gargoyle trotted over.

"Congratulations, Zorb. Looks like you are the acting Chieftain. I'm sure you're anxious to prove your leadership of the eyrie at the next Third Circle battle."

Although perhaps a trick of the light, Stefan thought the gargoyle's face paled despite the creature's dusky black skin. By no means the largest of the male gargoyles in the eyrie, Zorb would have no shortage of challengers to fill the vacuum left by Krall's death.

A cruel smile crept across Stefan's face. He could use the gargoyle's fear to his advantage.

Stefan pointed at Krall. "What do you suppose happened?"

Zorb scratched one of his bat-like ears. "Krall was killed by his own blade."

"I can see that, you fool! Tell me something I don't know." Cold anger crept into his voice.

"Krall was a mighty warrior, very strong," Zorb hastened to answer. "Only one mightier still could have turned his blade back onto him."

"Ah, my thoughts exactly." Stefan wrenched the dagger free, dried purple blood coating the obsidian blade. "Come closer." He motioned with the dagger and Zorb edged nearer, fear following each step.

Stefan threw an arm around Zorb's shoulders and pulled him close. He held the blade beneath the gargoyle's two diagonal scars. "Here's what we are going to do. The woman my mother sent me to fetch is gone." He chuckled and waved a hand at the wide swath of downed, splintered trees. "But not before she left a rather impressive calling card. We are going to follow the trail of magic she has so conveniently left. And Zorb?"

"Yes, Lord Stefan?"

"You and your eyrie are going to help me find and capture her."

Stefan traced an imaginary line with the dagger's tip beneath Zorb's scars. "In return, I'll carve your third mark myself. You'll be my choice as eyrie Chieftain without a Third Circle fight. All will know if they oppose you, they oppose *me*."

Stefan released the gargoyle and flipped the blade. He handed Zorb the dagger, hilt first. "Do we have an understanding?"

Zorb nodded vigorously, his ears flapping. "Yes, Lord Stefan."

"We have a bargain then!" Stefan paused. "Oh, one more thing. Someone helped this woman escape. Someone powerful enough to kill Krall and his entire flock. I'm going to want this person dead."

He turned to Zorb, eyes hard. "No matter how many of your eyrie have to die to accomplish this."

Zorb swallowed. "Ye-yes, Lord Stefan."

Stefan clapped. "Good! Gather your flock.

"Let the hunt begin."

Another day of food, water, and rest did wonders for Alex. With the exception of occasional bouts of fatigue, her strength and stamina returned almost to normal. With her recovery, her thoughts turned to other matters.

Like Tell.

She sat at the table and grief shook her. Tears pooled on the wooden slats, her last image of Tell holding his sword high in salute.

Let me guard your way one last time.

She sobbed, her face cupped in her hands.

The door opened and Tal walked in. "What's wrong?" He moved a chair next to Alex and sat down.

Alex removed her hands and turned to face Tal. "He's dead, isn't he?"

"Your companion?" Tal's grim voice asked. Alex nodded.

"Yes. I buried him here at the edge of the glade."

Even though she knew Tell to be mortally wounded, the confirmation of his death still left her unprepared. A wail escaped her lips and she hugged herself, lost in misery. Tal hesitated then scooted closer.

He put his arms around her. The chair squeaked as Alex clung to Tal like he was a piece of driftwood on a rising tide.

"My-my fault," she hiccuped between sobs. "He died because of me." A fresh wave of tears followed and she buried her face in Tal's chest.

After several minutes, Alex forced herself to push away, a damp patch on Tal's shirt. "I need to see his grave."

Tal nodded and helped Alex to her feet. He opened the door and led her outside. Her first time outdoors in days, the bright sunshine blinded her. Shielding her eyes, she followed Tal to the edge of the dell. Vivid, colorful flowers clearly outlined the grave's oval mound.

"An ancient enchantment infuses this entire meadow and cottage," Tal explained. "It has accepted your companion to be part of its magic."

Alex knelt beside the grave, then fell prostrate across the flowers, her arms spread wide. Fresh sobs shook her. "I'm sorry, Tell," she whispered in a voice thick with grief. Numb, she lay unmoving until Tal gently picked her up. He carried her a short distance and set her on her feet.

"I'm sorry about your friend. Proof of his bravery can be found in the number of gargoyles he slew before his injuries overcame him. I wish we had more time for you to mourn, but you are still being followed. We must leave and soon…today if possible."

Alex whirled. "I'm not going anywhere. Someone has to tend to Tell's grave. Besides, I'll—I'll just get you killed too. You're better off without me."

Tal grabbed her shoulders. "Did you not hear me? You are *still* being followed. And the enchantment holds sway here. Tell's grave will be protected."

"I don't care. No one else is going to die because of me."

"Well, I *do* care, and I'm not leaving you here to the tender mercies of the Veil filth."

"Just leave me alone!" Alex cried.

"You so easily dismiss the sacrifice he made for you? The very death you mourn? Are you so shallow you would let his death prove meaningless?"

Alex slapped Tal, the stinging impact leaving a red mark. "*Bastard*! You can't make me go with you!" she screamed.

Tal touched his face. His eyes narrowed. "Then I'll tie you up and strap you to the saddle like a bedroll if need be. Get this through your head. *I am not leaving you here!*"

Alex's hand moved in a blur to slap Tal again. In a flicker of movement, he caught her wrist and held it in a viselike grip. "So, shall you be packed like baggage, or will you ride in normal fashion?" he asked through gritted teeth.

A rollercoaster of conflicting emotions thundered through Alex. Grief over Tell's death, guilt she had been the cause of it, regret she hadn't allowed him to make love to her, and finally, shame—shame that the love he so desperately sought, she felt for another.

She wiped her eyes. "You don't understand," she whispered. "The one who deserved saving lies buried, not me."

Tal took both her hands in his. The anger in his eyes softened, and he gestured with his chin at the mound of flowers. "What would Tell have wanted?"

Alex swallowed. She knew what he would have said. "To go with you. To be safe."

The feel of his touch distracted her, and she pulled free to sit beside the grave. Her fingers brushed the flowers. They rippled and waved following her touch.

"Goodbye, Tell. I love you…and I'll never forget you." More tears dripped from her eyes. Where they fell on the blooms, the flowers quivered…and turned the color of snow.

She stood and followed Tal back to the cabin.

***

At the foot of a large oak near the cottage, Tal dug with the tip of his dagger until the hole he excavated was deep and wide. He dropped the black, swollen blood truffle into the hollow, then kicked soil into the hole to fill it up. Finished, he wiped his blade on the grass, and walked to where Alex stood beside Della.

"Time for us to leave. The problem is your mare is injured. She flew here, but when I checked her wing joint earlier, it's still swollen. She needs time for the wing to heal. I'm afraid if we are chased and forced to flee, her wing won't hold up to the strain."

Tal patted Della's neck. "A week, maybe longer before she can fly normally. Our horses will have to stay grounded until then." He helped Alex into the saddle. Both horses had packs secured and ready to go.

"We'll head into the wilderness and get as far from this place as possible. It will mean rough camps, sleeping on hard ground— probably not what you're used to—but its only temporary. When Della's wing is sound again, we'll head home."

"And where is home?" Alex asked.

Tal hesitated. "I-I can't tell you that…at least not right now."

A sad smile appeared on Alex's face. "Secrets. That's okay. I'm used to secrets."

Tal swung into the saddle. Before he could urge the storm mount forward, a familiar voice sounded in his head.

They come.

CHAPTER 34

STEFAN ALIGHTED IN THE MEADOW.

A cottage stood near the tree-line. He hopped off the squark and immediately sensed the enchantment which pervaded the entire area. He found it abrasive like a bothersome rash in constant need of scratching. The woman he pursued, Alexandria Duvalier, had definitely been here. Her own magic, immersed within the enchantment, left only a faint trace.

Which meant the trail ended here.

Fortunately, he planned for all contingencies. Unlike his brother, Rodric, whose cruel impulses led to this situation—Alexandria fleeing Wheel—he could control himself...at least until after the job was done.

Then he could indulge in his own vicious fantasies...such as prolonged torture of the one helping Alexandria.

He motioned Zorb over. "Move your flock near the cabin and out of the way." Zorb barked an order, and the gargoyles led their squarks away from the meadow.

Stefan tossed a small, cube-shaped object into the air. Rather than fall, it remained suspended and began to rotate. Four protrusions, ebony and viscous, hardened to form razor-sharp points. As they spun, the claws cut the air like a jeweler's lapidary. A high-pitched squeal filled the glade. After a complete turn, the circular incision fell away to reveal a dark hole.

Raiders on horseback poured out of the opening.

Stefan chuckled at the surprise and fear on Zorb's face. "It's always good to have a mother in control of the orb. One can take advantage all sorts of shortcuts, including artificial gateways."

A Dark Brother was the last to emerge. The sorcerer led a strange creature by the leash. Doglike in shape and form, the similarity ended there. Lacking eyes, pink fur covered the blind beast. Two large plumes of feathery antennae grew from each side of the creature's head. They waved back and forth, a long reptilian tongue slithering from the beast's mouth. The melded animal made soft *hooting* grunts as the Dark Brother directed it across the dell.

Uneasy, Zorb asked, "What manner of beast is that?"

An evil chuckle spilled from Stefan. "Ah, Mother is nothing if not creative. And to answer your question, the creature is called a Sniffer. It can track even the tiniest residue of magic. *That's* how we'll find Alexandria."

As if in confirmation, the Sniffer froze, both antennae pointed toward the thick tree line. It strained against the leash and hooted loudly.

Stefan rubbed his hands. "It has the scent." He turned and cried, "Peters!"

A rail thin raider trotted over. Greasy, blonde hair hung limp from the *horde* leader's head, a scraggly beard covering a pockmarked face. Watery blue eyes peered from above a nose broken so many times, it bent slightly to the side. "Yes, Lord Stefan."

"We'll lead the search from the ground. Have your men follow the Sniffer."

He turned to Zorb. "Get into the air and circle above us. Let me know immediately if you see any sign of the woman."

Zorb blinked. He swallowed and asked, "But-but we can see nothing except wilderness. The trees block our sight."

"I know that you fool!" Stefan snarled. "But she has a flying horse and may try to escape by air. There are also occasional clearings where you *can* see."

Stefan scratched his chin. "I'm surprised Alexandria hasn't already flown away from here. Why stay on the ground if you have a flying horse? Is she or her mount injured?" He tapped his lips. "We'll find out soon enough."

He mounted the horse Peters brought to him and circled his finger high in the air. "Let's go." Stefan ran his tongue over his lips. "I can't *wait* to meet my brother's future bride."

They disappeared into the trees.

###

They traveled for several hours before Tal called for a stop. Alex swayed in her seat, grateful for the respite. Fatigue clouded her thoughts, and the next thing she knew, Tal's arms had lifted her up and out of the saddle and onto the ground. He did so with ease, her weight no more substantial to him than if she had been a feather.

He rummaged through his pack and handed her a hard biscuit and a leather bladder of water. "Rest a moment while I climb a tree."

Puzzled, Alex asked, "Climb a tree? Why?"

Already at the base of a tall hardwood, Tal answered over his shoulder, "To see if we are being trailed." With that, he scurried up the branches with the dexterity of a squirrel.

Alex sat by another tree, and leaned against the trunk. She munched on the biscuit. Filled with nuts and dried fruit, each bite carried with it the sweet taste of honey. She quickly finished it and took a long drink from the bladder. She closed her eyes.

A gentle shake awakened her.

Tal peered at her, a grim look on his face. "We have to leave." He helped her up and back into the saddle.

"Wh-what's wrong? Are we being followed?"

He nodded and vaulted onto his horse. "I counted more than a score of gargoyles circling above us. There is almost certainly another group, probably on horseback, searching on the ground."

The breath caught in Alex's throat. *Does this never end?* Her fear must have been evident, because Tal urged his mount next to hers.

"Don't worry. We'll lose them. I know ways to put them off our trail."

A sense of déjà vu filled Alex and she found it hard to keep from shaking. "That's what Tell said, and I got him kill—"

Tal's hand shot across the space between them and settled on hers. "Look at me!" She forced herself to face him. "I'm *not* Tell."

His gaze never left her. Slowly, the knot of panic in her dissolved. She swallowed and managed to nod. "All right."

It occurred to her then that she knew nothing about Tal other than his name. Yet here she was, her life in his hands. The normal alarm bells which should have gone off in her mind remained silent. She felt safe with Tal but didn't trust her feelings—not when they were still so raw over Tell's death. Though only with him a scant few days, she couldn't deny her attraction to Tal, making things even more complicated.

And she didn't trust these feelings either.

He turned the storm horse. "Follow me."

They resumed their trek into the wilderness.

CHAPTER 35

TAL CALLED A HALT.

A storm had blown down a large tree down and created a natural windbreak and shelter. The hole scooped from the forest soil when the roots were ripped free, made a good place for a campsite.

Tal checked the sun. Although difficult to tell through the dense forest canopy, he estimated several hours of sunlight remained. They should continue to travel, but Alex, still weak from the debilitative effects of the poison, could barely stay in her saddle the last few leagues. She needed more days of rest and recovery, but their pursuers had forced his hand.

"We'll stop here for the night."

Alex, head and shoulders drooped, managed only a bare nod. Tal dismounted then lifted Alex off Della and helped her to the deadfall. He removed a blanket from her pack and laid it across the ground. She collapsed onto it, asleep almost immediately.

Tal squatted beside her still form. A long strand of golden hair lay across her face. He reached for it and tucked the errant strand behind her ear. Slow, even breaths escaped from her pursed lips, the rise and fall of her chest evidence of a deep slumber.

Despite tousled hair and the smudges of dirt on her face, Tal had never seen a woman so lovely.

A strange feeling welled up inside of him. His fingers and toes prickled, his thoughts muddled. *What is this?* Distracted, he stood and forced his mind from Alex and back to the matters at hand. His first priority was to shake their hunters. Then find a place for them to stay until Alex could more fully recover. Next, check the mare's injury to determine when she could fly without complications, and finally, take Alex with him and rejoin the legions advancing on Markingham. The last would necessitate contacting Bozar and apprising him of their plans. Tal fully expected a tongue-lashing which would make the last conversation with his *Eldred* seem like jolly fun.

He decided to put it off as long as possible.

Bozar knew Tal had an injured woman on his hands which gave him several days before he reported in again. He *didn't* know they were being chased, and Tal planned to keep it that way…at least for the time being. By the time he contacted his *Eldred* again, he hoped to be free of the pursuit.

Maybe it would lower Bozar's ire.

◈

The stallion picked its way across the hard ground.

For the past two days, they had followed a path which rose steadily in elevation and brought them closer to the rocky peaks thrusting upward in the distance. Hills and valleys appeared, the soil thinner and filled with stones. Several times, the open ground had forced Tal to double back to find a path which kept them under the cover of trees.

They topped a steep hill and Tal tugged on the reins to bring the storm horse to a halt. Large areas of open land lay below them, meadows, streams, and small lakes forming a patchwork pattern.

Tal scrubbed a hand across his face. He took this route toward the mountains specifically so the rocky soil would leave no evidence of their passage. Yet despite every trick he used, they were *still* being followed. Confident of his woodlore, he shook his head. *Why haven't we lost our pursuers?*

Something was wrong.

In a way unknown to him, a dark sorcery must be in use to track them. There could be no other explanation. Frustration fueled a growing anger inside him.

Time to visit our hunters.

Tal scanned the area, particularly the large meadow ahead. He smiled. *Perfect.*

He turned the storm mount and they traveled for several more leagues. Less than an hour of daylight remained when Tal stopped in a small clearing near a brook. He helped Alex off Della, then prepared their camp. In a now familiar routine, he spread a blanket and Alex immediately lay down and fell asleep.

Tal tucked another warm blanket around her. The nights grew colder the closer they drew to the mountains. He studied her still form with a knitted brow. Although Alex regained enough stamina to ride for a longer period each day, she looked haggard and thin. His anger at those tracking them grew. He scowled.

By the end of the night, there would be far fewer of them.

Alex woke with a start. She sat up, groggy and thirsty. Her mouth felt like it was stuffed with cotton. A glow came from the Dragon Stones Tal had taken from the cabin, the only light on the moonless night.

Tal appeared at her shoulder. "Would you like some water?" She nodded and groped for the leather bladder. His warm fingers covered her eyes followed by a pleasant tingle. When Tal removed his hand, the darkness disappeared to be replaced by a clarity of vision.

Amazed, Alex asked, "How did you do that?"

Tal shrugged. "It is an easy trick." He handed her the water skin, and she drank deeply.

He moved to the Dragon Stones. A pot rested on them, and he dipped stew into a wooden bowl. He handed her the bowl and a spoon. "Eat. You need to regain your strength."

Alex greedily attacked the stew, scraping the last of it into her mouth. Tal refilled the empty bowl and handed it back to her. The second helping dulled her hunger, and she declined more. She released a sigh and decided she felt more like herself than she had in days.

"I'm going to pay a visit to our 'followers' tonight," Tal told her. "I'll have to leave you alone for a while."

All the vibrancy she felt fled in a second. She sat up straighter. "Why? Isn't that dangerous?"

"Somehow, they continue to shadow us despite everything I've tried. I need to find out how. As for dangerous," a wolfish smile appeared, "it will be indeed…but for them, not me."

Alex's heart pounded. "No. Don't leave me. Don't go!"

Tal shook his head. "I don't have a choice. We must find out how they continue to follow our trail. Also, I need to slow them down and keep them from trailing so closely."

Alex leaped up. "You—you're going to attack them? That's insane! You could get hurt, or—or worse."

"I can take care of myself," he assured her.

All the air left her lungs. Tell killed, and now Tal foolishly putting his life at risk—all because of her.

He seemed to sense her unease. Tal put his hands on her hips and drew her closer. "I told you before not to compare me with your companion."

Alex tried to get her emotions under control. "Then who are you, Tal? What makes you so certain you won't end up dead or wounded?" She grabbed his arms. "I want to know why I shouldn't worry every second you're gone."

"I can't—"

"No, not good enough!" Alex cried. *"I want to know!"*

A thick silence filled the clearing. Tal tried to pull away, but Alex refused to let him go. "Answer me, damn you," she hissed.

Tal glared at Alex. "Very well," he spat. "You want to know? Here it is. I happened upon you by accident. I saved your life. I've kept you out of the hands of what are undoubtedly agents of the Veil Queen. This diversion has cost me dearly, and I may never be trusted with another mission. You're welcome!"

Alex felt her cheeks warm. "I-I didn't mean to be ungrateful. I'm just concerned about you. I don't want you to get hurt." She released her grip.

"I just…" Alex shook her head. She dropped her arms to her side. "Be careful, Tal. Don't take any unnecessary risks." She sat down on the blanket and hugged her knees to her chest. After a moment, Tal squatted beside her.

He studied her, the anger lines on his face evaporating. "I'll do what needs to be done and no more. I promise I'll take no foolish chances. That's the best I can do."

Their eyes locked. An unspoken communication passed between them, and Alex knew he meant to keep his promise. Her unease ebbed away. "Okay. But I'm going to wait up for you."

Tal stood and retrieved his weapons. He reached the edge of the campsite and looked back at her.

The he turned and melted into the night.

CHAPTER 36

TAL SLIPPED THROUGH THE MIDNIGHT FOREST WITH EASE. Loping along in a ground-eating pace, he eventually reached the edge of the large meadow they crossed earlier. A fierce thrill coursed through him.

As he hoped when he first spotted the field, a large encampment was spread out before him. He knew it would prove to be a favorable campground. Tents and campfires dotted the area, a mix of men and gargoyles moving about. Squarks were tethered on one far edge of the bivouac, horses on the other.

A quick tally put the force to be around one hundred, roughly split between men and gargoyles. His sharp eyes detected the sentries guarding the perimeter and more importantly, the squarks and horses.

He felt his smile grow wider.

Only a few guards walked the camp perimeter, fewer still near their mounts. They ambled about with little discipline, and Tal spotted one sentry stop to relieve himself. The entire camp appeared to have no fear of being attacked—an error he would take full advantage of.

Tal circled to where the squarks were secured. He stifled a curse at their vile smell, a combination of the rotten meat they were fed, and excrement. He studied the long leather tether. It looped around each bird's leg and was threaded through iron rings. Hammered into the ground, the rings were spaced at wide intervals. It would be a simple matter of cutting the tether to free the loathsome beasts.

Tal slipped out of the tree-line and crouched among the carrion birds waiting for the sentry to draw near. He didn't wait long before a gargoyle appeared. Obviously bored, the guard didn't even glance at the squarks, and instead turned his back to retrace his steps.

Tal attacked the gargoyle before he could take a single stride. The sentry never saw him come up from behind. Tal grasped the gargoyle's head in both hands and twisted. With a *crack*, the neck snapped, the sentry dead instantly. Tal dragged the limp body to the trees and hid it within the thick brush.

He returned to the squarks and cut the main lead. Then he moved among the birds severing the loops attached to their legs. Satisfied with his work, he moved to a safe distance. The other sentries were still far away, oblivious of Tal's deadly work.

With both hands cupped around his mouth, Tal mimicked the growl of a mountain cat. The squarks, undisturbed before, began to mill about, the clack of their beaks a sign of their uneasiness. The giant carrion birds roosted in crags and cliffs, and mountain panthers were among the few predators they feared.

Tal growled again. More bird heads shot up, their clacking even louder. He took a deep breath and released a long feline scream. Feathers shook, the squarks colliding with one another in panic. Free of the tether, one flapped into the air.

That was all it took.

With an explosion of wings, the entire flock took flight. Their raucous cries filled the air as they disappeared into the night. Men and gargoyles rushed about chaotically.

Tal raced through the woods and emerged behind them near to the horses. Not bothering with subtlety, he cut down the lone sentry gawking at the empty area the squarks once occupied. He slashed the picket line and shouted. The horses bolted and scattered.

He returned to the safety of the trees and kept moving. Full-blown pandemonium reigned. Horses, men, and gargoyles burst in all directions. Using the confusion, Tal slipped unnoticed back into the deserted camp. He searched until he came to a large cage placed between two tents. He looked inside, where a strange creature covered in pink fur hooted in alarm. Antennae like that on a moth waved, the aura from the melded creature assaulting his magical senses.

Another beast created by Marlinda's dark arts.

He spat in an attempt to rid his mouth of the foul taste. He knew with certainty the creature must be the reason why they were still being tracked. He drew his sword to kill the obscene creature, when a sharp pain at his side caused him to cry out. A javelin quivered, the tip buried at his feet. An inch closer and it would have impaled him.

He whirled, blood seeping from his tunic. Some distance away, a dark-haired man stood, cruel eyes locked on Tal as he hoisted another spear. Tal dodged behind the cage, then sprinted away. Amid the scattered tents, Tal flitted from one to another until he had put enough distance to be safe from any hurled javelin.

He darted back into the dense woods, and moved at an angle so his position couldn't be fixed. Already, some semblance of order had been restored and men and gargoyles were moving to where he disappeared into the trees.

Blood raced through his veins in savage anticipation. He pulled his bow from the case slung across his shoulders and strung it. Placing the quiver beside him, he nocked an arrow, took aim, and released the shaft. The nearest man fell, clutching at the arrow lodged in his chest.

He released missile after missile, reaping a bloody harvest. Those who survived the initial hail of arrows broke and ran. Their leader, the man who hurled the spear at him, shouted and gestured angrily. Soon arrows started to pepper the area near him as archers in the camp shot back. Tal moved in a circular retreat. Shafts remained in his quiver and he was determined to make every one count.

Then he recalled his promise to Alex. He gave her his word to take no foolish chances. One could argue that he had already broken the vow when he entered the encampment. To stay in a stubborn attempt to use every arrow, however, would mean he certainly lied.

With a sigh, he picked up the quiver and flitted back into the wilderness.

Alex sat by the Dragon Stones fighting drowsiness.

Determined to stay awake until Tal returned, Alex was surprised when he emerged soundlessly from the darkened forest. She leaped to her feet and rushed to him. Unable to help herself, she threw her arms around him. Tal grunted in pain.

He held a hand at his side, blood staining the fabric.

"You're hurt!" she cried.

Tal snorted. "Just a scratch." A ferocious smile came to his lips. "I did far worse to the scum chasing us. They won't be so eager to follow anytime soon."

"Get your shirt off, you stupid oaf!" Alex ordered.

Tal grunted again as he pulled the tunic over his head. Alex pushed him closer to the light of the Dragon Stones. They revealed a clean slash, fresh blood leaking from the wound.

Alex used the water skin to wash away the blood. "It looks like a shallow cut," she said. "Where are the bandages?" Tal indicated one of the saddle bags, and after rummaging in it, she returned with cloth gauze and a flask of antiseptic.

Tal hissed when Alex dabbed a generous amount on the laceration. He sucked in his breath again when she tightly bound his wound. "You're bedside manner leaves something to be desired," he quipped. "I think you're enjoying this."

Alex stepped back and shook a finger at him. "You promised."

"I kept my vow!" Tal replied hotly. "Well, sort of." He spread his hands. "I had to find out how they were able to follow us. I discovered this odd creature—*ouch!*"

Alex pulled the cloth binding tighter. "Shut up!" One hand lay against Tal's ribbed abdominal muscles, the other on the gauze. The touch of his warm flesh on her fingertips distracted her. Relieved he suffered only a minor laceration, she held his arm.

"Don't make promises to me you can't keep," she said and pushed him away.

Tal's face contained a mix of anger, surprise, and….something else. The glare he wore melted away, and his eyes softened. Alex tried to avoid Tal's gaze, but his effect on her was hypnotic. She reached for him again.

Their hands met and intertwined. An odd sensation, the same one which heralded the release of the strange power within her, trickled out of Alex's mind.

"Ow," Tal grimaced.

His cry broke the moment. Alex shook her head to clear the dizziness. Worried, she asked, "What's wrong?"

Tal touched the bandage. "It feels strange. My wound developed a maddening itch, but now—now the itch is gone."

Weariness settled over Alex. She pointed toward Tal's bedroll. "I think we've both had enough excitement for one night." With a yawn, Tal nodded and headed for his blankets.

Alex stretched out on her own bedroll and pulled the coverlet tight about her. One thought percolated through her mind before sleep took her.

What would it be like to have Tal to keep me warm instead of a blanket?

CHAPTER 37

"R EPORT!"

Stefan's black eyes smoldered and speared Zorb and Peters with a gaze filled with white-hot rage. Behind them, the entire camp was assembled to witness the proceedings.

The gargoyle and man shifted uneasily from one foot to the other, neither wanting to speak first. At last, Peters cleared his throat. "Five men dead, two wounded so severely they can't ride. We managed to recover most of the horses."

Stefan shifted his attention to Zorb. The gargoyle leader swallowed and said, "Eight of my flock were slain."

"And what of the squarks?"

At the question, Zorb stiffened, immobilized with fear.

Stefan took a step closer. "How many squarks do we have?" he hissed.

"None, L-Lord Stefan," he stammered. "They have returned to their roosts at the eyrie."

"I see." Stefan paced back and forth. Two men and a lone gargoyle stood next to Zorb and Peters. Stefan stopped in front of them.

"You were on sentry duty last night," Stefan stated, "but you let someone slip by you and free our horses and squarks. How do you explain this?"

The three quaked with fright. The first man nearest Stefan lost the battle to control his fear. A wet stain appeared in his breeches.

With a blur of motion, Stefan whipped his sword from the scabbard. The blade whispered through the air and through the unfortunate raider's neck. Lopped off like a ripe fruit, the severed head spun end-over-end to tumble to the ground. Blood sprayed in a geyser from the severed arteries, coating Peters, Zorb, and the remaining sentries. The body toppled over to join its head on the grassy soil.

Stefan stepped over the corpse. He dipped a finger in the blood dripping from Peters' face and sucked it into his mouth. "Hmm. Tasty."

He wiped his hand on Peter's tunic, then turned to address the entire camp. "I will execute every man or gargoyle derelict in their duty!" he roared. "Pray I don't have to make another example!"

He whirled on Zorb and Peters. "Break camp. We take up the chase at once. Zorb's flock will ride double with the men on horses."

When they hesitated, Stefan stepped closer. "You might be thinking that gargoyles don't ride horses or men don't ride with gargoyles," he said in a low, dangerous voice.

He pointed at the headless corpse. "Any who feel this way can stay behind."

Zorb and Peters scrambled to carry out his orders.

Alex awoke to see Tal cutting a sapling down.

Using his dagger's sharp tip, he formed two holes in the wood. Next he pounded sharpened stakes through each hole so the spikes pointed outward. He tied the end of the spear-length sapling five feet up the bole of a nearby tree so it extended like a branch in a horizontal position. Grunting, Tal pulled the branch back until it was bent into a U-shape. Another vine, tied to the end of the sapling, held it in place while Tal pounded a notched stake into the ground. The vine had a knotted end which Tal placed in the notch. He hid the stake under a pile of forest detritus, then stood back to admire his work.

"What are you doing?" Alex asked.

Tal flashed her a grin. "Leaving our trackers an unpleasant surprise."

Alex stood and stretched, thrusting her breasts forward. Tal stared at her profile, and then quickly turned away when Alex glanced at him. His reaction brought a smile to her face.

The dried blood on his tunic reminded her he had been injured. With pursed lips, she gestured to Tal. "Come here."

He ambled over and Alex pulled up his shirt. "The last thing you need to do is any strenuous activity." Brow wrinkled, she studied the bandage she had placed the night before. "If you're not careful you'll start to bleed again."

She shook her head. "This dressing probably needs to be replaced any way." In the early morning light, Tal's bare torso looked even more enticing. She swallowed. *How can he be so slim and muscular at the same time?*

Before her thoughts could take her in a dangerous direction, she unwrapped the cloth gauze and pulled it free. Her mouth dropped.

Where Tal's flesh had been opened by the javelin, only smooth skin lay. No sign of an injury existed.

"What? How?" She leaned closer. "You were hurt. I saw it with my own eyes." Alex pointed at Tal. "What did you do?" she asked.

Tal looked down and his mouth fell open. He pawed at his skin. "It's gone. My wound's disappeared."

Tal pulled his shirt down and took a step back. "I didn't do anything. *You* must have done something."

"But all I did was bandage your wound."

Tal rubbed his chin. "Wait. I remember an odd itch. It happened—"

He stopped a look of wonder on his face. "It happened when you held my hand last night."

The memory rushed back to Alex. The fissure in her mind, the dizziness heralding the release of the strange power within her.

Tal stepped toward her and gripped her shoulders. "What are you hiding? When I found you, an entire section of the wilderness had been laid flat, trees splintered into kindling."

"What? I did what?"

"You were lying unconscious. A path of destruction started at your feet and stretched for over a league."

"You never told me that!" Alex cried. She ripped free of Tal's grasp. *Destruction? Trees leveled? What did it mean? Was she becoming like Rodric?*

She turned back to Tal. "I don't have any answers. I don't know what's happening to me." Arms rigid, fists clenched, she added, "Maybe you should have left me to die. I don't want to turn into one of *them*."

Tal moved closer. He grasped Alex's arms and gently pulled her to his side. "If by *them*, you mean the Veil scum, you need not fear. You're nothing like them, nor will you ever be. As for saving your life, I count that the best thing I've ever done."

He flashed her a crooked smile. "Although, according to my family, my poor choices far outweigh the wise ones."

Tal's touch caused her flesh to goosepimple. It began to muddle her thoughts. She couldn't help herself, and slid her hand onto his. "How can you be so sure?"

"Because—" Tal bit his lip. Warring emotions flitted across his face, and Alex could tell he fought some sort of internal battle.

He tightened his grip on her. "Do you trust me?"

For once, Alex's head and heart were in agreement. Even though their companionship could be counted in only mere days, she knew the answer before it left her mouth.

"Yes."

Tal carefully chose his words. "I'm part of something far larger than you can imagine, something wonderful. I am familiar with magic, and I would have detected the stain of the dark arts within you if it existed. This unique power or magic you have is unlike anything I have ever come across. But I *do* know it is clean and without taint."

Alex searched Tal's face, his expression one of concerned honesty. Relief coursed through Alex. She squeezed his hand. "Thank you."

They stood inches apart, and for long moments, neither spoke. Alex found herself wishing Tal would pull her closer.

He released her and stepped away. Her disappointment must have been obvious to Tal because he quickly said, "We'll have plenty of time later to learn more about each other."

He handed her a strip of dried meat and started to pack up their things. "It's a poor breakfast, but the Veil filth will eventually get themselves organized. Then the pursuit will begin again. We must travel as far as we can before then."

A short time later they were on the move.

CHAPTER 38

THE DAY TURNED DARK AND GRAY.

Before noon, it began to drizzle. Tal called a halt and removed waterproof oilskins from his pack. The slicker he handed to Alex covered her like a tent. After a cold lunch of dried fruit and water, they resumed their trek toward the mountains. By early afternoon, the temperature had dropped and the drizzle turned to sleet.

Tal's eyes constantly searched the sky, but not a single squark appeared. Even with the weather, he was certain if any remained with the pursuing party, they would be in the air searching for them. The horses were another matter. While a few might have scattered, most would have been recaptured. Regardless of the number of mounts left, by now he was certain the pursuit would have been rejoined with a vengeance.

Although he caught only a glimpse of the man who wounded him with the javelin, it was enough. Undoubtedly the leader of this band of men and gargoyles, the filthy stain of the Veil marked him as clearly as a hilltop beacon on a moonless night.

The sleet came down harder, bouncing off his face and hands with stinging intensity. He glanced at Alex, whose teeth were chattering, wet hair plastered to her head, and lips tinged with blue. Warm clothes had not been part of their inventory, and she was clearly suffering from the cold, wet weather.

He tugged on the reins and stopped, then dismounted and helped Alex off Della.

"What are you doing," she managed to ask through clattering teeth.

"You're going to ride with me." Tal led Alex to the storm horse and removed her oilskin. While he rolled it up and repacked it, she danced from foot-to-foot and rubbed her hands trying to keep warm.

Tal boosted her up into the saddle then took a seat behind her. He draped his own slicker over the both of them and pulled her tight to add his body heat to hers. He mumbled a word and the oilskin's hood expanded to allow room for both of their faces. With a flick of the reins, they continued on.

Tal kept one arm firmly around Alex's waist and the other hand on the reins. The shared saddle proved a tight fit, her body molded against his. Soon, the combination of his added warmth and the rocking motion as they rode lulled Alex to sleep. Her head lolled from side-to-side against his chest. At times, one of her damp tresses tickled his chin, and he would have to rub the maddening itch. Being so tightly sandwiched together meant every time he scratched, his hand or arm would brush against the swell of her breasts. It proved a powerful distraction, and he had to fight to keep his attention on their route.

The land grew steeper, and pines started to appear interspersed among the hardwoods. Ahead, he saw the beginning of an expanse of conifers. Dwarfing all others around them, the massive trees each reached over a hundred feet into the air. As they drew nearer, he discovered the trunks of the mighty trees were so wide, it would take ten men standing fingertip-to-fingertip to span their perimeter.

They threaded their way through the forest titans, the gray sunlight dimming and the sleet dwindling under the mass of limbs and needles. Tal craned his neck searching each colossal evergreen. After traveling another half a league, his sharp eyes discovered a darkened hole halfway up the trunk of one of the trees.

Tal stopped and woke Alex. Disoriented, she clutched at his arm around her waist. He squeezed her and said, "It's okay. I may have found a place for us to camp for the night."

He relished the feel of her body against his, and with great reluctance, released her. Slipping out from under the oilskin, he dismounted. A coiled rope hung from the saddle and he unwound a length of it. He touched the end of it and a blue glow flowed from Tal into the rope. He dropped it to the ground where it rippled and then began to crawl up the tree. Farther and farther the cord traveled up the smooth trunk until it reached the opening Tal spotted earlier. The rope went taunt.

Tal took a firm grip on the line. "Rise."

Up he went pulled by the cord until he reached a hollow. The size of a small cave, the interior was littered with a drift of brown needles and other forest detritus. The bones of a small animal lay near the entrance, but other than the old remains, the cavity looked deserted.

Perfect.

Tal descended quickly. "There's a hollowed out area in the trunk about halfway up the tree," he told Alex. "We'll stay there tonight."

Alex looked doubtful "How am I supposed to get up there?"

Tal grinned. "I'm going to carry you."

He removed the saddles and gear from the flying horses. With a twirl of his finger, he directed the rope to snake through the tack and their packs, and then lift them up and into the space.

Tal motioned to Alex. "Put your arms around me and hold tight." He slipped one arm around her waist while his other hand wrapped around the cord. Alex squealed when they rose into the air and the ground dropped away. Moments later they both stood in the hollow bole.

Alex looked around. Tal could see she was pleased to be out of the weather and not facing the prospect of another night on the hard ground.

She turned and beamed at Tal.

Her smile lit up her face and Tal's breath caught in his throat. There had been precious few moments for Alex to smile about since he found her unconscious, and this simple act transformed her in a way which tugged powerfully at his heart.

He forced himself to prepare their camp for the night's stay. But he couldn't keep the same thought from surfacing over and over again in his mind.

What she would be like if truly happy.

***

"This is good."

Alex dipped her spoon in the bowl for another mouthful of hot stew. She sat cross-legged on a blanket beside the Dragon Stones. Tal arranged the magical rocks in a semi-circle above which the small pot of stew simmered. Their heat felt glorious after the day-long travel in the cold and wet weather.

Tal grinned. "It's amazing how a few spices and some water can make even dried meat and vegetables taste good."

"Where did you learn to cook trail rations?"

Tal paused, then stirred the pot. "I had good lore masters. And I spent a lot of my youth in the woods."

"Youth? You don't look much older than me."

"I'll be twenty-one on my next name day." Tal brushed the pine straw off his pants. "What about you? How old are you?"

Alex blinked. The question took her by surprise. Then she realized in all the time since she awoke to find herself on Meredith, she had never asked about her age, nor had anyone told her.

Tal took her silence as a sign of reluctance. He waved his hand. "Never mind. I didn't mean to pry."

"No, I'm also, uh, twenty-one." *I think.*

She quickly changed the subject. "Will the horses be all right since they're on the ground by themselves?"

Tal nodded. "I took off Della's wing net so she can fly if need be. She'll follow the stallion, and they'll browse around for grass. No matter how far away they are, he'll come back when I whistle."

He sat next to her. "We've been traveling together for days now, and I still I don't know anything about you. Don't you think it's about time to tell me something about yourself?"

Alex hesitated, then set her bowl aside. "What would you like to know?" she asked in a guarded voice.

"How about starting at the beginning? Why were you being chased by gargoyles? How did you come to be stung by that vile creature? Someone wants you badly enough that we are *still* being followed."

Alex stared at Tal, mesmerized by his green eyes. *I want to tell you everything. But I can't.*

Quickly, she turned away. Guilt from Tell's death still weighed on her, and she knew even less about Tal than he did about her. Both combined to make her reluctant to share any information about herself.

She shook her head. "I'm sorry. Can we talk about something else?" She bit her lip at the look of disappointment on his face.

He shrugged. "Of course."

Anxious to change the topic, Alex pointed at the hollow. "Is this a redwood tree we are in?"

Tal raised an eyebrow. "What's a redwood?"

Alex froze at her Mona slip of the tongue. *Idiot! Redwoods are an earth name. They call them a different name on this world.* "They are, uh, trees from where, ah, I'm from."

"We call them sentinel pines," Tal said coolly. "Odd they would be called by such a different name...wherever it is you're from."

Alex felt her cheeks warm. Tal saved her from further embarrassment by producing a small, reed-shaped object. "What's that?" she asked.

"A faerie flute. I always bring one with me when traveling through the wilderness."

Alex tilted her head. "Why?"

"Because they never fail to lift my spirits."

Alex frowned. "I don't understand. *Who* lifts your spirits?"

With a chuckle, Tal brought the reed to his lips. "I'll show you."

He blew on the flute, and musical notes filled the hollow. The timbre, soft and melodic, stroked Alex's ears. Her hand slipped to her mouth. "It's so beautiful," she breathed.

Tal nodded and continued to play. Alex gasped when motes of blue drifted from the reed to float about them. Each produced a musical pitch, and she clapped with delight.

Tal stopped and took a small leather bag from their supplies. "Hold out your hand." Alex reached out and he poured brown sugar crystals into her palm. "Now we wait. But be ready."

After a few moments, Tal pointed out toward the dark, rainy night. "Here they come."

"Who—"

Alex's mouth snapped shut when a multitude of tiny, fast-moving lights whizzed into the hollow. Green, red, yellow, purple, and blue—every shade of color—the miniscule points of light moved at breakneck speed. Buzzing and giggling, followed by brushes soft as butterfly wings, stroked her neck and face. Her hair, lifted and pulled, was twirled round and round.

Tal nudged her. "Hold out the sugar. The only way you can see them is if they slow down long enough to eat."

The tittering laughter increased when Alex held out her hand. Her skin tingled as tiny, doll-like figures with translucent wings perched on her palm. Each was distinguishable from the others only by the different-colored nimbus of light emanating from them. Though she looked closely, they moved so fast Alex could never see on any of the diminutive faeries longer than a moment. Tiny hands shoveled crystals of sugar greedily into their mouths, and then they were moving again in a blur of speed.

Too soon, the sugar disappeared, and the faeries zipped around the hollow bole in one last colorful display. One-by-one, they shot out of the tree and back into the forest.

Alex jumped to her feet and ran to the opening. She waved at the disappearing lights which rocketed away like super-charged fireflies. Hands clasped to her chest, she said, "They tickled me!"

She laughed and sat back down next to Tal. "I could only see them for a second. Are they fairies?"

Tal nodded. "We call them faerie imps. If you don't have something sweet for them to eat, they'll pinch, pull hair, and get into all kinds of mischief."

He cupped her chin with his hand. His finger traced a line along the curve of her mouth. "You need to smile more often."

Tal's touch set off a wild thumping of her heart. Alex's hand crept up to his. "Why?" she whispered.

"Because it reveals who you really are. Not this fear or sorrow, and not the pain."

Alex closed her eyes reveling in his touch. When she opened them, his own emerald eyes held hers. They contained no wariness or deceit. Her resistance disintegrated, the bond she felt for him growing stronger by the second. She wanted, *needed*, to be honest with him. The time for secrets was past. The words tumbled from her mouth before she even realized she was speaking.

"My name is Alexandria Duvalier, and I am the Duke of Wheel's daughter."

CHAPTER 39

TAL'S MOUTH DROPPED.

Having poured over the old maps, he knew to be Wheel the capital of Dalfur, the largest province within the territory trapped behind the Veil.

Before he could scant digest this, Alex continued. "My father, the Duke, arranged my marriage to someone who is evil and cruel. Tell helped me escape so I wouldn't have to marry him. We were fleeing to Markingham to start a new life. You know the rest."

Stunned, Tal sat back trying to absorb it all. The sadness returned to Alex's face. Bright with joy moments earlier, his heart ached to see her in such a state.

"Did you love Tell?" He immediately felt like kicking himself. *Why did I ask such a question?*

Alex's head dropped, hands twisting in her lap. "Yes. But not in the way he wanted. Not in the way he deserved."

Relief filled him, followed quickly by a feeling of shame. He barely knew Alex, but Tell had been killed, a terrible thing regardless of their relationship.

"So these men and gargoyles were sent after you by the Duke?"

"No!"

The vehemence in her reply startled Tal. "Fine, so if not your father, then who sent them?"

"I don't know, but it was probably Dorothea and Rodric."

"Who?"

Alex clutched his arm, eyes flashing. "My stepmother and the man I'm supposed to marry! She is poisoning Father so he can't think clearly, and Rodric wants to marry me so they can use me for this, this Veil Queen's purposes. I hate them!"

"What!" Tal cried. He jumped to his feet. "How do you know this?"

"I—I just do." She got to her feet, eyes pleading. "Please. I'm telling you the truth. If they catch me and I'm sent back to marry Rodric…" Her hands dropped to her side. "Then you should have left me to die. It would have been a far kinder fate."

Tal's mind raced. *The Veil Queen is involved in this?*

The thought of Alex coming to any kind of harm caused his heart to clench. He gripped her shoulders. "Listen to me. I'm not going to let anyone catch us or send you anywhere you don't want to go. You have my word."

Tal pulled Alex to him and held her tight. She eagerly threw her arms around him and pressed her cheek against his chest. "Thank you," she murmured.

The feel of Alex folded in his arms sparked heat to rise within him. Starting with his toes, it spread to the rest of his body. Molded against him, she felt good, a perfect fit, like they were two pieces of a puzzle interlocked together.

As if the pieces were tailored to pair together.

His jaw tightened. The only safe place for Alex was to remove her completely from Dalfur. It would mean transporting her back through the Veil and to Lodestone Castle. Only there would she be safely beyond the reach of Marlinda. The small matter of explaining all this to Bozar and his mother he would worry about later.

He needed to concentrate now on keeping her out of the hands of their pursuers.

With great reluctance, he pushed Alex away. He tilted her chin with his finger and cast a wry grin. "Enough excitement for one night. We have a long day tomorrow and need to turn in. But before we do, I want you to do something for me."

Puzzled, she asked, "What?"

"Smile...just once more."

Slowly, her lips stretched into a smile. Her face brightened and her blue eyes sparkled. Tal nodded. "That's more like it."

With a sigh, he released her, and they busied themselves spreading bedrolls near the warmth of the Dragon Stones. Alex used a saddle bag for a pillow and pulled her blanket up to her chin. Minutes later, the sound of her deep, even breaths came to Tal's ears.

He stepped to the edge of the hollow and leaned against its edge. The rain, now no more than an intermittent drizzle, dripped from needles and branches. He stared off into the dark, damp night. The breathtaking display by the faeries, though bright and glittering, paled in his mind. Tonight he had discovered something far more brilliant and vivid.

The Duke of Wheel's daughter.

The next day dawned clear and warmer. The sky, scrubbed clean by the rain, appeared a cerulean blue. The air, crisp and fresh, carried a sharp tang of pine sap.

They continued their trek and around noon, came to a fast-moving stream. Alex eyed the water longingly. "Can we stop here?" she asked Tal. "I haven't bathed since we left the enchanted cabin."

Tal grinned. "Why not? The horses need a rest and there is plenty of grass along the banks."

Broken rock, including large boulders, were strewn at intervals alongside the stream. Some were lodged in the shallow river slowing the water's flow and forming natural pools. Alex picked a quiet pool upstream far enough away she could have some privacy and undressed. She scrubbed her sweat and dirt-stained clothes at the water's edge the best she could, then laid them across a rock to dry.

Naked, she paused beside the deep pool, then jumped in. She surfaced with a scream. The water, bone-numbing cold, shocked her, and she splashed and sputtered in an attempt to get her feet under her. Just when she managed to get close enough to the bank to stand, water dripping from her prickled skin, Tal rounded the boulder and skidded to a stop. He stared at her, mouth working but no words formed.

The surprise of the cold water was trivial compared to Alex's realization she stood unclothed before Tal. With a squeak, she dropped back into the frigid stream.

"Why are you here? Go away!"

Chuckling, Tal crossed his arms and leaned against the mound of stone. "I heard you cry out. But you shouldn't worry. Remember, I've already seen your lovely body...many times."

His forehead wrinkled. "I seem to recall this one mole strategically located near your—"

"Stop it!" Alex cried through chattering teeth. "Will you please leave?"

"Hmm. I don't know. I'm curious to see how long you can stay immersed in the water. It looks bracing."

Before she could provide a retort, Tal laughed and raised his hands. "I'll leave you to your bath." He turned and disappeared.

Fuming, Alex finished washing. Although still damp, she put on her clothes and finger-combed her hair. Then she set off to find Tal and give him a piece of her mind. Their camp was deserted except for the horses cropping grass, so she picked her way down the riverbank to find him.

Climbing around and in some cases, over, rocks, she rounded a curve. His back to her, Tal stood waist deep, in the middle of the river. The cold water seemed to have no effect on him, and he scrubbed vigorously. Alex started to turn away, but the sight of his bare torso caused her breath to catch in her chest. It drew her eyes like a magnet.

His skin, smooth and tanned, rippled with the movement of muscle. She marveled at the definition of his body. Tal didn't appear to have an ounce of fat anywhere. The cage-fighters back on earth that Bud and Elaine liked to watch, had big, bulging muscles that always seemed artificial. There was nothing fake about Tal's physique. He looked like a chiseled sculpture.

Lost in her musings, she was slow to realize that Tal had turned around to make his way back to the riverbank. By the time this dawned on her, he was in water so shallow, the rest of his body was revealed. Alex blinked, unable to tear her vision away. Tal, as if sensing someone watching, cast about and stopped.

His eyes locked on hers.

Alex stumbled backwards and fell. Picking herself up, she fled. Her face on fire, she raced back to the camp. She fell several more times in her haste, her clothes muddied anew. She collapsed on a saddle pack, and buried her face in her hands. Embarrassment flamed her cheeks, but still she couldn't purge the sight of Tal's bare body from her mind.

And then another kind of blaze rose within her.

CHAPTER 40

WHEN TAL RETURNED TO THE CAMPSITE, HE FOUND ALEX sitting stiff and frozen as if afraid to move. Digging around in their supplies, he handed her a hard biscuit and a piece of dried meat. She took them but kept her eyes averted.

Amused, he decided to have some fun. Chewing on the hardtack, he said, "Well, I guess the scales are balanced between us."

Without looking up, Alex replied. "Huh? What do you mean?"

"You know. You showed me yours, and now I've shown you mine."

Alex's face went from pink to sunset red. She jumped to her feet. "It was an accident! If you hadn't barged in on me while I was trying to bathe, I never would have gone looking for you."

Tal fought to keep a solemn expression on his face. "I see. In the future, we need a better partnership." He turned, pulled up his shirt, and pointed to the small of his back. "I can never reach there. I say we go back to the river so you can scrub—"

A biscuit flew through the air and bounced off Tal's shoulder. "Bastard!"

Unable to contain himself any longer, Tal roared with laughter. Furious, Alex watched him with hands on her hips.

"It's not funny."

Tal held his side and tried to catch his breath. He finally straightened and noticed the hint of a smile lifting one corner of Alex's mouth. He reached for her.

"Ah, but your face tells a different story."

"Liar!" Alex tried to wrestle out of his grip, but her left leg became pinned behind his. Losing her balance, she fell against him and both toppled to the ground. She lay atop Tal, her face inches from his. Her eyes softened, the weight of her warm body an exquisite agony.

"What story do you see now?" she whispered.

Tal threaded his fingers through her hair and pressed her lips to his. A current coursed through him like a charge of lightning. Every nerve ending in his body came alive with a vibrancy that left him feeling like he might explode.

"What have you done to me?" he breathed.

Alex kissed him again, her lips soft and pliant. "How funny. I was about to ask you the same thing."

Another stroke of energy surged through Tal. His passion rose to such heights, spots appeared before his eyes. He had never felt anything like—

Abruptly, Tal sat up, Alex tumbling off him. "That's it! That's how they track us!"

Alex rubbed her rump and looked at him in confusion. "What are you talking about?"

"You leak!"

***

Alex tossed her hair. "You kiss me and the next thing I know you're throwing me off to say I leak?"

"You don't understand. It's not like that."

Alex stood and shook her finger. "I *understand* I'm a fool for ever trusting you. But don't worry, it won't happen again!"

Tal skipped to his feet. "No, I need you to kiss me again."

"Forget it!"

"Don't you see," Tal pleaded, "if we don't recreate what just happened, I won't know if that's why the magic trickles from you."

"I don't believe you. I have no idea what *leak* you're talking about, and I'm not going to be your guinea pig."

Tal frowned. "I never called you a pig. Why would I do that?"

Alex crossed her arms, her foot beating a tattoo on the ground. Finally, she threw up her hands. "Okay! Explain what you mean!"

Tal released a deep breath. "I haven't been able to discover how we are still being followed. Despite using every trick I know to disguise our trail, nothing has worked."

He shook his head. "But it should have worked. And then there is the strange creature I came across in the enemy's camp. I know it's Marlinda's abomination, but what is its purpose? I think the beast tracks magic—magic which even I haven't detected. That is, until now."

Despite herself, Alex's interest was piqued. "Whose magic?"

"Yours."

Alex stared at Tal. "Nonsense. I told you before, I don't have any magic."

"You leveled an entire section of forest. I'd say that qualifies you as someone with great power."

Shaken, Alex closed her eyes. Her governess's hands, scalded when she tried to pry into Alex's mind. Darcy's Rodric-controlled body hurled off of her, the dormant Staff of the Test suddenly coming alive in Pandathaway's shop, and now, the destruction of the forest. No random coincidences, but all proof of an undeniable pattern.

Of something uncoiling inside her.

When she opened her eyes, Tal was studying her closely. With a sigh, she asked, "What do you want to do?"

He took her hands in his. "I want to try and draw this—this

essence out of you again. I didn't recognize it before because I've never experienced anything like it. But it ran through me with such force, I can still feel it."

"You can't be serious. You're making this all up and it's just an excuse."

"An excuse for what?"

"You—you know what I mean!"

Tal cupped her face in his hands. "To kiss you? Do I need a reason? I *know* what I felt…and it was you. Every bit of it."

Alex wanted to stay angry with Tal, but at his touch, her resistance crumbled. She wanted him to kiss her again. *If I could be a cat, I'd be purring right now.*

"See? It's happening again." He pulled her close, his mouth covering hers. After long moments, they broke and his hands slipped down to her hips. "You're leaking again."

Alex swallowed. She managed to say, "So *you* caused this reaction within me? Don't flatter yourself."

Tal chuckled. "You still don't understand. It's like part of you leaves to become part of me. This seepage is why we continue to be followed. It leaves residue, a path."

The humor left his face. "What an odd feeling. It's almost like we are separate strands which entwine to become…" His words faltered.

"One." Alex finished for him.

Her hands flew to her mouth. *What did I just say?* "No! That's not what I mean."

Tal's eyes bored into her. Alex knew then she was in trouble. Her life on Meredith just took another sharp turn because one of Diana's future possibilities was coming to pass.

I'm falling in love with Tal.

CHAPTER 41

THE RAIDER SCREAMED.

Impaled on the sharp stakes, he struggled to free himself. Annoyed by the wounded man's shrieks, Stefan pulled his sword and thrust it through the unfortunate raider's heart.

The screams stopped.

Wiping the blade on the dead man's tunic, Stefan motioned to Peters and Zorb. "That's the third member of our party to fall prey to a trap. Pass the word. Any whose carelessness causes them to spring an ambush on themselves or others won't have to worry about being injured."

He grabbed the gargoyle by the tunic with one hand and the human leader with the other, then viciously pulled them to within inches of his face. "Because I'll kill them myself!"

He shoved them away. "I will allow nothing to slow our pursuit. Now mount up!"

The Flock Chieftain and *horde* leader rushed away to carry out his orders.

Stefan's scowl transformed into black hatred. *When I catch Alexandria, I'll make her watch while I peel the skin off whoever is helping her.*

One slice at a time.

The rest of the day went by uneventfully.

Thankfully, Tal didn't bring up her leaky magic. She was especially grateful he didn't mention her "one" comment.

What a dumb thing to say.

Since then, their conversations had been brief. For the most part, they rode in silence, Tal leading them deeper through hills and valleys that grew more numerous the farther they traveled. Alex studied Tal in an attempt to divine what he was thinking, but he gave no obvious clues. Back straight, eyes ahead, he seemed oblivious to her.

They crossed another stream and entered a copse of woods. Although thick with trees, they were not as densely packed as the earlier woodlands, and speckled sunlight peppered the ground with spots of sunlight. Tal called a halt.

"We'll take a break here before we continue."

He helped Alex out of the saddle, his strong arms lifting her easily to place her on the ground. In what was now a daily ritual, he rummaged in a saddle bag and handed her one of the crunchy biscuits and a piece of dried meat. *If we ever get out of here, I'll never touch another cracker, biscuit, or piece of jerky ever again.*

Retrieving the water bladder, Tal retreated to the base of a large tree and sat down against it. Unsure what to do, Alex stood frozen. *Do I sit next to him?*

Tal solved her problem by patting the ground beside him. "I'm not going to bite you."

Alex walked over stiffly and sat cross-legged. She nibbled on the biscuit without enthusiasm. When Tal placed his hand on her knee, she jumped. "What—"

"Shhh," Tal said, finger to his lips. He cocked his head. "Do you hear it?" he asked in a low voice.

Alex turned her head and strained to hear. *There*, a low buzz, barely audible. She cast about trying to fathom the location it came from. It seemed to come from—

Above.

Tal pointed up. Her eyes followed his finger and came to rest on an egg-shaped object the size of a small house. Constructed of sticks and leaves, it hung from a sturdy limb some forty feet above their heads. A hole, the entry into the structure, was located at the end pointing to the ground. She bit back a gasp when a bronze and yellow creature crawled out of the mouth and clung to the side. Compound eyes were mounted on a head that swiveled from side-to-side, its segmented body divided into a head, wings, legs, and abdomen.

It looked like a wasp with wings and stinger. However, this insect was the size of a dog. Its wings vibrated and the buzz they had been hearing was much clearer now.

Tal leaned closer and hissed into her ear. "Don't make any sudden movements. We need to stand, then carefully make our way back to the horses and lead them away. Watch your feet. Don't step on a dead branch or cause any loud noises."

Alex nodded, barely able to breathe. Tal gripped her arm and helped her to her feet. He steered her toward the flying horses browsing for grass near where they entered the thicket. Alex searched the ground to make sure of her steps. The journey to the horses seemed to take forever. When she finally clutched Della's bridle, her tunic was damp with sweat.

They led their mounts a safe distance away and into the bright sunlight. Alex blurted, "What are those things?"

"Emperor wasps—wild ones. The gnomes long ago domesticated them and bred them to the size of horses. They use them rather than flying horses for transportation. They are also valuable in times of war as battle mounts."

He cast her a grim look. "But in the wild, a colony of Emperor wasps will protect the nest at all costs. Their mandibles can tear a man's arm off, and the stingers can even pierce armor.

We are fortunate it's early spring, and they are still groggy from hibernation."

A gleam came to his eye. "I have an idea. Stay here." He turned to make his way back to the hive.

Alex grabbed his arm. "What are you doing?"

Tal flashed her a fierce smile. "To set up a greeting our foul hunters will never forget."

"What? Are you crazy? You just said we were lucky to get out of there alive."

Irritated, Tal tried to shake free. "Don't worry. I'm going to put them back to sleep."

"Worry is all I'm going to do!"

Tal huffed. "Okay. Follow me and I'll let you watch—but only from far away."

Alex never released her grip on Tal as they made their way back into the grove of trees. They entered the mottled gloom and the nest appeared some distance away.

"Stay here," Tal commanded, his tone brooking no argument.

He slipped away, feet padding soundlessly on the forest floor. Alex, heart in her throat, watched Tal swarm up the trunk and out onto the limb from which the hive hung suspended.

"You idiot, what are you doing?" she whispered to herself.

Tal cupped his hands around his mouth and blew. His breath formed a cloud of fog and enveloped the hive. He did this several times then climbed back down. He motioned for Alex.

Joining him, Alex pointed a shaky finger at the nest. "What did you do?"

"I told you. Put them back to sleep. The cold temporarily triggers their return to hibernation. It should last long enough to for me to construct the trap. All I need now is you."

The air carried a chill. Alex, head spinning, said, "I don't understand."

"I need your trail to lead here."

Alex swallowed. "I still don't...*oh*. You, you want to—"

"Stir a reaction within you," he finished for her.

So far Tal's had no problem doing that.

Alex shook her head. "I don't think this is a good idea."

She backed away. "Why not?" Tal asked following her.

"Are you kidding? There's a nest full of giant wasps hanging above our heads. The only reaction you're going to get from me is 'let's get out of here'." She continued to retreat until her back fetched up against the bole of the tree.

Tal grinned. "I accept your challenge." He leaned against her, his warm breath on her cheek.

"Look, this is stupid. I'm not in any mood—"

The air left her lungs in a rush as Tal's lips nuzzled her neck. He blazed a trajectory to the sensitive flesh by her ear, then started the process anew beside her other ear.

She draped her arms around him.

The day had turned warm and earlier she had unfastened the upper buttons on her tunic to allow some relief from the heat. Tal's mouth reached her cleavage, and her heart threatened to explode from her chest. No matter how many heaving gasps of air she took, she couldn't seem to get enough oxygen.

Tal stopped and leaned his forehead against hers. "I win. Your leak has turned into a flood." He traced a finger alongside her chin. "If we keep going, maybe we can cause the entire dam to break."

Reluctantly, Alex pushed him away. Part of her wanted him to continue no matter what. The rational side of her, hanging by a tenuous toehold, argued for caution. They were still being chased with no time for pleasant fantasies.

Tal swooped in for a final kiss. He stepped away and rubbed his hands eagerly.

"Time to prepare for our guests."

CHAPTER 42

TAL MADE ALEX WATCH FROM A SAFE DISTANCE WHILE HE searched for his materials.

He cut a green sapling, slightly larger than the diameter of his thumb, into a six-foot length. Vines grew in abundance in the thicket, and he used a section to secure a dagger to the end of the pole. When finished, the sharp blade extended from the end of the slender length of wood. Tal secured another length of vine around each end of the sapling and slung it across his back.

Coiling the vine he collected, Tal scrambled up the tree and onto the limb the wasp colony was attached to. Shinnying along the bough, he measured the distance to the thick cord the hive hung from. With an axe, he chopped a parallel groove roughly aligned to the cord. When finished, he had excavated a channel approximately half the length of the dagger-tipped sapling. He took the length of wood and fixed it within the indentation.

It fit snugly.

He then wrapped the tough vine around the tree limb securing the shaft in the groove. With more vine, he triple-wrapped and tied to the dagger-end of the pole. Tal tugged on it and nodded, satisfied it would hold. He dropped the rest of the line to the ground and scrambled down the tree.

With a wooden stake he fashioned into a "Y"-shaped notch, Tal used the flat end of the axe to pound it into the ground. He pulled on the vine with both hands. Grunting with effort, his muscles bunched, the front half of the green sapling curved back until bent almost double. The sharp blade of the dagger hung scythe-like above the thick cable holding the wasp nest to the limb. When triggered, the dagger would whip forward and sever the nest from the limb.

Tal tied a knot in the vine and, struggling to hold it in place, secured it to the notch on the stake. He slowly eased the tension until he finally released it.

Taunt as a bowstring, the line held.

Tal concealed the vine and stake by scattering forest leaves and detritus over them. He stood back and examined his efforts. A savage thrill ran through him. Only the sharpest of eyes would detect anything amiss. The trap was set. *I only wish I could be here to see it triggered.*

After a last look around to make sure he left no sign of his work, he trotted out into the open where Alex waited with the horses.

Mounting, they continued on toward the mountains.

Stefan scanned the landscape ahead as bedraggled men and gargoyles rode by.

He had pushed them relentlessly in an attempt to overtake the woman and her companion. Some looked ready to drop from the saddle, but they knew better than to grumble and face his wrath. His anger and hatred had abated little, and he spent the long hours fantasizing on the different and unique ways he would torture the man who helped Alexandria.

If he could ever catch them.

Stefan knew they were getting closer. Having discovered the tree hollow they stayed in earlier, the Dark Brother assured him they were within a half-day of overtaking their prey. Although slowed somewhat by the cold, wet weather, Stefan pressed on even during the night. Peters finally worked up the courage to tell him they would kill the horses if they didn't stop and allow them to rest and forage. Stefan relented for *that*. He could afford to lose men and gargoyles. He couldn't afford to lose the horses.

He wiped sweat from his face with the cuff of his tunic. The weather had gone from cold and wet to warm and humid. He longed to return to the comforts of his fortress. However, as much as he wanted to leave the cursed wilderness, he wanted the man and Alexandria more…much more.

He cursed under his breath. Even though his brother Rodric was to blame for Alexandria fleeing Wheel, their mother would hold *him* responsible if he didn't recover the Duke's daughter. The Veil Queen had little patience with failure—even from her son.

Stefan checked the sun. Low in the sky, dusk was less than an hour away. They would push on for a few more hours and then make camp. As he was making these plans, a shout came up ahead. He spurred his horse toward the commotion. When he reached the front of the column, a Dark Brother rode up to him.

"Lord Stefan! We found another place where they stopped," he said excitedly.

"Take me there!"

Nodding, the Dark Brother turned and galloped away, Stefan hard at his heels.

They reached a clearing within the forest a short time later. Stefan looked around but could see nothing remarkable about it. Mindful of the traps previously set for them, his suspicions intensified as the clearing filled with men and gargoyles.

He barked a warning. "Be careful you fools."

The Dark Brother dismounted and walked to where the Sniffer was tied to a tree. He grabbed the leash and led the creature toward Stefan. Snuffling, its feathery antennae waving, the Sniffer hooted loudly.

"The base of the tree is where Lady Alexandria's scent is the strongest," the Dark Brother said pointing.

Stefan carefully examined the area. Nothing seemed amiss. Then he noticed a vine rising vertically from the forest floor. His eyes flew open at the realization it wasn't just straight.

It was stretched tight!

Before he could open his mouth to shout a warning, one of the men on horseback blundered across the vine. A *twang* resonated in the clearing and the line went slack.

Stefan followed the loose vine as it whiplashed upward. In a blur of motion, a bar of wood whipped forward. A *thwack* echoed from above, followed by a large, oval object plummeting to the ground. Bouncing, it broke open. Angry buzzing ensued and dozens of enraged emperor wasps emerged from the damaged nest.

They began attacking anything within sight.

In seconds, the clearing was filled with the screams of men, gargoyles, and horses. They all tried to flee at once, blundering into one another in blind terror.

Caught in the struggling, bucking mass, Stefan, in desperation, used his sword and cut a swath through his own men in order to escape. A wasp landed on a terror-stricken gargoyle beside him and stung the eyrie dweller. The stinger went all the way through the gargoyle's chest and protruded out the other side. A brief scream of agony followed, and the dead body fell off the madly bucking horse.

The same wasp chose another victim, a mounted man in front of Stefan. It landed on the horse's rump, and quickly made its way to the man's back as the horse kicked trying to rid itself of the insect. The horseman clung desperately to his wildly rearing mount. Moments later, the raider lost his grip when the wasp's sharp mandibles severed his arm at the elbow. He screamed in agony, blood spraying from the stump as the horse-man tumbled from the saddle.

Stefan's own horse, eyes rolling in fear, reached the edge of the clearing, and charged through the underbrush. They reached the edge of the stream before Stefan finally reined in his mount. He turned back, red rage building at the sight of the unfolding debacle.

Pursued by wasps, horses exploded from the trees going in all directions. Most were riderless. Those men and gargoyles who managed to stay saddled, became tempting targets for the enraged insects. One after another were overtaken by the swift wasps. The lucky ones were simply stung followed by numbness and a quick death. The unlucky lost parts of their arms, legs, and other appendages to the wasp's massive mandibles, then bled to death.

One of the wasps spotted Stefan and veered off from the others. It sped unerringly toward him. Stefan waited until the insect was almost upon him, then twitched his hand. A purple nimbus of magic met and swallowed the wasp in mid-air. The insect disintegrated, showering the ground in front of Stefan with its dust-like remains.

Although he managed to kill a score or more of the giant wasps with withering blasts of magic, they were too numerous, and the slaughter continued all around him. Molten hatred rose in him like lava. He renewed his determination to catch the one helping Alexandria and make him suffer.

And this time, he included Alexandria in his list.

CHAPTER 43

TAL KEPT THEM MOVING UNTIL WELL PAST DARK.

If all went as planned, the wasps would be keeping the Veil Lord and his lackeys busy for some time. However, he was under no illusion the insects would stop the foul sorcerer. As soon as he could collect and organize his militia, the chase would be taken up again. Tal planned to use this time they were disorganized to put more distance between them.

When Tal finally called a halt, they had been riding in darkness for two hours. Alex slipped off Della, bone tired. After a quick supper, they slid into their bedrolls and went to sleep.

The next morning, they were up and on the move again before the sun even peeked over the horizon. The day was cloudless, and they made good time. Following the stream that ran through the mountain valley, they traveled most of the morning. After a brief stop for lunch they continued.

They spoke little during this time, and Tal found himself sneaking glances at Alex. An awkwardness had grown between them, and he wasn't sure why. The intimacy they shared earlier had vanished as suddenly as it appeared. He pinched his lips, certain she responded to him with the same eagerness he had to her.

Didn't she?

The question followed him over the leagues they traveled. He racked his brain for a reason why she remained so quiet and aloof. The pent-up frustration built to the point he could take it no more. He moved the storm horse to block her progress.

"Alex, what's wrong?" he blurted.

Surprised, Alex stopped Della. Tal moved beside her. "Besides your usual irritation with me, have I done something to upset you?"

She remained silent for so long, he feared she was refusing to answer. Then she looked at him, eyes bright with tears.

"No. You saved my life and kept me out of the hands of that evil dark lord Rodric sent after me. I'm so grateful, Tal."

She wiped the tears from her eyes. "But so much has happened in just a matter of days. It seems like yesterday I fled Wheel with Tell. Then he's killed, and I'm stung and almost die. You find me, help me recover, then off we go, chased across the wilderness. I find out the reason we can't escape, the reason we keep being followed, is because of me. Some mysterious power, magic, whatever you want to call it, oozes out of me, especially when you—you touch me. I lose all perspective, and I can't help it."

She stopped and looked at Tal. "This is all my fault. I should have never left Wheel. Tell would still be alive, and your life wouldn't be in danger."

Tal shook his head. "I have no regrets. None." He nudged his horse closer and covered her hand with his. "And I'm going to see you safely away from here." He leaned closer. "Do you trust me?" Alex nodded.

"Good. Then believe me when I say I'm going to get *both* of us out of here."

Although she still had the look of someone standing on the edge of a precipice, Alex nodded.

It saddened Tal to see her in such a state. He wanted desperately to see the happy Alex, the one whose bright smile could warm the coldest winter night.

Reluctantly, he turned his attention from her and studied the sun's position. "Let's keep moving."

It was late afternoon when they came across the remnants of a road. Long disused, it had almost disappeared under weeds and second-growth forest. Since it ran in the general direction they were traveling, Tal decided to follow it. A short time later he spied the remains of an abandoned village. He urged the storm horse to a trot, and they entered what at one time must have been the village square. The remains of numerous buildings were evidence of a once bustling community.

The long-abandoned township was the first evidence Tal had seen of the former population of Dalfur.

Cobbled streets ran down the main thoroughfare of the village and through side avenues. Passing by abandoned houses and shops, some two or three stories high, the *clop* from the horses' hooves echoed eerily off the buildings. Doors leaned drunkenly on rotting doorframes, shattered windows like broken teeth exposed the dark shadows within.

They came to the main square. A once grand fountain dominated the plaza. A water nymph, head conspicuously missing, crowned the top of the multi-tiered fountain. Water trickled from the headless nymph and collected in the green, scummy water filling the fountain's basin. Slime coated the sides of the bowl, and even the horses, though thirsty, refused to drink from it.

Tal and Alex dismounted and studied the deserted village. Weeds grew everywhere. Here and there, trees thrust upward through collapsed roofs. Dead silence covered everything, relieved only by the occasional moan of the wind through exposed rafters and accompanied by the scratch of scurrying rodents—the new residents of the hamlet.

"Where is everyone?" Alex asked softly, afraid to speak too loudly.

"Gone. Long gone by the looks of it," Tal replied.

"But where?"

Tal shrugged. "A good question…and one that continues to go unanswered." He clenched his jaw. "This whole region appears abandoned. Men, women, gnomes…where they've gone, what's happened to them, I don't know."

Alex clutched his arm and he felt a shiver grip her body. He slipped his arm around her shoulders. "Let's not tarry here any longer."

She nodded eagerly, and soon they were remounted and on their way again through the silent village.

They reached the outskirts, and the road soon faded again into grass and bushes. Enough remained to reveal a faint outline, so they continued to follow it. Abandoned farmsteads passed by. In various stages of neglect, some were still standing, while others had long since collapsed. They became fewer and fewer the farther they traveled.

Near dusk they came upon yet another derelict homestead. Unlike all the others, this one held a house and barn that seemed curiously well preserved. With darkness falling, Tal thought it might be their last chance to find a place with an intact roof over their heads. Pleased after a brief inspection of the house and barn revealed them to be reasonably sound, he determined they would spend the night.

He unsaddled the horses leaving them to graze on the new spring grass, then carried their camp supplies into the house. The door creaked as he pushed it open, the interior of the house bathed in darkness. Tal dug into the Deep Pocket and pulled out several light crystals. Activating them, he carried one and handed another to Alex. The last one he placed on the middle of a scarred and dust-laden kitchen table. Dropping the saddle bags, he embarked on a more thorough examination of the farmstead.

Nothing looked out of the ordinary. Filled with the kind of practical, well-worn furniture one would expect on a farm, dust and disuse permeated everything. Several bedrooms occupied the house, each with large beds resting on rusty, wrought-iron frames.

Alex sat on one of the beds, a groan escaping from her lips. "It feels so good." After spending night after night on the cold, hard, ground, Tal could hardly disagree.

Alex got up and stood before a cracked mirror. "Look at me. What a mess."

Tal came up behind Alex, his arms slipping around her waist. He peered over her shoulder. "Your 'mess' is a fair sight to me." He felt her stiffen. Disappointed he said, "I didn't mean to startle you." When he tried to move his hands, she held on to them.

"I'm being foolish again. Don't let me go." Even in the uncertain light cast by the crystal, her blue eyes seemed larger and clearer. She turned and pulled Tal closer. "Don't ever let me go."

The top of her head came to rest below his chin, and she pressed her face against his chest. A lump rose in Tal's throat. "Never," he answered softly.

His long arms enveloped her warm body. Turbulence and conflict marked most of his young life, none of it preparing him for what he felt now. It was like they occupied a quiet eddy in the midst of a raging river.

Just the two of them.

They stood locked in their embrace neither willing to let the moment pass.

With a sigh, Tal tilted her chin up to face him. "I don't know what spell you have cast on me, but it is powerful indeed."

Alex smiled. "I have no power, remember?"

Tal laughed, and soon she joined him. Arm around Alex's shoulder, hers around his waist, they prepared to spend the night in the farmhouse.

CHAPTER 44

ALEX SAT ALONE AT THE KITCHEN TABLE.

Although Tal had left earlier to go check on the horses, he still occupied her thoughts. Her emotions roiled inside her. One minute his stubborn, childish nature was angering her, the next he was holding or kissing her, and all rational thinking flew from her mind. The feel of his flesh on hers, like a drug, lifted her to an incredible high, something she couldn't escape or get enough of.

She shook her head. She ought to be more concerned about their precarious position and her "leak".

But all she could think about was Tal.

The front door banged open and Tal entered holding a pair of geese. They had already been gutted, plucked, and cleaned. "There's a pond behind the barn. There was just enough light left to spot and shoot them," he announced.

He put the waterfowl on the table along with his quiver and bow. Alex doubted the lack of light hampered Tal. He could see like a cat in the dark.

Gesturing at the pair, Tal said, "We will have roast goose tonight." Just the prospect of anything but trail rations caused Alex's stomach to growl.

He soon had the Dragon Stones arranged in the fireplace and the geese turning on a spit. Fat dripped from them, the aroma of roasting meat filling the kitchen. Alex found plates and cutlery. She used a bucket of water Tal had fetched from the well, and washed the dust off the dishes. Then she set the table and they sat down to eat. Famished, she picked the bones clean.

Later, her head on Tal's shoulder, his arm around her, they basked in the heat of the Dragon Stones. Warm, full, and sleepy, her eyelids felt like heavy weights. With a yawn, she said, "Maybe we should turn in for the night. It's been so long since I've slept in a real bed, I've almost forgotten what it's like."

Tal nodded and they retreated to their bedrooms, each adjacent to one another. Since the quilts covering each bed were hopelessly gritty and dusty, they simply spread their bed rolls on top. Alex kicked off her boots and loosened her bodice. She took the light crystal and placed it beside her on the wood-plank nightstand, then lay down and stared at the ceiling.

What would it be like to be in the same bed with Tal?

The image of him standing naked in the stream flashed through her mind. Unwinding like an old-fashioned reel of film, one frame pictured him bare to the waist, another the play of his muscles as he scrubbed his body. The last frame had him facing her in ankle deep water his entire body exposed—

She bolted upright, her drowsiness gone in a flush of desire. Slipping out of bed, she tiptoed to Tal's bedroom and peeked in. He lay with arms behind his head, eyes closed. The hilt of his dagger protruded under a pillow, his sword unsheathed and leaning within easy reach against the nightstand. Her breath caught in her throat at the sight of his bare chest.

"Are you going to just stand there or join me?" he asked with eyes still shut.

Alex felt her face warm. "I—I just wanted to say goodnight," she stammered.

Tal cracked an eyelid. The corner of his mouth curved with the hint of a smile. He patted the bed. "You could say it better from here than there."

Alex spun to flee back to her own room. She hesitated…then turned back and boldly walked to Tal's side and sat on the edge of the bed.

She leaned down and pecked him on the cheek. "Goodnight."

When she tried to stand, he pulled her back. Forced to place both hands on his chest to keep from falling over, her face hovered inches from him. Before she could take another breath, Tal crushed her lips to his. He tasted of mint and wild goose. Heart thumping, she fought the overwhelming urge to climb on top of him. Pushing off the bed, Alex staggered away.

She stopped at the doorway and looked back. Tal's frustrated expression caused her to smile.

Now he knew how *she* felt. Triumphant, she went back to her own bed and blankets.

Sleep came easily.

Within the barn, a trap door cleverly recessed into the floor creaked open.

A thin figure rose into the air from a cellar concealed by the trap door. It hovered a few inches above the floor and pivoted in a circle. Rotting clothes hung from its gaunt frame. Red, feral eyes gleamed with hunger. A pair of sharp incisors protruded from its mouth. Long, jagged nails grew from the fingers of each hand, its flesh a deathly, corpse-white color.

The figure glided slowly across the floor to stop at the open barn doors. Three similar creatures rose silently from the hidden cellar. One, comparable in size to the leader, had long hair and emaciated breasts. Two smaller versions hung motionless in the air behind the female. All had red eyes burning with the same overwhelming hunger, a craving only blood could satiate.

Always it drove them from their lair every night.

The foursome glided silently into the clearing. The horses looked up and snorted at the sight of the creatures. When the two smaller creatures eagerly began to pursue them, the leader raised his clawed hand. The two halted, a mewling coming from wasted lips. The lead creature sniffed the air and rotated soundlessly. A long talon pointed at the house.

As one, they all floated toward it.

White, pointed, tongues licked teeth and lips in anticipation of the feast. Reaching the door, they silently entered the house. Whispering across the floor, the creatures entered a bedroom. A woman slept on the bed, head askew. Throat exposed, the lead creature hovered toward her, sharp fangs posed at her juggler. The woman's blood called to him, the soft pulsing of the vein in her neck an irresistible song.

Careful, so as not to awaken the prey prematurely, the creature grasped the woman's shoulders and prepared to plunge its teeth into her soft throat. When it's cold flesh came in contact with the woman, a ghostly luminescence rose from her and into its wasted hands.

The creature paused, dormant memories long forgotten, began to flow like water through it. A distraction from its rapacious hunger, the leader shook its head to rid the unwanted memories. Frozen above the woman's throat, whines of craving came from the others who waited their turn to feed. More memories flowed, and it remembered.

For the first time over the long ages, it remembered…

CHAPTER 45

ALEX DREAMED.

She was standing outside the derelict house they were sleeping in. Only the farmstead wasn't abandoned. A mother and her two children, a boy and a girl, were on the porch. The mother mended a tear in a pair of trousers, while her children played. The peaceful, happy scene brought a smile to Alex's lips.

The woman's husband approached from the barn with a pail of milk. Reaching his wife, he kissed her and handed her the pail. The children crowded around his feet and he picked them up accompanied by their screams of laughter.

As if watching snippets from a movie, one scene from the farm family after another rolled by. These scenes flashed by with increasing speed, until they stopped to present Alex with a familiar image—a nighttime view of the current abandoned farmhouse.

A strange, out-of-body sensation gripped Alex. She found herself floating toward the farmstead. Reaching the door, she entered and moved to a bedroom. A woman lay fast asleep. She had a certain familiarity about her, and puzzled, Alex moved closer. Movement caught the corner of her eye, and she looked up.

A creature of horror stared back at her from the cracked mirror.

Pale, dead flesh covered its face. Bestial red eyes and a pair of long, pointed teeth protruded from its mouth. The horrible sight triggered a return to the movie-like clips.

The farmer and his family appeared again. A vampiric creature was at the farmer's throat, his wife and children its next victims. Unable to close her eyes or block the awful vision, each in turn was drained of blood and life. Then the worst scene of all.

Their transformation from a happy family full of life and hope, to the red-eyed creatures of burning hunger.

The gruesome sight proved too much, and Alex forced herself to wake up. Opening her eyes, she thought the nightmare still lingered—because the face of the horrendous creature was still there, and only inches from her face. It struggled to speak to her.

"Help…me…Help…us…Release…us…Release…us," it pleaded in a rasping voice.

The effort to talk produced a tortuous effect upon the creature, every word causing spasms of agony. It looked briefly away from Alex, but when it turned back, its eyes were seared with blood-hunger.

It bared its sharp incisors in preparation to sink them into her throat.

Alex screamed in terror as the vampire struck at her like a snake.

Its teeth never reached her skin.

A blinding flash exploded from her. Lifting the vampire off Alex, its body flew through the air and slammed into the ceiling. As it fell back to the floor, magic cocooned the vampire and continued to crackle like lightning. It writhed in agony, unable to escape.

The remaining vampires hissed in hunger and fear. They scuttled away from contact with the lightning-like magic. Regrouping, they bared sharp teeth and crept toward her.

Alex continued to scream with raw-throated horror.

Tal rolled out of bed with sword in hand before Alex's first scream had faded.

No vestige of sleep remained as he sprinted to her room. Bursting through the door, a kaleidoscope of light and magic greeted him. The pulsing illumination revealed Alex huddled in a corner, an undulating, writhing creature on the floor in front of her. A keening from multiple mouths raised the hair on Tal's neck. He turned and quickly spied three figures advancing on him. Like flies, they crawled along the ceiling upside down, hungry mouths open to expose sharp teeth.

"Night Walkers!" Tal shouted. He leaped over the creature on the floor and placed himself between Alex and the advancing vampires.

He spied the light crystal on Alex's night table. He fumbled for it, his eyes warily on the vampires. Before he could reach it, one of the smaller Night Walkers could no longer contain its hunger. With a screech, it launched itself at Tal with mouth agape. The unnatural quickness in the vampire's attack allowed Tal only time to bring his sword up in a defensive blow.

His blade and Night Walker met in midair.

The vampire catapulted from the sword in a shower of magical sparks. Bouncing off the wall, it landed on its feet. The impact with the wall had no effect on the Night Walker, but the sword left a scorched and blackened streak. It mewled and keened in pain. The other vampires, recognizing the threat the sword represented, hissed in fear and frustration.

Changing tactics, they split up, the smaller Night Walkers crawling to the left on the ceiling, while the larger vampire scuttled to the right.

Tal watched in grim silence as the vampires tried to flank him. He had been fortunate to get his sword up in time to knock the first Night Walker from him. It would take more than luck a second time. Desperately, he rooted again for the light crystal.

His hand closed on the crystal. "Close your eyes!" he shouted to Alex just as the Night Walkers coiled their bodies to launch another attack. He hurled the crystal as hard as he could against the floor.

It shattered. Dazzling sunlight exploded, so bright, that even with eyes closed, Tal's eyelids couldn't stop the seepage of the intense light. Inhuman shrieks of agony accompanied the brilliant illumination. They ended abruptly. Numb silence filled the aftermath, with only Alex's muffled sobs breaking the hush.

Tal opened his eyes. He waited while sparks of light danced in his vision. When he could see clearly, four mounds of ash lay on the floor—the remains of the Night Walkers. With a last flicker, Alex's magic sputtered and died. The bedroom was left in darkness.

"I'm going to retrieve the other light crystal," he said and turned to go back to his bedroom.

"No!" Alex screamed. "Don't leave me here alone!" She streaked to his side and clung to him. Tal put his arms around her shaking body. Realizing she was completely undone, he made no move to leave.

When the worst of the quivering left her, Tal said, "We'll go together." She nodded, her grip on him never slackening as they walked to the other bedroom for the light. When Tal turned to go back to her room, Alex refused to budge. "No! I'm not going back there."

Tal activated the crystal and they sat on the bed. "Okay, we can stay right here."

Eyes wide in fear and shock, Alex clung to him. "I saw them, I saw them, I saw them!" she repeated, her voice edged with hysteria.

"I saw the Night Walkers, too," Tal answered softly.

"No, you don't understand. I saw them before they turned

into—into those things. They were a normal, happy family before some vampire-like horror transformed them."

Alex turned a tear-streaked face to Tal. "One of them asked me to help him, to release them. Then he tried to attack me. If you hadn't come when you did…" She left the rest unspoken.

A shaky laugh erupted from her. "I'm piling up the thank yous for saving my life. I don't know how I'll ever be able to repay you."

Tal used his thumb to wipe away her tears. "You're safe and unharmed. That's payment enough." He stood. "But I need to make sure there are no more of them."

"No, Tal, no!" Alex cried. "Wait until morning."

Tal shook his head. "And wait for another attack? Night Walkers hunt silently. We would never know until their fangs were at our throats."

He dug into the Deep Pocket and retrieved a handful light crystals. "The magic of the crystals store sunlight, an anathema to the Night Walkers. You saw what it did to them." He hefted his sword with grim purpose. "But if any are left, they will die one way or the other."

Angry, Alex jumped up off the bed. "If you won't listen to me, then I'm coming with you."

Tal regarded her with hooded eyes. "No, you're not. It's not safe and besides, you'll get in my way."

A harsh laugh bubbled from Alex. "And I'm safe here? Alone?" She grabbed one of the crystals. "I can throw one of these just like you can. Let's go!"

By her tone, Tal knew it would be useless to argue with Alex. Short of tying her to a chair, she would just follow him.

They left the room…together.

CHAPTER 46

A THOROUGH SEARCH OF THE HOUSE REVEALED NOTHING.

Tal, light crystal in one hand, sword in the other, moved outside. Alex followed behind with a firm grasp on the waist of his pants. She never released her grip and repeatedly stumbled into him when he stopped. Although he liked the feel of her nearness, he knew it would definitely slow him should he have to defend them.

The light of the triple moons lit their way, the soft luminosity bathing the entire area with a velvety glow. He approached the barn, senses on high alert. The doors were wide open and he immediately spotted the trapdoor. Cautiously, they made their way to the edge. The fetid smell of death and decay rose from the black pit below.

They had found the Night Walker's lair.

He backed away. "Cover your eyes." Tal hurled a light crystal. It struck the bottom, ruptured, and blinding light followed. He waited a moment, then using another crystal, illuminated the inside of the hidden cellar. He leaned over the edge and looked down.

Nothing. No pile of ash or any other evidence another Night Walker existed.

A thorough inspection of the barn also proved fruitless.

They headed back to the farmstead.

Tal used the rest of his supply of the magical crystals to illuminate the house's interior. Knowing the nightmarish ordeal Alex had gone through, he wanted the place as bright as possible with little or no shadows. Still, she followed him closely wherever he went, much like a puppy he had as a child. He didn't blame her. To awaken and find a vampire inches from your throat would give anyone a case of screaming hysteria. That she had recovered so quickly was amazing.

He decided Alex contained an inner strength he had given her little or no credit for.

An idea came to him while they were making their search. The more he turned it over in his mind, the more certain he thought it would work. They went back to Alex's bedroom, and he sifted through a pile of ash.

"What are you doing?" Alex asked.

"Looking for the fangs."

"Why?"

"Because I think I can use them to set another trap. One I believe will finally free us from our hunters."

Tal continued to paw through the gray powder. "Ah. Here!" Tal triumphantly held up a pair of ivory fangs. Sharp and curved, they glinted in the light. He dropped them into a wooden cup he took from the kitchen.

He moved on to the next mound while Alex searched another. Soon they had four pairs of vampire incisors. Tal dug through the Deep Pocket and pulled out a mortar and pestle. He dropped the teeth into the mortar and ground them into a fine powder with the pestle. More digging around in the magical bag produced a glass vial and stopper. Tal poured the entire contents of the mortar into the flask. He sealed it tightly with the cork stopper.

A fierce thrill ran through him. "They'll never know until it's too late."

He held the flask before Alex. "The teeth are the part of a Night Walker most resistant to sunlight. That's why they endured while the rest of their bodies turned to ash. However, when you grind them to powder, they lose part of this resistance. Then the dust reacts to sunlight in explosive fashion. It becomes highly flammable."

"What are you going to do with it?"

"Bury it. C'mon." Tal grabbed Alex's arm and they went outside.

Tal cast about and found a suitable place in front of the porch. He dug a shallow hole with his dagger, and wrapped the vial in a rag he took from the kitchen. Then he dropped it in the hole and covered it up.

Dusting off his hands, he motioned to Alex. When she reached him, he took her in his arms and kissed her. "Need me to leak some more?" she murmured.

Tal chuckled. "No. You've already left enough residue they'll have no trouble finding this place. I just wanted to kiss you."

Alex aimed a playful slap at him. "How can you think about such things after what we just went through?"

"Oh, it's easy enough." Tal pulled her tighter. "Especially since I find myself thinking about you all the time now."

She stroked his cheek. "My own personal Prince Charming."

Tal frowned. "Another Prince? Which Kingdom does he rule?"

Alex went silent. "Just a silly saying. That's all," she finally said.

Arm-in-arm, they returned to the farmhouse.

❈

Alex lay on top of Tal's bed while he occupied a space on the floor beside the bedstead.

She refused to return to the other bedroom, not after her blood-chilling experience with the Night Walkers. Nor was she willing to sleep anywhere without Tal close by. But it was more than fear which drove this feeling within her.

She needed him.

Like food and water, she needed him.

At first, she thought her feelings foolish and simply a flight of fancy driven in large part by the danger they always seemed to be in. Diana's possible futures notwithstanding, Alex didn't really believe love to be inevitable. Such things were straight out of an earthly pulp fiction romance novel. They never really happened in real life...or in her case, her alternate life on an alternate world.

Yet here she was, her yearning for Tal a physical ache which continued to grow in intensity.

She turned and peeked over the edge of the bed. "Tal?"

"Hmm?" came his muffled voice.

"I know this is, well, a strange thing to ask, but can you sleep beside me tonight?"

"I don't know. This hard floor is so comfortable."

"I won't ask again."

Blankets flew, and Tal jumped up. He quickly slid under her bedroll next to her. "What took you so long?" Alex asked.

Tal chuckled and put his arm around her. "A sense of humor as well? Is there no end to your surprises?"

Alex climbed atop Tal, straddling him. "I have a few more," she whispered. She ran her fingers over his chest. Her lips followed her hands and laid a trail of kisses on his bare flesh. She felt him respond, and worked her way up to his broad shoulders. By this time, Tal was squirming beneath her.

She sat up and pulled his hands to her breasts. Her breath came in sharp gasps, and she felt herself approaching a point of no return.

Alex paused. *What am I doing? If I don't stop now, I won't be able to.*

With a heavy sigh, she leaned forward and kissed Tal. Then she rolled off and lay by his side. Her head on his chest, she ignored his groan of disappointment. "Good night, Tal."

Then she added one more silent thought.

I love you.

CHAPTER 47

"What's the final count?" Stefan asked through clenched teeth.

"Fifty men and gargoyles still able to ride with about as many horses," Peters replied grimly.

Fifty! They had started with over a hundred. Their only luck had been that the Dark Brother was able to conjure a protective shield over the Sniffer. Without the melded beast, the hunt would already be over. His hatred for Alexandria's companion, the orchestrator of this disaster, consumed him to the point he couldn't think clearly. No matter how much time or effort it took, he vowed to have his revenge.

"I'll get you," he hissed to himself. "Then you'll wish you never laid eyes on Alexandria."

Stefan gripped the reins in white knuckles. "Move out!" he barked to the survivors. "We'll pick up the trail again, and this time we don't stop until we find them."

He leaned forward, his dark eyes daring any to challenge him. "Any questions?" No one moved.

With the Dark Brother and Sniffer in the lead, the survivors formed a loose column and resumed the chase.

Tal woke early with Alex sprawled partially across him.

He lay motionless reveling in the feel of her soft body.

As a popular, if reluctant, figure at many of his mother's court functions, he had attracted the attention of many a nobleman's daughter. Some shamelessly flirted with him, while others, more subtle, tried to use the formal occasions to arrange intimate "meetings". Most were beautiful, some breathtakingly so. No fool, Tal knew as the Prince and Heir, he could have had his pick of any of them. But all paled in comparison to Alex.

And none held his heart like she did.

How it happened, why it happened, made no sense. They were on the run, chased in a life and death hunt. However, in less than a week's time, she had turned his life inside out. His feelings for her were already so deeply rooted that no matter what happened, he didn't think he would ever be the same. He blinked at a sudden realization.

Could I be falling in love?

From the time of his father's death at the hands of Veil raiders to the present, his focus had been spent on one singular objective—killing any and every man and melded creature issuing from the Veil. Nothing else mattered, nothing else held any interest for him.

Not until now.

He tilted his head so he could see Alex's face as it lay against his chest. Lips parted, her breathing slow and easy, he smiled at her peaceful expression. Deep inside him, the tightly wound coil of hate and rage loosened. So much a part of him for so long, the release felt like a heavy weight dropping from him.

With a sigh, he brought his mind back to their present situation. They needed to be up and off with the rising sun. At some point he also needed to talk to Alex again about her magic. He chose not to last night because of the frightening ordeal she had endured. But the power she claimed to lack had manifested itself again. And this time it protected her by covering and trapping a vampire. No random burst of magic, no "leaking", but something else entirely.

A deliberate use of her power.

He woke Alex.

❖

Crisp morning air caressed Alex's face as they left the farmhouse. She watched Tal reach into his mystical bag and pull out a small brass ring.

Puzzled, she asked, "What is it?"

"A communication Artifact. I'm going to use it to spy on our hunters."

Alex squinted at the Deep Pocket. "How can that small bag hold so much?"

Tal shrugged. "Because of the Artifact's magic. A Deep Pocket can contain a lot. It can also conjure items, though that tends to exhaust magic faster."

He climbed a nearby tree and firmly lodged the ring in the crook of two branching limbs. He jumped down and dusted off his hands. Squatting, Tal scrutinized the line-of-sight from the ring's location to the front of the farmhouse.

He turned to Alex and flashed a fierce smile. "Perfect."

Tal helped Alex onto Della then mounted his storm horse. "Your power has saturated this entire area. The small amount of magic I used to activate the ring won't ever be noticed."

Alex found Tal's comment bewildering. She knew he possessed magic—and suspected it to be formidable. Why would he be worried about anyone noticing it?

Unless he is hiding something.

The realization she still knew so little about Tal caught her off guard. It started an ache inside her. Her feelings for him continued to grow even as he kept the details of his life to himself. His prolonged reticence hurt, almost like a betrayal.

How can I feel this way about someone who doesn't trust me?

Tal, oblivious to her discomfort, led them away.

They traveled for over an hour before Tal called a halt. He helped Alex off Della then removed the net restraining the horse's wings. Della snorted, wings flapping. Tal stroked her neck while he examined the injured joint.

He turned to Alex with a look of triumph. "The wing is completely healed." He lifted Alex into the air and swung her around. "We can finally go home!" Laughing he lowered her into his arms and hugged her.

Alex stiffened and when Tal released her, she turned away. Tal frowned. "What's wrong?"

Alex whirled around, arms crossed. "And where is 'home'? Where are we going? And why do you feel the need to hide your magic?" She felt tears spring to her eyes. "I told you everything about me, even about Tell and why we left Wheel. I trusted you, but you don't trust me...not even enough to give me a hint of who you really are."

Tal's mouth opened and closed several times before he found his voice. "I told you before I was—"

"I know, I know, part of something!" Alex cried. "Which means it could be anything. So really, you told me nothing. I just thought..." her throat tightened, and she stopped.

Tal gripped her by the shoulders. "What? You thought what?"

Alex shook her head, but Tal persisted. "Tell me!"

Her voice barely above a whisper, Alex said, "Because I thought your feelings for me were the same that I feel for you."

Dejected, Alex stood while Tal's eyes bored into her. Finally, he said, "You don't know how hard this has been for me. Not the chase, not these hunters or their vile leader, but trying to separate my feelings for you from my real purpose."

He shook his head. "I have an obligation, a duty I must follow. This burden transcends everything else…even you. It leaves me twisted like a knot I can't loosen. But whatever you feel for me, I swear, I share the same and more for you."

Tal's words brought little comfort. Alex understood a conflict raged within him, but she bared her soul, told him she was the Duke of Wheel's daughter and why she fled the city. In return he gave her only excuses.

Alex swallowed her bitter disappointment. "What will happen to me when we reach this 'home' you speak of?" She followed with the question she dreaded to ask. But everything depended on his answer. "What becomes of us?"

Tal, face frozen like stone, struggled to answer. His jaw clenched and unclenched, and he kicked at the ground in frustration. With a sigh, he looked up. "I don't know. Had you asked me a week ago, the answer would have been simple. But now…now I don't know."

"Why?"

His arms slipped from her shoulders to her waist. He pulled her closer. "Because I want you near me. The thought of you far away even though it means you'll be safe, is something I can't even bring myself to consider."

The raw emotion in Tal's voice pricked her heart. Like a salve, it acted to soothe her own tattered feelings. She reached up and cupped his face.

"Then keep me near."

CHAPTER 48

STEFAN'S MEN SPREAD OUT AS THEY CAME UPON THE ABANDONED farmhouse.

Alexandria's path of magic led straight here. In fact, her lingering magic was so powerful, the Sniffer hooted and hopped repeatedly—as if the creature had gone mad. Stefan had been forced to have the Dark Brother cage the beast. The potent scent made it obvious something happened here, something which had triggered a powerful release from Alexandria.

His greatly reduced force picked their way across the premises, and thoroughly searched the grounds, then the house and barn. He was pleased to see they moved with care. After all the deadly surprises, their dull brains must have finally gotten the message.

The Dark Brother approached him. "The barn has a cellar with a trap door. It appears to be a lair of some sort."

"Lair? For what manner of creature?"

The Dark Brother shrugged. "I am unsure, Lord Stefan. The stink of death permeates the den like that of a crypt. But it's empty."

Brow furrowed, Stefan mulled over this discovery. He urged his horse into a trot to see for himself. Dismounting, he inspected the cellar. The waft of decay assaulted his nostrils. A familiarity danced at the edge of his mind, but he couldn't quite grasp hold of it. Frustrated, he remounted and made his way back to the farmstead.

A group of gargoyles and men stood around a section of freshly turned soil. Peters and Zorb stood nearby, giving the disturbed loam a wide berth.

"What of your search?" Stefan barked.

"We found evidence Lady Alexandria and her companion spent the night here, Lord Stefan," Zorb answered.

The Veil Lord gritted his teeth. "I know that you fool. Tell me something I *don't* know!"

Peters pointed at the ground. "We found this. It looks like they may have buried something."

Stefan examined the loose soil. Although suspicious it could be another lethal trap, he didn't see how. He wracked his brain but couldn't come up with anything buried that could pose a threat. Nevertheless, he would take no chances. He motioned to the Dark Brother.

"See what it is. Tread carefully."

One of Peters' men tossed the sorcerer a shovel. The Dark Brother, face pale, extended the shovel at arm's length. He removed the dirt bit-by-bit. After only a few minutes of digging, he uncovered an object wrapped in a rag. Eying the bundle as if it were a poisonous serpent, the sorcerer managed to get the shovel underneath. He lifted it up and plucked the bundle out of the dirt. When he held it up, part of the rag fell off to reveal the glint of glass.

"It looks like a vial of some sort," the Dark Brother commented. Emboldened he removed the rest of the tattered cloth. A shaky laugh came from the sorcerer. "That's all it is. A glass vial."

Stefan stared at the flask and wondered if it was somehow related to the death-scented cellar. Again, something nibbled at the edge of his mind. Suddenly, his eyes widened in recognition. Night Walkers! The stench from the cellar came from the blood-sucking creatures. But their lair proved to be empty. Where were they?

Dread realization struck the Veil Lord.

"Stop!" he cried. "Cover the—"

He never finished the sentence.

Sunlight reflected off the flask's contents and it shot into the air. While Stefan's men and gargoyles watched slack-jawed, the vial exploded, hurling its powdery residue in all directions. Floating back to the ground like motes of dust, the sun's rays struck the particles and they burned with an incandescence so bright, many of Stefan's band were instantly blinded.

Stefan barely had time to hurl a spell of protection over himself, when the first fiery particles began to land. The burning dust broiled a hole through whatever it came in contact with. Men, gargoyles, and horses thrashed in agony, smoke rising from the holes eating into their flesh. Helpless to intervene, Stefan watched his band being decimated by the incendiary powder.

Those blinded by the initial explosion collided with one another as they tried to escape the agony. Beating at their scorched bodies, driven mad by the pain, men and gargoyles clawed at their flesh, leaving long, bloody furrows, their nails peeling back ruined skin. One raider, his arm smoking like a fat sausage, hacked the appendage off in a spray of blood.

Total chaos reigned, the smell of roasted meat a heavy pall in the air.

Stefan watched the decimation in silence. He choked back the defeat which rose in his throat like a bitter bile. They couldn't capture Alexandria now. Even if any of his band survived, the handful would not be enough. Alexandria's companion had proven to be a resourceful, formidable opponent. To continue the chase with less than a full complement of men and gargoyles would be suicidal.

Stefan was patient, however. He would bide his time and wait for the next opportunity. Eventually, his path would cross this man's again, the one responsible for his humiliation. Accounts would be settled then. In the meantime, he would plan the tortures he would employ when that glorious day arrived.

Oblivious to the screams around him, he smiled in anticipation.

◈

Horrified, Alex watched men, horses, and gargoyles immolate.

Their screams pierced her soul.

Earlier, Tal had taken another of the communication Artifacts he removed from the Deep Pocket and placed it on the ground. The entire scene played out in front of them, every gruesome detail in loud, living color. She turned away and covered her ears.

Blessed silence finally came to the clearing. Alex stood, turned, and wiped her wet cheeks. Her attention came to rest on Tal who danced with joy.

"Did you see that?" he crowed. "We did it! We killed almost all of them!"

At first, the "we" didn't register with her. Then she realized she had helped Tal recover the vampire teeth and assisted him while he ground them to powder.

She aided and abetted in the murder of these men and gargoyles.

Tal stopped his celebration, frowning at her tear-stained face. Perplexed, he asked, "What is it?"

Alex stared at him. "You don't know? How can you be so happy? Didn't you see them burn to death? Didn't you hear them?"

"Of course, I saw and heard it all. So what?" He paused and peered at her. "Surely you bear no sympathy for those vile creatures?"

"Yes, I do! Any normal person would."

"They would have done the same or worse to you and me."

"Then that makes us no better than them."

Tal, his face a mask of fury, stalked to Alex and grabbed her shoulders. "You compare *me* to the Veil foulness?"

"I didn't—"

Tal shook her. "Your mind can't conceive of the things I've seen. Whole families decimated, villages with bodies scattered from one end to the other. Women raped, children carried off to slavery or worse, men tortured to the point they beg for death. Then comes Marlinda's special touch, the cruelty of reuniting mothers with children she has turned into abominations."

Tal's outburst sparked anger in Alex and she tried to push away. "So you become a monster to kill a monster?"

Eyes narrowed, his face a mask of fury, Tal spat, "Don't you dare pass judgement! You who have led a sheltered life where the hardest decision is which pair of shoes to wear!" His fingers dug into her flesh.

Alex tore herself from Tal's grip. "You have no idea what I've seen or what I've been through!"

"I know your unhappiness with an arranged marriage cost Tell his life."

The *crack* of her slap across Tal's face echoed in the clearing. "You incredible bastard!" Alex screamed. "To think I was falling in love with you. What a fool I am."

Silence, broken only by Alex's sobs, bruised the air.

Tal rubbed the red handprint on his face, his anger melting away. "I'm sorry. I—I don't know why I said that."

When he reached for Alex, she pushed him away. "Don't touch me! Don't you ever touch me again!"

Tal stiffened. After a moment, he pivoted and stalked to the flying horses. He repacked the few items he removed, then mounted his storm mount. He motioned for Alex.

Pulling herself together, Alex approached Della, put her foot in the stirrup, and swung into the saddle. Securing the safety strap, she nodded at Tal.

Wings beating, the storm horse soared into the air, followed shortly by Della.

CHAPTER 49

IDWAY THROUGH THEIR SECOND DAY OF TRAVEL, ALEX SPIED A long column of men and supplies. It stretched for miles appearing and disappearing in the thick stands of trees.

As they drew closer, she realized it was a military operation of some sort. From her observation point high above, the size and scope of the entire force was staggering. Thousands of soldiers, wagons, draft animals, and other personnel were involved. What was happening here wasn't clear, but even to her untrained eye, the effort required to carry out such a task must be monumental.

Of course, Tal could have told her what to expect, but they had hardly spoken since their falling out. What little talk they did engage in involved only the mundane tasks required each day. She found herself sneaking surreptitious glances at him. But he always kept his eyes straight ahead.

He never looked her way.

Despite his cruel comment about Tell and his celebration at the horrific slaughter of the Veil Lord's forces, she couldn't get him out of her mind...or out of her heart.

She still loved him.

He was stubborn, impetuous, had a quick temper, and his blunt words could cut deeper than the sharpest knife. But when he held her in his arms, when he kissed her, when his beautiful green eyes gazed into hers, his every flaw disappeared. Although his hatred for all things associated with the Veil often disguised it, there was a tenderness to Tal—and those roots ran deep. Unlike any person she had ever met, it was impossible to fit him into any box or category.

Her thoughts were interrupted when a company of flying cavalry intercepted them. Although she couldn't hear the conversation, it quickly became evident Tal was a person of some importance. Their leader saluted Tal, followed by all the cavalrymen who touched their hands from head to heart.

The next thing she knew, they were surrounded and escorted to the ground below.

No sooner had Della's hooves touched ground than they were met by a group of men. Two had a military bearing, and one looked like he just rolled out of bed with frumpy red hair and beard. The pair that stood out, however, were a tall, robed figure with snow-white hair, and a black man, who from the deference shown to him by the others, must be their leader.

He didn't look happy.

When Alex glanced at Tal, his face was lined with tension. He helped her off Della and quickly introduced her.

"My *Eldred*, this is Lady Alexandria."

The black man stepped forward and placed her hand to his lips. "Bozar Ali Shehem at your service. Welcome, Lady Alexandria."

The shabby, red-haired man shouldered his way through the others. With an exaggerated bow, he boomed, "Artemis Thurgood." A broad smile split his face. "Tal said he found a sparkling gem in the midst of this godforsaken wilderness." He winked at her. "The lad has a way of understating things."

Completely disarmed, Alex laughed at his comment.

The next to step up was the white-haired man. "John Fedders, although around here I am better known by 'Pulpit'." He also put her hand to his lips.

His touch produced a sensation within her. Although it felt

odd, it wasn't unpleasant. Pulpit's eyes widened and he stepped back. "I look forward to our meeting later."

Puzzled by the comment, Alex said, "Meeting?"

Bozar cleared his throat. "We would like to talk to you…after you have rested and refreshed yourself of course."

An uneasiness rose within Alex. Tal must have sensed her discomfort, because he moved to her side. "I'll be there with you. All you need to do is tell them what you've told me." It was his longest speech to her since their fight.

The rest of the introductions were made, and Tal led her deeper into the sprawling encampment. They came to a pavilion which dwarfed the other tents.

"My humble abode," Artemis Thurgood stated. "No need for you to sleep on the hard ground or eat tasteless trail rations the military passes off as food." As they entered the tent, two sentries took positions outside the entrance. The similarity to Wheel and her lack of freedom was uncanny.

Her life just came full circle.

Tal's eyes lingered on her. "I have to go. You'll stay here with Artemis. Just let him know any of your needs. He's…very resourceful."

When Tal turned to leave, a trunk resting inside the tent stood up on stubby legs. With much clanking, it waddled over to Alex. She squeaked in surprise and clutched Tal's arm. In a blink, he caught her and pulled her close. His scent drifted to her nostrils, along with the familiar throb he always seemed to produce in her.

"My pardon, Lady Alexandria," Thurgood apologized. "I should have warned you about Daisy. She didn't mean to startle you."

Alex placed her hands on Tal's chest to push away. Their eye's locked momentarily. In that one brief moment, everything she felt about Tal came roaring back.

He leaned close to her ear and whispered, "I'm a fool…and I'm sorry."

He turned and walked away.

She watched him disappear among the sea of tents, her sense of loss so profound, she couldn't move.

Rooted to the spot, an, "Ahem," finally caused her to stir.

She swallowed and noticed Artemis Thurgood beside her, his hand extended. "Let me take you on the grand tour." She nodded and he led her through the voluminous pavilion. When finished, Alex was impressed.

"But I only noticed one bed," she said. "You're not giving that up for me, are you?"

Thurgood chuckled, a pleasant, deep bass sound. "Oh, no, Lady Alexandria. I am a creature of comforts, I admit. No, all we need is a little expansion."

With that, he took a pinch of powder from a bag at his waist. Mumbling words of power, he tossed the dust into the air. Immediately, a portion of the tent rippled and billowed. Seconds later, another section appeared. This included a large bed with pillows, thick quilts, and a soft mattress.

Amazed, Alex walked to the bed and sat on it. Then she lay back and closed her eyes, reveling in the luxurious comfort. More clanking came to her ears. She sat up and at her feet was the trunk.

"Daisy has taken quite a liking to you," Thurgood observed.

Alex tilted her head. "What *is* Daisy?"

"An enchanted chest. She tends to be underfoot, so just let me know if she becomes a bother."

Alex slid off the bed. She dropped to her knees and put her hand on top of the trunk. "Daisy. What a sweet name." Daisy waggled her tasseled end so vigorously, her contents jangled nonstop.

"Uh, oh. She'll follow you everywhere now."

Thurgood rubbed his hands together. "I've saved the best for last. Follow me."

Alex stood and trailed after him to another part of the tent. He pulled back a curtain to reveal a large tub filled with steaming water. "I imagine it's been awhile since you've had a proper bath."

Alex squealed in delight. She threw her arms around Thurgood. "It looks wonderful! Thank you."

Thurgood beamed. He pointed to a nearby table. "Towels and robes are stacked there. Push your clothes under the curtain and I'll have them cleaned while you bathe."

After Artemis Thurgood left, Alex quickly stripped, folded her clothes and placed them under the curtain. She stepped into the water, goosebumps of pleasure appearing on her skin from the silky-hot water.

Closing her eyes, she sank into the water up to her chin. She let her mind drift, her thoughts coming back to Tal's whispered comment. "I'm sorry" he said. But did that mean 'sorry' as in an apology, or did it have the ring of a finality? The latter would mean whatever they had between them was now over. Even though immersed in the hot tub, a shard of ice pierced her heart at the thought.

She would find out soon enough.

CHAPTER 50

T HE BATH AND CLEAN CLOTHES DID WONDERS FOR ALEX.
Ready as she was ever going to be, Artemis Thurgood
led her through the enormous encampment to another tent,
this one larger than the others. Inside, arranged around a table,
were the same men who met her earlier. Two chairs were placed
to face the small group. In one sat Tal.

The empty chair was for her.

She sat down next to Tal. He glanced at her, a troubled look
on his face.

Not a good sign.

For the next hour, she answered their questions, Tal filling in the
spaces she didn't know or wasn't sure of. While their queries started
off innocently enough, they evolved into a grilling, particularly
toward the end. One man, Lord Gravelback, was especially blunt.

"So, you claim to be the Duke of Wheel's daughter?"

"Yes."

"What proof do you have for this assertion?"

"I—I don't have any," Alex stammered.

"And you expect us to believe you?"

The chair next to her fell over as Tal jumped to his feet, his face
red. "Do not badger her, Lord Gravelback!"

"Tal," Bozar warned, "the Lord Commander is asking a legitimate
question, and an important one." Tal opened his mouth to provide
a retort, but was interrupted by a voice from the back of the tent.

"She has answered every question truthfully."

Alex stared in surprise at Pulpit. He had not said a word the entire time.

Until now.

Heads swiveled. "And how can you be so sure, monk?" Gravelback asked.

Pulpit shrugged. "How can one explain why water is wet, Lord Gravelback? As a Monk of the Order of the White, I just know."

That seemed to settle the matter. Alex slumped in her chair, a sigh of relief escaping from her.

"I think that is enough for now," Bozar announced. The others stood, and one-by-one, filed out until only Tal remained with Alex and Bozar.

"I would like to talk to Lady Alexandria, Tal."

When Tal made no move to leave, Bozar added, "Alone."

Tal looked ready to argue, but instead, said, "Very well." He turned and stalked out.

Bozar took the chair next to Alex. "You and Tal have been through quite an adventure."

"Yes, I suppose we have," she agreed.

"Sometimes, such life and death circumstances produce a closeness, a camaraderie not experienced at any other time."

Alex felt her face flush. "I—I guess that could happen."

"For example, when the suggestion was made to escort you back to Wheel and to your father, the Duke, Tal went berserk. He threatened to break the arms of any soldier who touched you. Even for Tal, it was quite a display."

"He did?"

"Oh, yes. He is quite taken with you."

The ache returned with a vengeance. Fighting to control her emotions, Alex asked, "Is he in trouble because of me?"

Bozar nodded. "Tal disobeyed explicit orders."

"But he saved my life!" she blurted. "Not once, but twice. He kept me out of the hands of the dark lord chasing us. Doesn't that count for anything?"

Bozar shook his head. "I'm afraid it's a bit more complicated than that."

"You don't understand. He didn't tell me anything! He said he had a duty and responsibility, and, and..." her voice trailed off.

Bozar cocked his head. "Go ahead. Finish."

Alex dug her fingernails into the soft flesh of her palms. The pain helped to steady her nerves. "He said his duty was more important. Even more important than me. Than us. Then later, we had a big fight and haven't really spoken since."

Bozar frowned. He leaned forward. "So, Tal hasn't told you who he is?"

Miserable, Alex shook her head. "No."

Bozar sat back tapping his lips. He released a deep sigh. "Then let me clear it up for you. Tal is a Blood Prince, the Heir to the Throne of Meredith. He will one day rule the Empire."

The room wobbled.

Bozar's hand shot out to steady Alex. "What?" she managed to choke out. "But that's impossible. The Veil—"

"Has finally been breached," Bozar finished for her. "We are part of the Imperial army invading Dalfur. Our intent is to destroy the Veil and to find and execute the Veil Queen and King. I tell you all this, because you would have eventually found out anyway. By being up front, we can avoid future misunderstandings."

"What misunderstandings? What do you mean?"

"I mean this; you will be escorted back through the Veil. You will stay at Lodestone Castle for the duration of the war as a ward of the Empire. There you will be safe. On this, at least, Tal and I agree."

Alex's thoughts galloped through her mind. *Safe.* Since arriving on Meredith, only once had she ever really felt safe.

The night at the abandoned farmstead when she slept wrapped in Tal's arms.

"Will Tal come back too?"

Bozar shook his head. "He is needed here." Bozar's implication was obvious.

I'm not to see Tal again.

She covered her face. This time she couldn't stop the tears.

Bozar gently squeezed her shoulder. "I know this isn't what you wanted to hear. But Tal is right. The stakes are too high, and countless lives depend on our success."

Alex wrenched her emotions under control. She removed her hands and used her sleeves to dry her eyes. "When?" she croaked.

"Tomorrow. You'll rest tonight and get an early start in the morning."

"I see." Alex turned to Bozar. "Can I at least see Tal before I leave?"

He shook his head. "I'm sorry. I don't think that would be wise."

A strained laugh escaped from Alex. "It's probably for the best. Tal might do something reckless. He can't help himself sometimes."

"You're very perceptive, Lady Alexandria." Bozar studied her. "Despite your short time together, you've come to know Tal well."

He took her hand and escorted Alex to Artemis Thurgood's pavilion. Every step felt wooden, unreal, a bad dream she couldn't wake up from.

Because each step took her farther away from Tal.

CHAPTER 51

ARTEMIS THURGOOD SERVED A SUMPTUOUS BREAKFAST.

Ham, bacon, fried eggs, and biscuits dripping with butter and honey were piled high before Alex. A steaming mug, whose look and smell were similar to coffee, sat by her hand. The delicious aroma alone should have left her salivating. Instead, she nibbled, the food tasteless, her appetite nonexistent.

Numb, her senses dulled, she moved about like a zombie. After breakfast, she completed the task of packing her few belongings for the trip to Lodestone Castle. An hour later, a young lieutenant, the leader of the escort taking her back through the Veil, came to retrieve her. Most of the tents within the military encampment had already been struck, the soldiers joining the train of men and supplies headed for Markingham.

Markingham. The city she and Tell were headed for when they escaped from Wheel. Now his grave rested under a flower-covered mound somewhere in the trackless wilderness. She would probably never see it again.

The same might be true for Tal as well.

They were met by a column of winged cavalry, and a groom led Della to her. The flying horse nuzzled her hand, and Alex patted her neck. "Here we go again," she whispered to the mare.

The lieutenant helped her into the saddle, then mounted his own steed. He waved his arm forward, and the escort broke into a canter in preparation to take off.

They had gone only a short distance when a commotion erupted behind them. Shouting and drumming hooves shook the ground. Alex stopped and turned.

Her jaw dropped.

Tal, bent low over the saddle, galloped toward them. In pursuit were a group of men led by Bozar and Lord Gravelback.

Tal came to an abrupt stop beside Alex, his horse throwing a shower of sod and gravel. He leaped from the saddle.

"Hold!" he ordered the lieutenant. "You are not to move without my leave!"

The officer, his face a mask of confusion, nodded. "Yes, Sire."

Tal approached Alex and lifted her off Della.

"Is this what you want?" he demanded.

Alex's pulse raced. "What? I don't understand. I thought I had to leave."

Tal's eyes softened. "I don't care what they told you. What I *do* care about is you. Is this what you want?"

Stay with Tal and all the possible danger that comes with him, or live in comfort and safety at Lodestone castle?

She stood on her toes and rested her head against Tal's. "Don't you remember? I already answered your question."

Tal's arms tightened around her. "Refresh my foolish mind."

"I said always keep me near."

Bozar, hands resting on the pommel, watched Tal crush Alexandria to him, her feet lifted off the ground in his desperate embrace. She returned his affection with equal passion.

"Shall I order Lady Alexandria's escort to proceed?" Gravelback asked.

The First Advisor shook his head. "It's too late for that now."

Puzzled, Gravelback growled, "The morning's early yet. Plenty of good light left to travel in."

A bemused chuckle spilled from Bozar's lips. "Do you remember all the countless hours spent planning this invasion? How we went over every detail innumerable times? Days and weeks it took until we accounted for every contingency, no matter how small."

"Aye," Gravelback agreed.

"It seems we left one out."

Gravelback snorted. "Impossible! What could we have missed?"

Bozar turned his mount to join the legions bound for Markingham.

"Tal falling in love."

ABOUT THE AUTHOR

Journey into realms of magic and mystery

Michael Scott Clifton, a public educator for over 38 years, is a rapacious reader and movie junkie. He currently lives in Mount Pleasant, Texas with his wife, Melanie and family cat, Sallie. An award-winning author, his books include The Treasure Hunt Club, The Janus Witch, Book I in the Conquest of the Veil Series, The Open Portal, and the Teen/YA novel, Edison Jones and the Anti-Grav Elevator. Google him at authormsclifton, or visit his website at michaelscottclifton.com

Printed in Great Britain
by Amazon

23886427R00171